MAGIC BY STARLIGHT

TERRA HAVEN HOLIDAY CHRONICLES

BOOKS 1-3

REBECCA CHASTAIN

Copyright © 2023 by Rebecca Chastain
The Stolen Solstice Copyright © 2023 by Rebecca Chastain
The Mistletoe Crown Copyright © 2023 by Rebecca Chastain
The Midnight Sleigh Copyright © 2023 by Rebecca Chastain
Excerpt from *Flight of the Gargoyles* copyright © by Rebecca Chastain
Cover design by JoY Author Design Studio
www.rebeccachastain.com

Mind Your Muse Books
PO Box 374
Rocklin, CA 95677
ISBN: 978-1-7344939-8-6

ALSO BY REBECCA CHASTAIN

NOVELS OF TERRA HAVEN

GARGOYLE GUARDIAN CHRONICLES

Magic of the Gargoyles

Curse of the Gargoyles

Secret of the Gargoyles

Lured (VIP bonus)

Flight of the Gargoyles

TERRA HAVEN CHRONICLES

Deadlines & Dryads

Leads & Lynxes

Headlines & Hydras

Muckrakers & Minotaurs

TERRA HAVEN HOLIDAY CHRONICLES

Magic by Starlight (Books 1-3)

THE MADISON FOX ADVENTURES

A Fistful of Evil

A Fistful of Fire

A Fistful of Flirtation (VIP bonus)

A Fistful of Frost

Madison Fox Novella Box Set

❄

STAND ALONE

Tiny Glitches

Never miss any novel news:

Join Rebecca's VIP List to receive emails regarding future releases,
bonus content, and behind-the-scenes goodies.

https://www.rebeccachastain.com/newsletter/

For Cody,
Every holiday is made magical
because I share it with you.

Constructive Elements

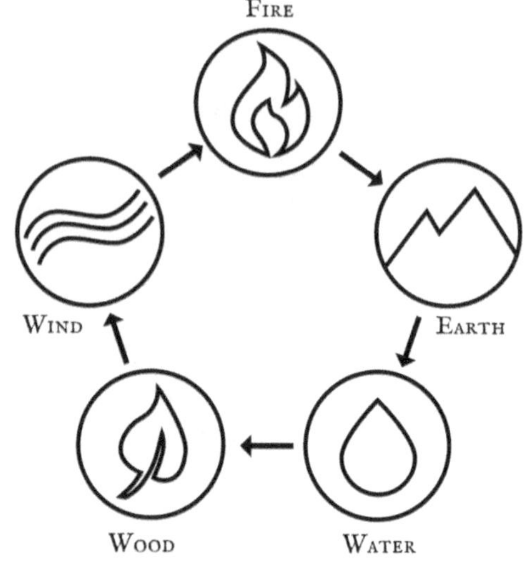

Destructive Elements

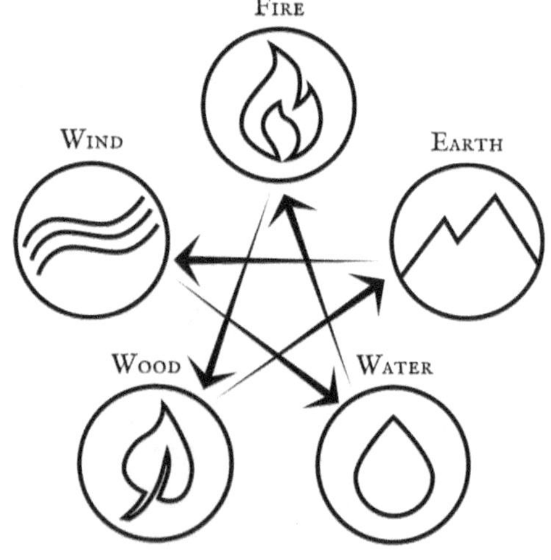

TABLE OF CONTENTS

THE STOLEN SOLSTICE

TERRA HAVEN HOLIDAY CHRONICLES
(BOOK 1)

1

I hummed an upbeat tune as I sank quartz-tuned earth element into a brilliant green aventurine seed crystal. The solid stone stretched like clay, forming a multifaceted star larger than my hand. I blunted the tips of each point, then pushed a small hole through one spoke and threaded a red ribbon through the opening. Lifting the ornament by the ribbon, I studied my handiwork. Muted midday sunlight refracted off the quartz's angular planes, chasing green light down the white sleeve of my angora sweater. The shape of the ornament was simplistic compared to my normal gargoyle-inspired figurines, but it was more fitting for the winter solstice party Kylie, Ms. Zuberrie, and I were hosting today.

"Oh, that's beautiful, Mika!" Kylie said.

She pushed through the Victorian's back door, balancing a platter of food in each hand. The delicious aroma of warm cheese, rosemary, and butter swirled into the crisp air, making my mouth water. Kylie bustled to the wooden table off to one side of the yard and arranged her cheesy herb cookies and a tray of assorted fruit among a growing selection of celebratory foods.

"I really like the way they're turning out too," I said, spinning in a slow circle to admire the decorations.

Yesterday, Marcus and Grant had strung cables in a zigzag pattern across the backyard above our heads—an easy feat for my boyfriend and Kylie's fiancé, since they both stood over six feet tall and could enhance their reach with platforms of air when needed. I had spent the last hour adding decorative lanterns and my own quartz artwork, using a step stool to reach the cables since I didn't possess the same elemental strength as the men.

I climbed atop the stool once more, tied the latest star in place, and then hopped to the grass. Seed crystals clacked in my skirt pockets. Brushing my hands across my hips, I marveled at the transformation of our ordinary backyard into a solstice wonderland. In addition to the decorations suspended overhead, cedar garlands threaded with silver ribbon and strung with brass ornaments and a few of my quartz creations hung along the walls. Red velvet banners draped among the garlands, artistic renditions of amaryllises, hellebores, and poinsettias stitched down their lengths in golden thread. Once I finished adding another dozen or so ornaments to fill in the gaps in the cables, and a couple more to spruce up the dormant plum and apple trees growing along the fence, the yard would be party ready.

"I think you could sell these." Kylie plucked a hollow rose-quartz sphere from a garland, rolling the ornament in her palm. The thin carnelian piping spiraled around the quartz seemed to dance as the light hit it. "Anywhere that sells your current work would be delighted to add these to the mix, especially in the months leading up to the solstice. Something to think about next year."

"I put a few samples out at the Eclectic Emporium," I confessed. My calling as a gargoyle guardian and healer paid my bills these days, but quartz artistry remained a passion. Besides, working with delicate quartz every day kept my skills honed.

"Good for you! Why only a few, though?"

"I ran out of time."

Kylie snorted. "We've had a busy year, haven't we?"

"Busy but wonderful." This year had brought Marcus into my life—and Grant into Kylie's. It had also pitted us against more danger than either of us had encountered in the twenty-some-odd years we had lived prior, but I wouldn't change a moment of it.

"Speaking of wonderful"—Kylie tipped her head back to check the peaks of the Victorian's roof—"where are our gargoyles?"

"Lydia and Anya are attending the midday winter solstice ceremonies at the capitol, and Oliver, Quinn, and Herbert wanted to fly around the city and take in the sights."

"They know the party starts in . . ." Kylie checked her pocket watch. "Oh crap! Less than two hours? We've got to get the sourdough in the oven, and I wanted to soak the cherries in bourbon for at least an hour." Her hand went to her head, where a soft braid held her white-blond hair mostly in place. "I still need do my hair, and—"

"The gargoyles will be back soon. No one wants to miss the party. And you look . . ." I scrunched up my face as I eyed her up and down, unable to resist teasing her. "Well, it's nothing a cleansing spell or three won't fix."

Kylie's eyes widened. "It's not that bad, is it?" She rushed to the nearest window, using the faint reflection to examine herself. Her fingers fluttered around her hair, but she stopped herself before touching the berry-stained tips to her white tresses. Her eyes narrowed at me in the reflection. Planting her fists on her hips, she turned the full force of her glare on me.

I grinned. Kylie loved a good solstice party, and she always cooked too much, but this year had her wound extra tight. I couldn't tell who she wanted to impress more: her new fiancé or her parents, who would both be attending.

"You look beautiful," I reassured her. "Fit for a high-society party."

She made a face, but I was right. Her hand-tailored navy tunic with its embroidered pale-blue flowers that perfectly matched the aquamarine of Kylie's eyes looked as if it had been designed specifically for her. Soft brown pants and navy suede boots completed her outfit. The cranberry-stained yellow floral apron protecting her clothing and a dusting of flour across her chin added charm.

"You know, Grant would probably prefer you like this," I said. "Smelling of cookies, cheeks flushed from the stove's heat, hair tousled."

A blush flashed up Kylie's neck to her cheeks, and she lost her imperious posture. I burst out laughing.

"I'm right, aren't I?"

Kylie patted her cheeks with the backs of her fingers. "No comment. Now come on. We've got more dishes ready to come out, and we could use your help."

I trailed Kylie into the house, my skirt swishing around my ankles, my stomach growling at the savory and sweet aromas wafting from the kitchen. A wall of heat enveloped me, and I propped the back door open. I didn't make it fully into the kitchen before Kylie loaded me down with a pie-sized quiche and a tureen of mashed sweet potatoes, both wrapped in warming spells.

"Come right back. I've got more for you," Kylie instructed, then disappeared behind the kitchen door.

"Remind me how many people we're expecting," I said over my shoulder.

"More than we invited. Everyone's curious about what goes on in this house," Ms. Zuberrie said, and since it was just the three of us, my landlady didn't bother to hide the satisfaction she derived from being the talk of the neighborhood.

"It looks like we're feeding a village," I said, mostly to myself. The table outside was already crowded. How much more were they making?

"People can't resist a well-thrown party," Kylie shouted.

"Maybe a few will," I whispered to the quiche as I snuggled its ceramic dish between an apple-shaped kettle of mulled cider and a vase of yellow and blue pansies. I preferred small, intimate parties, the kind where I knew everyone and didn't have to make small talk with strangers. Kylie and Ms. Zuberrie thrived on social interactions. At least Marcus would be coming, and maybe we could sneak away after we ate.

I pivoted toward the house, then paused to take a second look at the table. Something was off. The cheesy cookies hadn't been so haphazardly arranged when Kylie brought them out, had they? She was a talented cook, but she didn't have an artist's eye for design. Nevertheless, she wouldn't have bunched them into a pile on one side of the platter.

I rearranged the cookies into a pleasing fan—sneaking one that didn't fit right—and hustled back inside. When I returned with honey-and-ginger roasted turnips and a basket of garlic bread rolls, half the cookies were missing.

I plunked the turnip platter and basket onto the table and frowned at the cookie plate. Then at the ground. Three cheese-and-rosemary morsels appeared to have leaped off all on their own. More crumbs sprinkled the grass. I circled the table, checking the yard. Everything appeared to be in place and nothing—

There. The garland on the southern wall hung askew. The tigereye ornament nestled among the decorative cedar boughs was missing. I remembered that particular ornament because it had been difficult to find a position in which it was visible. The stone's natural brown-and-gold pattern camouflaged it, and I had decided against making another ornament with tigereye.

A rosemary bush grew beneath the garland, and I gently rummaged through its branches, double-checking that it hadn't simply fallen. When I didn't find it, I formed a quartz-tuned pentagram, refined it to tigereye, and swept it back and forth above the soil. Nothing.

"What's taking so lo— What are you doing?" Kylie asked. She set down a pitcher of orange juice and stalked to my side.

I didn't want to voice my suspicion out loud, but quartz ornaments—and cookies—didn't walk off by themselves.

"I think we have a thief."

Kylie barked a laugh, but her mirth faded when I didn't join her. "Wait. You're serious? What did they take?" She spun around, scrutinizing the yard.

I crouched to look under the table, then behind a gardenia bush. "An ornament and some food. Cookies, mainly."

"Cookies?" Kylie sounded as incredulous as I felt.

Who would sneak into our backyard just to filch a few treats? Not that they weren't delicious, but it was peculiar, especially since a pair of expensive silver candlesticks stood right next to the cookies. My ornament was another odd choice. Why not the heirloom gold, silver, and bronze ring-toss set leaning against the raised planter box beneath where the ornament had hung?

A trio of glowing beacons lit up inside my head, growing closer. Their abrupt arrival on the edge of my awareness flipped my attention inward to my mental map. A sprinkling of lights hung in my mind's eye, most of them static, each corresponding to an individual gargoyle. In Terra Haven, multiple gargoyles always lit up my unique guardian sense, but the only place they usually congregated in more than pairs was at home. Or when my gargoyles went on expeditions together, like Oliver, Quinn, and Herbert had today.

All gargoyle beacons were identical. A gargoyle's size or shape didn't change how they appeared on my mental map. Only their health affected the strength of their beacon, and all three incoming gargoyles glowed with good health. However, the movement of the lights in my mind made it easy to differentiate between the three. Oliver glided in smooth sweeps, his stone eagle wings built for soaring. Quinn's flight was similar, with more bobs, as his larger body forced him to flap more often. Herbert's beacon darted between them, the smaller gargoyle likely working twice as hard to keep up with his brothers.

Kylie squinted at the sky. "Quinn?"

I nodded. The gargoyles weren't in sight yet, but Kylie trusted I would sense them first. She created a simple arrow of light and launched it into the sky, letting the gargoyles know we were in the backyard. Seconds later, a dizzying rush of magic opened to me as three gargoyles offered me their elemental boosts at the same time. I swayed, bracing my fingertips against the gritty brick wall. Kylie bent her knees, absorbing a similar offering. In the kitchen, Ms. Zuberrie shouted out her thanks and called for Kylie to come help her. Rather than going back inside, Kylie formed a quick message spell and sent it in her stead.

"A *what*?" Ms. Zuberrie bustled out the back door seconds after her exclamation, dusting her hands on her apron. A spell swept the damp flour from the apron's magenta fabric into a small air-encased ball. Without looking, Ms. Zuberrie incinerated the flour ball. Her steely blue eyes swept the yard, taking in every detail. "A thief? Tell me I misheard your message, Kylie."

"No, I—"

Kylie's explanation was cut off when Quinn dove into the yard. Golden citrine from muzzle to tail, Quinn had the body of a lion, wings large enough to block out the sun, and an expressive face that was split wide with a grin. He slowed his descent with a couple of well-timed flaps, the clatter of his quartz feathers echoing off the Victorian's siding and drowning out Kylie's voice. Cold drafts gusted across my cheeks, blowing my hair into my eyes. By the time I batted the strawberry-blond strands aside, Quinn had threaded through the cables strung across the yard. The moment his feet touched down, he trotted to Kylie's side, making way for Oliver and Herbert.

A warm glow tinted the lawn as Oliver coasted over the peak of the roof and the sun refracted off his carnelian length. His sinuous Chinese dragon body didn't block as much sky as Quinn's lion form, but his wingspan was equally as wide. His tail snapped with excitement as he dropped the last few feet. The length of his body and his disproportionately short legs bunched his midsection together, then elongated it, as he bounded to my side.

"The snow makes everything look so different," he exclaimed. "And there are lights and decorations everywhere. The library looks like a wrapped present. And this looks amazing." He craned his head back and forth to take in the yard's transformation.

Herbert sailed in Oliver's wake, his pink toucan beak parted in his version of a smile. With an armadillo body, big bird eyes, and oversized lion paws, Herbert always looked like a cub, even when his much larger siblings weren't present. Sunlight splashed across his rose-quartz wings, highlighting the veins of deep-blue dumortierite speckling his feathers. More dumortierite ran through the bony plates of his back, providing a surprisingly effective camouflage when he curled up in the garden—or on my bookcase. Less so when he dropped into an empty spot on the table among all the food platters.

"Where is the thief and what have they stolen?" Ms. Zuberrie demanded over the final rasp of Herbert's wings settling against his back.

The gargoyles instantly stilled, only their heads swiveling soundlessly.

"A few cookies are missing and got knocked down," I said, indicating the disturbed plate.

"And one of Mika's ornaments is gone," Kylie said.

"Anything else?" Ms. Zuberrie stalked to the table to conduct her own examination, her lavender plaid skirt snapping around her ankles.

"Not that I can see," I said.

"Nothing's missing from over here," Kylie said from the far side of the yard, where she peered behind the oregano and sage. She squinted at our decorations from her new angle. "What about from the cables, Mika? There's a gap here."

"I haven't gotten that far. It seems like it was just the cookies and the ornament from this garland here."

We all turned toward the wall.

"The snow along the top is disturbed," Kylie said, jumping up to the edge of the planter box and standing on her tiptoes for a closer examination.

The latest winter storm had deposited several inches of snow across Terra Haven two nights earlier. I agreed with Oliver that it added an enchanting quality to the city, but it also would have turned the yard into a muddy mess during a party. Which was why yesterday, when Marcus and Grant strung the cables, they also cleared the backyard of snow, warmed the soil beneath the grass, and anchored a dome of fire and air above the yard. Their final touch had been the installation of a temporary spell to draw excess heat from the Victorian's chimneys out to the yard, capturing the warmth under the dome. Instead of being bundled against freezing temperatures, our party guests would enjoy a springlike oasis.

However, Marcus and Grant hadn't extended their spell to include the top of the wall, and a three-inch-layer of snow trimmed the stone coping. The only place the snow was missing was above the rosemary bush and mussed garland.

"This has to be a prank," Kylie said.

"Or it's Arlene," Ms. Zuberrie grumbled.

"Who is Arlene?" Oliver asked at the same time I blurted out, "Ms. Cartwright? Our neighbor?"

The curtains were closed across the upstairs bedroom windows of the two-story house next door, and I couldn't see the bottom floor. If Ms. Cartwright was watching us, she was being discreet. And if the sixty-something woman had hopped our shared eight-foot wall, nabbed a couple of cookies and an ornament, and sprang back to her yard in the short time Kylie and I were inside, I really wanted to see a repeat performance.

"Why her?" Kylie asked.

"Because she's a meddling busybody." Ms. Zuberrie glared at the quiet house.

I shot Kylie a questioning look. She lived for gossip of all kinds, a trait shared by our landlady and the foundation of their friendship. If anyone among us had insight into Ms. Zuberrie's seemingly illogical suspicions, it would be her.

Kylie gave me a small shake of her head, a suppressed

smile tightening the corners of her mouth. "I think this looks more like the act of children. A prank. Let's see if someone's kids are getting up to a bit of holiday mischief."

"Holiday mischief?" Ms. Zuberrie planted her hands on her hips. "Holiday mischief is putting mistletoe up to create amusing awkwardness. Holiday mischief is building a snow kraken in front of your neighbor's door to startle them when they step out. Holiday mischief is *not* breaking into someone's property and *stealing* from them. Stealing from *me*."

Kylie nodded as if she was listening to Ms. Zuberrie's rant. Meanwhile, she crafted a series of message spells, voiced a quick question into each one, and sent them zipping over the fence in every which direction.

"There. We'll know in a moment who our culprit is," Kylie said.

Ms. Zuberrie huffed. "Do you really think some child sneaked in past my wards?"

"You're not warding against friends, right?"

Ms. Zuberrie arched a pale eyebrow. "Friends don't steal—"

"Pull pranks," Kylie interrupted. "It's cookies that are missing, not the main course or even your famous chocolate truffle cake."

Ms. Zuberrie looked like she was going to continue arguing, but after Kylie mirrored her fists-on-hips, eyebrow-raised posture, our landlady deflated. Shaking her head, she said, "You'll see. Arlene is behind this somehow."

The first message spell returned, and Kylie activated it almost before it cleared the wall. The familiar voice of Larissa, our neighbor across the street, spilled into the air.

"Nothing missing here, Kylie, and my girls have been linked with me and in my sight all morning. Good luck finding your prankster."

Kylie and Ms. Zuberrie shared a look, and Ms. Zuberrie cracked a smile. "I told you Larissa keeps those girls linked with her as much as possible. She thinks it'll make them stronger in water, but they're both destined to be wood elementals."

The next two message spells arrived almost on top of each other. Kylie caught them both and activated them one at a time. Two more neighbors confirmed the same thing Larissa had: all children and belongings were accounted for.

I nibbled on a puff pastry, savoring the creamy honey-and-goat-cheese filling as the rest of the messages returned. No one else had been struck by our mysterious pranksters. No one else was missing anything, edible or otherwise. No one had seen anything or anyone suspicious.

"So where does that leave us?" I asked. A few stolen cookies—and a missing ornament—didn't warrant contacting the city guard, but their disappearance and the lack of a genuine suspect sparked my curiosity.

"It leaves us with Arlene," Ms. Zuberrie announced.

3

Ms. Zuberrie swept through the house and out the front door, leaving it open in her wake. I scurried after her, pausing to shrug on my coat while Kylie shut the door behind us.

"Hurry. She's not stopping," Kylie whispered.

I tossed my scarf over my neck and pounded down the porch stairs after Ms. Zuberrie, my work boots landing heavier than my slender landlady's determined stomps. Without the backyard's balmy spell, the winter air bit through my sweater and spread goose bumps up my arms. I gave my red-and-green plaid scarf a quick twist around my neck, then tucked the ends beneath my wool coat and buttoned it closed.

"You still haven't explained why you think Ms. Cartwright would want to steal a few cookies," I said to my landlady's stiff back. "I mean, isn't she coming to the party? Couldn't we talk to her then?"

Ms. Zuberrie stopped so abruptly I had to dodge to the side to avoid running into her. Kylie squeaked and grabbed the stair railing to halt herself. Taking a deep breath, Ms.

Zuberrie turned to face me. Wisps of fine white hair escaped her tidy bun to frame her face, but they did nothing to soften the stubborn jut of her chin.

"Arlene Cartwright has had it in for me for thirty-odd years now, ever since I took out the apricot tree."

"The, ah, apricot tree?" I repeated dumbly.

Three gargoyle beacons swung from ground level behind me to the sky, arcing to settle on the edge of the roof. If I glanced up, I would see Oliver, Quinn, and Herbert hanging over the edge, eavesdropping—literally. But I couldn't tear my gaze from Ms. Zuberrie's intense stare.

"It grew on Arlene's side of the backyard and shaded half the lawn. I wanted a garden. I wanted flowers. So I removed the tree to let sunlight in. Arlene took it personally."

"This was when you first moved in?" Kylie asked in a tone I recognized all too well. She was using her journalist voice, the one that coaxed facts out of witnesses and interviewees. No wonder she hadn't tried to stop Ms. Zuberrie from rushing next door. Kylie's insatiable curiosity was piqued. It didn't matter that whatever had happened to those cookies wasn't worthy of being written up for the *Terra Haven Chronicle*. Kylie couldn't resist a mystery or a story.

"It was the first improvement I made to the property," Ms. Zuberrie confirmed. "How was I supposed to know Arlene loved apricots and looked forward to all the fruit that hung across the wall into her yard? She thought I cut the tree down intentionally to spite her."

"And if you had known?" Kylie pressed.

Ms. Zuberrie's eyes narrowed. "I tried to make it up to Arlene. I bought her the first basket of fresh apricots available at the market. She pretended all was forgiven, but the next year, she planted a walnut tree on her side of the wall.

Do you know the roots of those trees kill most of the edible plants I enjoy growing?"

I nodded, as if I understood half as much about gardening as Ms. Zuberrie. I could identify healthy soil, and I had a few basic plant-wellness spells in my repertoire, enough to pass my classes in school, but I couldn't grow my own food. For that, I relied on Ms. Zuberrie's bountiful garden and Terra Haven's talented farmers.

"And yet, there's no walnut tree in Arlene's yard," Kylie said.

"It didn't survive. Must not have been enough sun." Ms. Zuberrie shrugged, failing to hide a quick smile.

"Josephine! What did you do?" Kylie asked, pretending to be shocked.

"That's not the end of it," Ms. Zuberrie continued, dodging the question. "Next, she put up that atrocious gazebo."

I had never seen the entirety of Ms. Cartwright's gazebo, only the patina-coated domed bronze roof and the tops of several pale pillars visible over the backyard wall. The Romanesque style didn't match the Victorian architecture of the neighborhood, but I thought it added charm.

"I kind of li—" I bit off my words when Ms. Zuberrie's gaze sliced to me.

"It's an eyesore, and Arlene knows it. Why else does she get the roof polished every couple of years? I decided that if she wants to assault the senses, two can play at that game. I planted a patch of aromatic hyacinths along the front blueberry hedgerow between our homes."

"Isn't Arlene allergic to . . ." Kylie began, her eyes widening when Ms. Zuberrie winked.

"A short-lived victory, though." Ms. Zuberrie appeared to finally notice the cold, and she slipped on the coat she had tossed over her arm. Kylie handed her a butter-yellow scarf, and Ms. Zuberrie wrapped it artfully around her neck. A quick flurry of practiced air spells, and her white hair smoothed into a chignon, not a strand out of place.

"We have blueberries?" I asked, wondering how I had missed seeing them.

"Not anymore."

"Let me guess," Kylie said. "She killed them."

"You're catching on. That crafty woman performed a warming spell for some bulbs she planted and *conveniently* fried the roots of the hyacinths *and* my blueberries. It took me two years to get those blueberry bushes established. Two years! And she killed them in twenty minutes. She claimed it was an accident, but I know better."

I nibbled my bottom lip, trying to be mindful of Ms. Zuberrie's emotions and choosing my words carefully. "I thought you two were friends."

Ms. Zuberrie tsked. "We are. That doesn't mean we have to agree on everything."

Apparently not, if she and Ms. Cartwright had nurtured a vegetation feud for longer than I had been alive.

"But cookies?" Kylie asked, finally descending the last two steps to stand on the flagstones with us. "Why would Arlene steal cookies and one of Mika's ornaments? That doesn't fit the pattern."

"It does if you've met the hellions that are her grand-children."

Finally, someone was making sense. Stealing cookies was the prank of a child, not a sexagenarian woman.

"You think this is a multigenerational grudge?" Kylie stage-whispered.

I thought Ms. Zuberrie might be offended by her gentle teasing, but my landlady surprised me with a jovial grin.

"Now you're getting it." She spun on a heel and squared her shoulders.

I reached for her, but hesitated. Ms. Zuberrie tended to behave toward Kylie and me more like an aunt than a landlady these days. The gargoyles and Kylie had softened her, and even if I didn't share the same level of friendship with her as Kylie, I had genuine affection for the older woman, and she for me. Nevertheless, the idea of gripping Ms. Zuberrie's coat to hold her in place elicited a cautionary surge of trepidation, and my fingers curled into my palm. I stuffed my hands in my pockets and tried logic instead.

"We can't march over there and accuse Ms. Cartwright of being a thief."

Ms. Zuberrie half turned, facing Ms. Cartwright's house more than me. "Why not?"

"Um, because it's not in the spirit of the solstice?"

Kylie snapped her fingers. "Mika's right. We should bring something. Hang on."

She jogged back up the porch steps and disappeared into the house, and I pretended not to hear Ms. Zuberrie mutter about gifting Arlene with a gazebo-demolishing phoenix egg.

"Herbert," I called, projecting my voice upward.

The small gargoyle dove off the roof and landed on the porch's round newel cap next to me. The rail creaked beneath his weight, but he was careful not to dent the worn wood with his rose-quartz claws.

"Can you hide in the backyard and keep watch in case our thief comes back?" I asked, keeping my voice down. I felt a touch foolish for making the request. This was about missing *cookies*. But I also didn't think Ms. Cartwright was our suspect, and I didn't want to broadcast my plan to anyone who might be listening. "Give a shout if you see someone. And please ask Oliver and Quinn to keep vigil from the roof."

"I can do that!" Herbert clacked his long beak together, producing a decisive crystalline chime.

I stepped back as he leapt into the air, flapping rapidly to the Victorian's high roof, where he relayed the message to the other gargoyles. Oliver gave me a talon-tipped thumbs-up before he and Quinn disappeared. In my head, their beacons separated to take positions on opposite corners at the back of the house.

"Good thinking. It will be better if we can catch them in the act," Ms. Zuberrie said.

I didn't ask if she meant Ms. Cartwright or her grandchildren. Considering the way she was glaring at the innocuous boxwood shrub dividing our front yard from Ms. Cartwright's, I thought she might have veered back to suspecting her friend-adversary.

Kylie trotted down the steps with a basket hanging from one arm. A slender bottle of Fireside Rocker sherry peeked over the top, and a maroon napkin covered the rest of the contents. Good. The winter solstice was a time for reflection and renewal. Maybe a bit of holiday cordiality would inspire Ms. Zuberrie to let go of the feud and embrace a new, better version of friendship with her long-time neighbor.

"Sherry?" Ms. Zuberrie asked, eyebrows rising.

"Alcohol and honesty are old friends," Kylie said. She lifted the corner of the napkin. "Plus . . . cookies!"

Ms. Zuberrie burst out laughing. "Oh, you're devious, Kylie. Let's go stir up some guilt."

Kylie linked arms with Ms. Zuberrie, their heads tipping together conspiratorially as they strode down the path to the sidewalk. Sighing, I followed. So much for my grand idea of spontaneous holiday harmony.

4

Ms. Zuberrie's third knock on Ms. Cartwright's door would have done Marcus proud. Her bony fist hammered the oak panel with the commanding authority of the Federal Pentagon Defense—an authority which my landlady did *not* have. I squinted at her pale hand. Was she using earth magic to add weight to her knuckles?

"I don't think Ms. Cartwright is home," I said, stating the obvious since Ms. Zuberrie's chin had that stubborn jut again.

"I think you're right," Kylie said, her face pressed to a window, her hand cupped around her eyes to shade them from the sun's weak light. "Not a single lamp or glowball is lit." She straightened. "Josephine, did Arlene say if she was spending the solstice with her kids?"

"The morning, yes. She was making her son take her to a livestock auction, the fancy one in the Copper District."

"There's somewhere in the Copper District that sells *livestock*?" I asked, trying to picture the residents of one of the city's wealthier neighborhoods allowing farm animals to be corralled—even temporarily—anywhere in their vicinity.

"Apparently." Ms. Zuberrie stomped down the steps and rounded the porch to peer in a side window.

I burrowed my hands deeper into my coat pockets, furtively checking our neighbors' windows to see who might be watching us. "I think it's safe to say that whatever happened in our backyard, Ms. Cartwright or her grandkids had nothing to do with it."

"Whatever happened? Now you don't think we had a theft?" Kylie shifted the gift basket to her other arm, frowning. "Cookies don't just disappear."

I quirked an eyebrow at her. "Don't you think we've wasted enough time on this? The guys are going to be here soon, and more party guests after them, including your parents. I haven't finished decorating, and I don't know what's left to do in the kitchen . . ."

"Everything is under the appropriate spells. Nothing will burn or get cold while we're gone. Why do you think I went back inside before we came over here?"

"I thought it was to retrieve a guilt-inducing bribe."

"That too." A hint of a dimple flashed in her cheek.

"Kylie."

"What?" She tried to look innocent but failed.

I lowered my voice. "You know Ms. Zuberrie better than me. Help her see that she's blowing this out of proportion. It was *cookies*."

"And your ornament."

"And I don't think—"

A shriek pierced my eardrums, stabbing an ice pick of pain through my skull. I clapped my hands over my ears. Kylie's face went ashen, her gaze darting skyward. The sound pulsed, repeated, pulsed, and repeated.

"Not a harpy," I yelled.

She nodded, her lips pressed into a bloodless line. Cups of dense air sprang into existence over her ears. I mimicked her, clapping earth-laced air over mine to dampen the deafening screeches.

"Alarm spell," Kylie shouted, sounding as if she spoke through a pillow.

Ms. Zuberrie.

We spun at the same time, pounding down the steps. I grabbed the railing with one hand, my skirt in the other, and flung myself around the corner of the house.

Ms. Zuberrie hung in a vise of air, her boots three feet above the ground, her arms clamped to her sides. In front of her, the gate to Ms. Cartwright's side yard hung ajar. The spell protruded from the opening, squeezing Ms. Zuberrie with malicious force. She squirmed, her fizzling magic as useless at freeing her as her thwarted kicks.

I slashed through the spell with blades of earth. By myself, I wouldn't have been strong enough, but with the enhancement of three gargoyles, my magic cut through the Cartwright house's defensive spell as if it were cobwebs. Ms. Zuberrie dropped. She landed off balance and would have fallen if Kylie hadn't caught her in a gentle grip of air. The alarm continued to blare.

"Link," Ms. Zuberrie wheezed. Still bent double, she thrust a shaking balance of magic toward Kylie.

I rushed to Ms. Zuberrie's side, offering an arm of support. She leaned heavily on me, gasping in lungfuls of air. Dense air ear plugs settled over Ms. Zuberrie's ears, then Kylie tapped my shoulder. I crafted a small balance of elements and gave it to Kylie, joining their link. My grip on Ms. Zuberrie tightened as a dizzying rush of our combined magic swirled through me. The link messed with my guardian senses, telling me nine gargoyles enhanced our magic, not three, but the beacons in my head didn't lie. It was merely Oliver's, Quinn's, and Herbert's boosts echoing through Kylie and Ms. Zuberrie.

Off-kilter, I focused on Kylie's magical signature. My friend and I had linked countless times, and the familiar feel of her magic, a summer breeze flecked with sparks that danced like fireflies, grounded me. Beneath Kylie's magic, I parsed Ms. Zuberrie's signature of lush green foliage after a rainstorm, and I was relieved that her magic felt solid. The defensive spell hadn't caused lasting damage to her elemental abilities.

Kylie wasted no time hacking the alarm spell to pieces. Crackling lines of electrified magic disintegrated from the house's windows and doors. The dreadful screeching cut off. I blinked, disbanding my earplugs and listening to Ms. Zuberrie's heavy breathing and a ringing in my ears.

Eyes widening, Ms. Zuberrie snapped straight.

"The safeguards," she exclaimed, wrenching control of the link from Kylie.

Dense walls of water enveloped the three of us, distorting the yard and house into wavering blurs of white, beige, and green. Seconds later, thick fire bolts pummeled the spell. I flinched and Kylie cursed. Heat burrowed through Ms. Zuberrie's wards as the fire swelled to engulf half the dome around us. Ms. Zuberrie gathered magic from the link, thickening the water ward and swallowing the flames. They extinguished in a hiss of steam.

I glanced around frantically for the next attack, but the Cartwright house remained quiet. Heart pounding, I straightened from my crouch. Beside me, Kylie waved to Oliver and Quinn, where they hung over the edge of our Victorian's roof, worry visible in both their expressions.

"Are you all right?" Oliver shouted, his legs bunched to launch. If the side yard could have accommodated his wingspan, I suspected he would already be at my side.

"We're fine," I said. *I think,* I added silently.

Ms. Zuberrie let our link disband and patted some wayward strands of hair into place. "Humph. I told Arlene her fire work was too weak."

I shared an incredulous look with Kylie. I wouldn't have been able to snuff out Ms. Cartwright's "safeguards" alone, and I doubted Kylie—or Ms. Zuberrie—would have been able to, either.

"Why does Arlene have spells in place to set fire to people who enter her backyard?" Kylie asked, jumping to the most important question.

"She doesn't. She has safeguards in place against anyone who annihilates her house wards."

"Oops," Kylie said.

"Oops?" I echoed.

"The alarm was woven into all the house wards. It would have taken twenty minutes to pluck it out without damaging the rest of the spells." Kylie shrugged. "I thought we might not want to wait for the guards to show up, so I cut through everything."

My gut sank. Were city guards already on their way? Breaking a house ward was illegal, the kind of illegal that had jail time attached.

"We need to fix this." I waved my hand toward Ms. Cartwright's house, visions of spending the rest of the winter solstice staring at the inside of a guard station flashing through my mind. "Before the guards arrive."

"Or Arlene," Kylie added unhelpfully. "She'll know right away that her spell is broken. But if we replace it . . ."

"Our magical signatures will be all over the spell," I finished.

"We're not wasting time replacing the wards," Ms. Zuberrie said. "Arlene will tear up anything we do, and besides, if she's up to her shenanigans, she deserves the headache of reinstating all those dreadful spells herself."

"And if she's not the culprit?" I asked, not quite believing I was using the term *culprit* for someone who filched cookies.

"Then she'll thank me for ousting a thief from her property." Ms. Zuberrie spun on a heel and marched through the open gate to Ms. Cartwright's backyard.

Working my jaw to massage the residual ringing from my ears, I checked either end of the street for incoming guards. "I think it's clear Ms. Cartwright isn't lurking back there, stuffing herself with stolen cookies." If she were home, our grand entrance would have brought her running, with flames shooting from her fingertips.

"No, probably not," Kylie said. "But we can't let Josephine search by herself."

"Are you sure?" Finding out who stole a few cookies wasn't worth getting arrested. I could be home in ten steps. Walking away was the smart decision.

My feet didn't move.

Kylie wrapped an arm around my shoulder, giving me a reassuring side hug. She tipped her head toward me and whispered, "Besides, whether we like it or not, I think we're part of this feud now."

5

I was so busy gaping at Kylie, I didn't think to stop her from dragging me across the threshold into Ms. Cartwright's backyard until the gate closed behind us.

"Wait, what are you doing?" I spun to grab the latch, ready to bolt. We had already destroyed the house ward. I didn't need to add trespassing to my list of crimes.

"I'm getting us out of sight before the feds arrive," Kylie said in a conspiratorial hush.

"The feds—" My heart rate spiked before I saw the humorous twinkle in Kylie's eyes and logic dampened my panic. The feds—the Federal Pentagon Defense—was none other than my boyfriend, Marcus, and Kylie's fiancé, Grant, neither of whom would arrest us.

"Focus, ladies," Ms. Zuberrie said. "Our burglar could be getting away."

The side yard was a tight corridor defined by the house on the left and our shared brick wall on the right. Aggressively pruned plants in mismatched clay pots clogged the narrow path. Ms. Zuberrie reached for one stunted stalk, tsking softly. I bounced on my toes. We didn't have time to critique Ms. Cartwright's terrible horticultural skills. Any minute, the city guard would arrive, and I didn't want to be caught back here on the flimsy excuse of "looking for a cookie thief."

Clutching my skirt close to my legs so it didn't brush against the muddy pots, I squeezed past Ms. Zuberrie. Snow crunched underfoot, and a whiff of something earthy and tart hit my nose. If Ms. Cartwright had a compost pile in the back, it needed to be turned. Taking shallow breaths, I paused at the corner of the house to survey the backyard.

Ms. Zuberrie was right; when seen in its full glory, the gazebo begged to be destroyed. It had begun its life as a replica of an open-air Roman-style seating area, with a domed bronze roof, marble columns etched with grape vines, and stone benches inset between the pillars. But then a teething cerberus or maybe a bored child with an iron fire poker had been left alone with the structure, because every surface below waist height was gouged and scratched dozens of times over. To make it worse, Ms. Cartwright had decided to enclose the rear of the gazebo. The work appeared to have been done with a hasty hand, or perhaps by someone blind. Clumsy lumps of earth element fused rough wooden planks to the marble columns, shadowing the back half of the structure. Floor pillows and colorful wooden crates cluttered the enclosed space, giving it the hodgepodge air of a kids' fort. I tried to picture elegant Ms. Cartwright lounging on the grubby pillows, but my imagination failed me. Tearing my gaze from the monstrosity took physical willpower.

Another building, this one smaller than the gazebo and made more of windows than wooden walls, crouched on the left side of the yard beneath the bare branches of a cherry tree. A small garden caged by a knee-high fence lay dormant beside the shed. Cobblestones covered the rest of the yard, the center dominated by a giant inlaid pentagram, with a brick fire pit taking pride of place at the center. Compared to our lush garden oasis, Ms. Cartwright's yard looked bleak and disjointed. Every attempt at greenery had failed—and there had been plenty of attempts. Ceramic and clay pots sprouted in the corners and hugged the brick walls, but only bare stalks or barren soil filled their depths.

"If a thief came this way—"

"Mika, don't say that word," Kylie hissed.

"What word? Thief?" I lifted my new skirt higher, stepping across a patch of mud-churned gravel. "Would you prefer I call them a cookie bandit?"

"Shh," Kylie said, her gaze darting around the yard.

I rolled my eyes. It was a bit late for caution. "Look, no one is here, no T-H-I-E-F or robber or poacher or—"

The gazebo unleashed an unholy scream and spat out a wild-eyed goatlike monster of miniature proportions. Speckled gray from nose to tail, with a splotch of white on its forehead and a single stiletto-sharp ivory horn in the center of its forehead, the beast didn't stretch taller than my knees. But what it lacked in height, it made up for in speed. It cleared the gap between the gazebo and the fire pit in two cloven-hooved leaps. Springing sideways off the raised bricks, it tore across the yard straight for me, murder emanating from its square pupils.

I shrieked and bolted for the back porch. Wood chafed my palm as I hauled myself up the steps, skirt hiked up around my thighs. Gravel peppered the side of the house as the homicidal goat spun to chase me. I thundered across the wooden planks and leapt to the ground on the far side. A staccato of death echoed behind me.

Whipping my hair from my eyes, I checked frantically

for Kylie and Ms. Zuberrie. They cowered by the corner of the house. Mud slid beneath my boots, and I twisted forward, but not before I caught the oddest expression on Kylie's face. It wasn't fear. It wasn't astonishment—

An ear-piercing bleat a half step behind me shot fear up my spine. The goat's horn wasn't long, but it was plenty sharp enough to skewer me. The gazebo loomed. I planted a foot on its low stone bench and launched myself into its shadowy depths. A blur of gray flew through the air on my left, landing atop a teal crate at waist level. My feet continued to churn, but I couldn't tear my eyes from the wicked horn as the goat careened up the crate ziggurat. At the pinnacle, the beast paused to glare down at me before throwing its head back to scream its rage.

Blindly, I shot a hand toward the nearest pillar, seizing an ice-cold grape vine and flinging myself from the gazebo. My grip slipped. Windmilling my arms, I shoved off the lip of the stone dais and turned my fall into forward momentum.

A blur of carnelian crashed to the cobblestones behind me. Oliver snapped his wings high, creating a quartz wall of protection. I spun, crouching behind him. The goat bleated its malicious mirth and charged. Before Oliver could react, the hellion sprang onto Oliver's muzzle, twisted sideways to land on the edge of an upraised wing, and vaulted to Oliver's humped back. Then it dove for me.

I yelped and tumbled backward over my own feet. A cushion of air caught me inches from the ground. Mid-leap, the goat tucked its head, angling to pierce me through the heart. Fear hollowed out my gut. I didn't have time to roll aside. Throwing up my arms to protect myself, I made a clumsy grasp for the elements.

The goat struck a barrier of air that materialized above

my chest. Undeterred, it reared up, bringing its sharp hooves down on my stomach. The cocoon of air cushioned me from the piercing blow. Bleating, the goat repeated its rearing attack. When nothing happened, it lowered its nose to sniff the elemental barrier, its malevolent golden eyes locked with mine. The muted weight of four tiny hooves pressed into the spell, bearing down on my midsection.

Oliver spun on a heel, one wing raised like a battering ram.

"Wait, *wait*," Kylie yelled.

The goat bucked, landing heavily on all four feet. Oliver froze, his wing poised to sweep the possessed beast from my chest.

Kylie stumbled into my line of sight, bent in half, clutching her stomach. My heart sank. Had the goat skewered her? She was breathing hard, her shoulders shaking, her face red . . .

"Are you *laughing*?" I demanded.

"Maybe?" She held up her right hand, her thumb and forefinger an inch apart. "Just a little."

"This isn't funny. This murder goat has it in for me." I tried to sit up, but Kylie's protective cocoon of air bound me in place.

Ms. Zuberrie's cackle split the air, and Kylie started giggling again. I gave her my best glare. With obvious effort, Kylie pulled her face straight. Ms. Zuberrie came into view next to her, fanning her flushed cheeks and blotting at tears.

"I'm glad you both find this so amusing," I said through gritted teeth. "Maybe you want to explain why this beast isn't trying to kill you."

"It's what you said. The T-word," Kylie said.

"The *T-word*? You mean *thief*?"

The goat whipped toward me and screamed into my

face. Kylie's air barrier took the brunt of its flying spittle. Oliver snaked his head forward, thrusting his snout between the goat and my face. His scowl was fierce enough to freeze a basilisk in its tracks. A low growl rumbled up his throat, releasing as a puff of air into the goat's face.

The tiny terror reared back, canted its head, and drove the tip of its horn into Oliver's carnelian muzzle. Oliver didn't flinch, but the impact rattled the goat's eyes in their sockets. Or maybe that was wishful thinking. The beast angled for a second assault. Oliver flared his wings, menace radiating from every quartz-hard fiber of his being. The goat bleated in his face.

Clearly this creature didn't have a brain in its head.

"Now would be a great time to let me up," I growled.

"Oh, um, yes, but . . ." Kylie waved a hand toward the goat.

"Whisper won't be satisfied until you redeem yourself," Ms. Zuberrie said.

"Whisper?" She couldn't be referring to this obnoxious beast, could she?

"Whisper of Integrity, or some such nonsense," Ms. Zuberrie said. "She's a xiezhi."

"A zee-she?" I glanced between Kylie and Ms. Zuberrie, wondering if I should know what that was.

"It's a Chinese animal, used in their courts." Kylie circled me to lay a soothing hand on Oliver's forehead. "Sort of like a lynx. Only instead of being able to discern lies, xiezhis can distinguish right from wrong."

"The real ones can. They also impale the corrupt and feast on their bodies." Ms. Zuberrie scanned the yard while she talked, her attention clearly not on her words. "You're never going to see a pure-blooded xiezhi stateside. The Chinese guard those like gold. But these mutts . . ." She waved a hand toward Whisper. "The smaller they get, the more the brains have been bred right out of them. Something Joey would have known if he'd done an ounce of research."

"This runt wants to kill and eat Mika?" Oliver asked, his voice sliding from a menacing growl to a squeak. "Why are you just standing there? Get it off her."

"What he said." I squirmed in Kylie's spell.

The upper protective layer flexed with my movements, causing Whisper to prance in place to keep her balance. She let out a disgruntled *baa* and pooped. Tiny black pellets cascaded off the spell blanketing me to land on either side of my hips. Ms. Zuberrie and Kylie took a coordinated step back.

"The only danger Whisper poses is to Arlene's poor plants," Ms. Zuberrie said. She pointed to a pot at the base of the hideous gazebo. "Look at what she's done to that lavender plant. It's just a nub. And that used to be the loveliest begonia."

I grabbed hold of the elements—something I should have done the instant I heard Whisper's murderous battle cry—and prepared to cage the mini xiezhi with raw earth element. Doing so would break Kylie's spells, inflicting a painful magical backlash on her, but I was fed up with lying here helpless.

Kylie must have seen my intention, because she knelt and rested a hand on Whisper's back. The xiezhi tossed her head, twisting around to snuffle Kylie's arm.

"She's harmless," Kylie assured me. At my glare, she added, "Mostly. Her horn wouldn't do more than bruise. See?"

Kylie pressed her finger to the tip of Whisper's horn. The xiezhi shook her head, soft ears flapping. Kylie held up her undamaged finger for me to examine. Embarrassment heated my cheeks. Terror had exaggerated my perception, but now it was clear Whisper's horn was as blunt as a carrot.

I had essentially been scared out of my mind by an excited baby goat.

6

———

"**I** want up," I ground out, certain I was as red as Oliver.

"If I let you up, Whisper's just going to keep charging you until you convince her you're morally virtuous," Kylie said.

"Morally virtuous? How am I supposed to do that?"

"Talk to her?" Kylie guessed.

Ms. Zuberrie nodded. "That's what Arlene has her grandkids do."

"Is that why she got Whisper? To help teach her grandkids right and wrong?" Kylie asked.

"Psh. Whisper was the latest in her son's schemes to improve business. Joey had the harebrained notion that bringing this twit to business negotiations would keep everyone honest. You can guess how well that went over."

"That sounds like a story I should hear." Kylie straightened, abandoning me to Whisper's baleful attention.

I tuned out Ms. Zuberrie's voice and locked eyes with the xiezhi.

"I'm a good person," I said.

Whisper didn't budge.

"I'm a healer."

Whisper cocked her head.

"I help gargoyles."

"Tell her you're a guardian," Oliver said.

"I'm a gargoyle guardian. A protector, you stupid mutant goat."

Whisper reared and drove her front feet into my ribs. Even with Kylie's spell protecting me, I was grateful my crossed arms protected my chest. The urge to cage this high-minded runt in an earth cage roared back to life, but Kylie's muffled laughter held it in check.

"You know who's not virtuous? Xiezhi who attack people and poop on them." Drawing in a deep, calming breath, I thought about what had set off the xiezhi: the word *thief*.

"I believe people should respect each other's property. It's wrong to steal."

Whisper launched off my stomach and sprang to the rim of the fire pit. Kylie disbanded the spell above me, then helped me to my feet before releasing the cushion of air that had broken my fall—and saved my outfit. Only a few flecks of mud marred the hem of my floral skirt, and a quick cleansing spell took care of those. Oliver stuck close to my side, and I brushed a reassuring hand across his forehead. A quick elemental check confirmed Whisper's hooves and horn hadn't so much as scratched his hard flesh.

"All that time with your fed man has improved your reflexes." Ms. Zuberrie brushed my hair off my shoulders. She smiled, then started to chuckle. "Your scareability, not so much. Your scream! And your expression when Whisper dove out of the gazebo." She made a face, throwing up her hands, and she and Kylie burst into fresh laughter.

Whisper pranced around the fire pit, looking annoyingly adorable. Perhaps I had overreacted. But after the scare of the house alarms and breaking all of Ms. Cartwright's wards, I was on edge.

"You could have warned me," I groused, not quite ready to share in Kylie and Ms. Zuberrie's humor.

"I tried," Kylie said. "You were on a mission."

"Because I'd rather not spend the solstice in jail."

"Oh, good point," Ms. Zuberrie said, sobering. "This would all be easier to explain to the city guard if we found the thief's tracks and—"

Whisper leapt for Ms. Zuberrie, and she used a sheet of air to redirect the xiezhi's charge.

"No, you twit," she said, shunting aside the xiezhi's follow-up attack. "I'm not a thief. None of us are. We are law-abiding citizens. I approve of following rules."

Whisper bounced to a stop, head cocked as she weighed my landlady's statements. Obviously the xiezhi didn't possess the refined senses of a lynx, because Whisper didn't appear to detect Ms. Zuberrie's lie. Law-abiding citizens didn't break into other people's properties.

"Good thing she doesn't understand the laws on trespassing," Kylie said, as if reading my mind.

Whisper pivoted to face Kylie and stomped her front feet in agitation. Kylie raised both hands in surrender.

"I think every person has a right to their privacy," she said. Her spine visibly deflated when Whisper lost interest and bounced away to her makeshift home inside the gazebo.

"Let's make this quick," Ms. Zuberrie said.

I beelined toward the wall between our properties, Oliver at my side. I could just see the lantern-studded cables crisscrossing our yard. My ornaments twisted gently on their strings, sparkling in the sunlight. The remaining gaps where I planned to hang a few more ornaments called to me. The sooner we finished this farce of an investigation, the better.

"Do you think someone climbed the fence while you weren't looking?" Oliver asked, craning his head to peer at different levels of the plant-like fountain anchored next to the wall.

"I don't see how." I gave the clay pots clustered in one corner a halfhearted examination. "Kylie and I weren't inside more than two minutes. That's not a lot of time to scale a wall with cookies in hand."

"And an ornament," Oliver said.

"And an ornament."

"Wouldn't our house wards have prevented someone from sneaking in?"

"Maybe."

Ms. Zuberrie and Kylie had softened our house wards yesterday in anticipation of guests moving around the property. It would be bad form for someone to get trapped in a spell we forgot to deactivate during the festivities. But Ms. Cartwright had made no such modifications to her grounds. For any person to pop over the wall from her side, they would have to be recognized by her spells. That left family and friends of Ms. Cartwright, or Ms. Cartwright herself. Feud or no feud, the proper and somewhat frail Ms. Cartwright wasn't a suspect, at least not in my head. I also couldn't imagine any of her family members had committed such a random theft and were now hiding in the house, watching us blunder through the backyard.

With a growing suspicion that we were focusing on the wrong kind of culprit, I took a better look at the dormant fountain.

Whoever created it hadn't attempted to replicate a specific plant. Instead, the fountain melded the structure of a tree with exaggerated trumpet flowers angled to arc water across wide lily-pad-shaped leaves. I brushed earth magic against a petal, testing the clay's strength. Despite the sturdiness of the fountain, it wouldn't hold a human's weight, especially not near the top.

I grabbed an empty pot and upturned it, stepping onto the flat base. Oliver held out a wing, and I gripped his stone feathers to steady myself. Snow dusted the cold clay of the fountain, and ice pooled in its leaves and dripped in finger-length icicles from the flower petals. A subtle earth spell insulated the lower levels of the fountain, likely to protect against Whisper's exuberance. There, the latest layer of snow was undisturbed. But higher, several clay leaves were missing their winter adornment. Leaning side to side, I traced a vertical path of broken icicles and missing snow. A smattering of tan crumbs was mounded among the frozen lily pads.

I stood on my tiptoes and reached into the top trumpet.

"Look what I found." I held up half a cheesy cookie like a trophy.

Ms. Zuberrie and Kylie joined me as I hopped down from the clay pot.

"So they came over here," Ms. Zuberrie said, eyes narrowing on the rosemary-crusted cookie like she was examining a murder weapon.

"There are more crumbs here," Oliver said, drawing our attention to the cobblestones.

"And here, another cookie," Kylie said, rushing toward the fire pit.

Together, we crossed the yard, following the trail to the many-windowed shed. Whisper sprang from her shelter and darted back and forth in front of us until a spell cordoning off the shed and its dormant companion garden stopped her. She bleated in frustration as we filed through the hip-high gate, the dull thump of her horn against a fence post punctuating her displeasure.

Ms. Zuberrie strode into the miniature garden, treading carefully along the stone path. An earth-tuned pentagram dove from her palm into the soil, and she shook her head at whatever she learned.

I went directly to a window, cupping my hands around my eyes to peer inside. A potter's wheel and short wooden stool sat in the center of the shed, both liberally splattered with dried gray clay. A couple of buckets were stacked against the opposite wall. Handmade ceramic pots crowded the top of a single low cabinet, their labels identifying the colors inside. Along the back wall, an impressive fire-laced heat spell wrapped a stack of deep shelves. Clay jars, vases, teakettles, bowls, and a series of xiezhi busts of increasing realism lined the shelves.

The excessive number of pots cluttering the backyard and the elaborate hand-molded fountain made more sense now. What Ms. Cartwright lacked in gazebo remodeling skills, she made up for in pottery enthusiasm.

Kylie tried the door handle. Ice cracked, and the door popped open. Nothing moved within the cramped interior.

"Well, it's clear no one was here before us," she said.

"I don't think we're looking for someone—or something—that can open a door," I said.

"An animal does seem more likely," Kylie agreed.

I circled the shed and peeked inside a squat brick kiln. Nothing lurked inside except the scent of ash and old woodsmoke. Closing the lid, I continued around the shed. Gravel gave way to mud, and I stepped softly, distributing my weight evenly on my boots, eyes on the ground. Oliver minced behind me, the saturated soil suctioning his paws and releasing each foot with wet pops. The interior heating spell had melted half the snow on the shed's roof, creating this quagmire. Tentatively, I patted the wood siding. Balmy heat radiated from it. If I were a small cookie-stealing creature, this would be a nice place to get warm on a cold winter evening.

"There's a broken ornament back here," Oliver rumbled, his head deep in the small opening between the back of the shed and the yard wall.

I squeezed next to his shoulder and peered into the gap. Soft heat bathed my chilled cheeks. Shadows darkened the narrow space, making it hard to see anything. I formed a plum-sized glowball and floated it over Oliver's head. The fiery ball burned through several cobwebs, and a flurry of arachnids vanished into cracks in the wall.

"Look, paw prints." Oliver pointed with one clawed toe.

I guided the glowball toward the ground, revealing a cluster of small mammalian prints. With a narrow pad and four toe indents, the prints could have been made by anything from a small dog to a jackalope or even a young kitsune. Shards of a former ornament scattered the ground among the prints, the amber-hued tigereye glistening like glass.

Kylie peeked behind the shed on the opposite side, and Ms. Zuberrie peered over her shoulder.

"What type of animal do you think we're looking for?" Kylie asked.

"Does it matter? We barged in here looking for a thi—" I glanced around for Whisper before remembering the spell holding her at bay. Nevertheless, I lowered my voice as I continued. "We solved the mystery. Perhaps we should head home now."

"We didn't solve anything. We found footprints," Kylie

said. "Aren't you at all curious what sort of animal this is? Why it wants cookies and your ornament?"

I wasn't about to admit to my sense of disappointment. Despite nearly being gored and trampled by Whisper, breaking house wards, and skulking around our neighbor's property in clear violation of trespassing laws, the puzzle of the cookie thief had been an interesting diversion. But now we had our answer. Plus, I didn't like the way Kylie was rubbing her thumb against her fingertips. She only did that when she thought she had a lead on an article for the *Terra Haven Chronicle*. Once she had a story in her sights, nothing would distract her, and we still had work to do to get ready for the party.

"I already know what type of animal it is. A hungry one," I said.

Kylie shot me an exasperated look.

"Kylie, we have guests arriving soon. You said you wanted time to clean up before Grant got here."

She snorted, and a soft cleaning spell tidied the hem of her pants. "There. Done."

"You two can head back. I want justice," Ms. Zuberrie declared.

"Justice? For a cookie?" Oliver asked before I could.

"It was more than one cookie. It was several." Perhaps hearing the absurdity of her statement, Ms. Zuberrie rushed on. "It's about more than stolen cookies. It's the principle. What if this seems like a prank, but it's something much larger?"

"Larger? Like what?" Kylie asked.

I wanted to reach across the gap between us and give both women a shake. They were terrible together, their vivid imaginations feeding off each other. If I didn't intercede, they would convince each other of something utterly ridiculous and nefarious like—

"Perhaps it's a test run of some lowlife hiding in the blight," Ms. Zuberrie said.

"Or . . ." I tried, but Ms. Zuberrie didn't pause.

"First they teach their animal to grab whatever's lying around, then they teach them to break into homes. No one wards against animals."

"Oh, that's ingenious. Or nefarious," Kylie murmured, crouching to examine the paw prints.

I thunked my head against the warm shed. Kylie glanced up at the sound, and I straightened.

"Or it could just be a hungry animal working all on its own," I said, knowing my logic wouldn't be enough.

"Shouldn't we find out?" Kylie asked with far too much innocence. She measured the print against the length of her finger. It didn't span more than one knuckle. With a fingernail, she stirred the broken remains of the ornament. "Oh no! Look."

A second glowball sprang into existence next to mine, bathing the tigereye in golden light.

Bright red blood beaded the tip of a quartz shard.

The animal was injured.

7

My glowball doubled in size with a thought. Scratches cut through a horizontal board halfway up the shed. Claw marks scraped the wood beneath it. Our animal had jumped to this nominal ledge, then had gone . . . I swung the glowball back and forth, scanning the shed and wall. There. A smear of blood marred a brick near the top of the wall.

"Oliver, may I?" I held up a foot.

He straightened his legs and flattened his wings, giving me a nod.

"Thank you." I stepped onto his back, careful to place my rough boot soles to either side of his spine, where his muscles were the strongest.

Two streaks of fresh blood smeared the damp capstones. The yard beyond was manicured within an inch of its life, devoid of snow, and completely quiet. Standing on my tiptoes, I searched in vain for any movement or small shapes huddled in the shadows. A purple-tinted ward flared a proximity warning, and I flinched away from it.

Reluctantly, I hopped to the ground, then verified with a

touch of magic that I hadn't bruised Oliver. I couldn't strike the image of an innocent animal limping around the city with an injured paw, all because it had hurt itself on my quartz. Unlike the gargoyles I treated, a scratch for a flesh-and-blood animal could mean death. The wound could become infected. The injured animal's ability to hunt could be compromised, as could their ability to defend themselves. A creature as small as these tracks indicated would already be vulnerable to predators. Add in a bleeding paw, and its chances of survival plunged.

"There's blood on the top stones," I said. "It fled this way. We need to go after it. We can't leave it to suffer." I headed for the side gate. I couldn't scale the wall, not in these clothes. Plus the neighbor's ward would be a problem. We would have to track the animal a different way.

"And here I thought we'd be dragging Mika along," Ms. Zuberrie murmured to Kylie as she bustled around the shed from the opposite side.

"More likely we'll be holding her reins." Kylie projected her voice toward me.

I didn't slow down.

Oliver shook mud from his paws and loped around me, jumping to perch on the waist-high fence and stopping me before I could push through the low gate. Whisper charged him, butting her pale horn against the wooden post and bleating loud enough to startle a pair of blue jays from the neighbor's maple tree. Oliver didn't flinch or even look at the xiezhi.

"A hurt animal can be dangerous," he said.

"All the more reason to find it quickly. We can't let it harm anyone." Or injure itself further.

Kylie and Oliver shared a look.

"What?" I asked, impatient at the delay.

"Well, a minute ago, you were ready to go home," Kylie said.

I crossed my arms. "Don't you want to get to the bottom of this mystery?"

Kylie held up a hand. "You don't have to convince me. Just consider using some caution."

This, from *Kylie*? She was the one prone to rushing toward danger in the name of a story, safety be damned.

"It's the healer in her," Ms. Zuberrie said. "Every one I've met has the same fire. Good thing she has us to balance her instincts with logic."

My eyebrows bounced toward my hairline. If these two thought they were the reasonable ones, we were in trouble. Or maybe Ms. Zuberrie was including Oliver in her calculations. My companion's serious eyes bored into me, and I didn't miss that he had placed himself between me and Whisper . . . and me and the exit.

"I'll be careful. We all will," I promised Oliver.

"How are we going to track the creature?" Kylie asked. "It's not like we can keep knocking out people's house wards and breaking into their backyards."

Ms. Zuberrie rubbed her palms together, eyeing the neighboring house. "Gerald is a lightweight on wards. It wouldn't be too hard to pick it apart."

Kylie's eyes widened, darting from me to Ms. Zuberrie. Her mouth formed an *O*, but no sound came out.

"But his aunt is staying with him for the solstice," Ms. Zuberrie mused. "She used to work at the Terra Haven Heritage Conservatory. She could have added something tricky. And if the creature kept going in that direction, it's headed into the blight. You never know what you're going to encounter there. No, you're right; bludgeoning our way through isn't going to work."

"No, I suppose not," Kylie agreed weakly.

I let out a pent-up breath. Ms. Zuberrie's promised logic prevailed. In any other situation, my landlady's disappointment at not going on a ward-demolishing spree would have been amusing. She was normally a law-abiding citizen, but having a thief pilfer from her backyard seemed to have sparked an unpredictable recklessness in her.

"Quinn or I can go through the ward," Oliver said.

"That's right!" Anyone on our street would be *thrilled* if one of my gargoyles—or any gargoyle—took up residence on their roof. No one warded against gargoyles.

I shaded my eyes to look at Quinn perched on the edge of Ms. Cartwright's roof. He stood with his front paws curled over the gutters, his head hanging between them. If his mane had been made of fur instead of golden citrine quartz, it would have fallen into his eyes.

"Quinn, have you spotted any suspicious creatures? Ones with feet about this big?" I held up my fingers, spreading them an inch apart.

He shook his head. "I think the house alarm spooked all the animals in the area."

"Good point. Oliver, do you mind going next door and looking for us?" I asked.

"If you find the animal, come get us," Kylie said. "We can use magic to keep it safe until we can get it to a healer."

"You'll wait here?" Oliver asked.

"I think it's time we left." Likely the only reason the guards hadn't burst through the side gate to arrest us was because they were understaffed during the holiday. I wasn't eager to wait around for them to show up, either. "We'll be out front. And I promise not to say anything to enrage Whisper on my way out."

Oliver finally nodded. With one last glare at the xiezhi

currently prodding his tail with her horn, he launched into the air. The three of us ducked reflexively. Ms. Zuberrie clamped her hands over her hair, holding the fine strands in place, and we all shivered from the blast of chilly wind.

In my mind, Oliver's beacon arched over the fence behind the pottery shed and dipped into the next yard. His feet touched down with muffled thumps. We waited, heads cocked as we listened to his progress across the yard. When the snap of Oliver's wings echoed off Gerald's house and the sound of his flight receded toward the next house, Ms. Zuberrie twitched her skirts and glanced around.

"Mika is right," she said. "No point in us waiting back here."

Kylie led the way to the gate, shooing Whisper out of her path. The little xiezhi bleated pitifully at us when we filed through the gate, her head drooping when she realized we were leaving her behind. Feeling bad for her, I backtracked to give her farewell scratches behind the ears. Whisper leaned into my touch, eyes closing in bliss. Her earlier aggression appeared to be forgotten.

"You're a silly little xiezhi, but you're not all bad," I whispered.

"Not bad, just a bit simple," Ms. Zuberrie agreed. She studied the xiezhi from where she held the gate. "And she's lonely. But not for long."

"The livestock auction?" Kylie guessed.

Ms. Zuberrie sighed and nodded. "I tried to convince Arlene to sell Whisper, but she's gotten attached. Instead, she's picking up a companion for Whisper today."

"Another xiezhi?" I asked.

"So help us, yes."

"Good, everyone needs a friend," I said, giving Whisper one last pat.

The xiezhi nuzzled into my skirt and tried to take a bite of the fabric. With a huff, I shooed her away. She bounded into the ugly gazebo and curled up on a pillow, and I latched the gate closed.

Quinn glided to the sidewalk. Slushy snow sprayed from beneath his paws when he landed, and Kylie tossed up a hasty air barrier. Grimacing an apology, Quinn minced toward us.

"What do you think the mystery animal is?" he asked.

"I don't know." Kylie tapped her fingers on her thigh. "It's not a weasel, not in the middle of the day. A house cat wouldn't have taken the cookies. A sunekosuri wouldn't have made it over the wall. I suspected a frost-crested pamolet, but the tracks are wrong for that. It's definitely a mammal, not a bird."

Ms. Zuberrie stood with her hands on her hips, glaring down the street in the direction Oliver had flown. I attempted a more nonchalant stance, acutely aware of the Cartwright house wards still faintly dissipating into the air behind us.

Nothing to see here, neighbors. We're just delivering solstice cookies to our friend. Pay no attention to the commotion.

My shoulders relaxed marginally when Oliver's beacon backtracked toward us, and I pivoted to face his direction. Seconds later, he sailed over the peaked gables. He landed in the middle of the empty street to avoid dodging tree limbs, then loped to our group.

"The tracks go over several fences that direction, toward the blight," Oliver said.

Dread coiled in my stomach. The blight was less an official Terra Haven district than it was a warren of run-down homes and dilapidated businesses—qualities that made it an ideal bolt-hole for lowlifes and criminals. Although, in this case, I thought the cookie pincher's path might be coincidental.

"Just what I thought." Ms. Zuberrie nodded as if the fleeing creature's trail confirmed her far-fetched theory of an animal-training thief.

"Can you continue to track it?" I asked.

"Yes."

My heart urged me to race after the injured animal before anything worse happened to it, but I forced myself to take a breath. How would Marcus approach this problem?

"Kylie, can you send Marcus and Grant a message telling them where we're headed?"

"I'm on it." Kylie stepped away from us and formed a message bubble around her mouth.

"Ms. Zuberrie, make sure the house is locked. I'm going to let Herbert know what we've learned and ask him to wait here in case the animal circles back. He can relay anything he learns through Marcus, when he arrives."

Ms. Zuberrie nodded, and we split up.

"Grant wants us to wait for him," Kylie said when we regrouped on the sidewalk.

"Is he close?" I asked.

"Since it's not an emergency, he has to stay at the park. He and Marcus are part of the team setting up the temporary event arena and its spells. They won't be free for another twenty to thirty minutes."

"That's too long." Those prints had been tiny, indicating a small animal or a baby of some kind. I couldn't stomach twiddling my thumbs while it was bleeding and vulnerable.

"You two are acting like I haven't been strolling these streets since before those boys were in diapers," Ms. Zuberrie said. "We can manage to track down one injured animal between two gargoyles and three competent women.

And if we can't, I might as well sell this house, and we can all move to a downtown loft, where the most dangerous thing we'll encounter is air-dropped road apples from the Pegasus Express."

"I was hoping you'd say something like that." Kylie made a face. "Well, not *that* exactly."

Ms. Zuberrie shrugged.

"Anyway," Kylie continued, "I already told my fiancé we would be back in time for the party."

We set out down the sidewalk. Oliver took to the sky, flapping clear of the street's trees to resume his aerial hunt for the injured thief. In seconds, he disappeared from view, his beacon dropping low into a distant backyard.

"Hang on," Kylie said, stopping me from jogging after him.

She darted up to Ms. Cartwright's porch and the abandoned basket of cookies. After wrapping half the cookies in a cloth napkin, she stuffed them in her pants pocket. The rest she left with the sherry bottle for Ms. Cartwright. We owed her an explanation, too, but it would have to wait.

"Remind me to ask Grant to add some FPD-grade wards to Arlene's house when we get back," Kylie said, jogging to fall in stride with us. "Maybe that will help soothe any urges to retaliate."

With an indelicate snort, Ms. Zuberrie shook out her skirts and took the lead, marching with purpose. Quinn trotted in the street, keeping pace with us while remaining far enough away for his footsteps not to splash muddy water on our solstice outfits. Oliver's beacon traced a bumblebee's path, bouncing up and down through the yards to our right. Distracted, I stepped off the sidewalk and tripped over a tree root. Kylie grabbed my elbow to stabilize me, then linked her arm through mine, silently keeping me on track.

"Which way?" Ms. Zuberrie asked when we reached the end of the block.

"Right," Quinn said. He pointed toward Oliver's out-of-sight location up the street moments before Oliver sprang over the property's back wall and flowed to the sidewalk.

He froze with the uncanny stillness only a gargoyle could maintain as he studied the ground. Against the bright white snow, Oliver's carnelian body glistened like a jewel and left a dark afterimage in my vision when he burst into motion. Snow squeaking beneath his quartz paws, he zigzagged across the cobblestones to the sidewalk on the opposite side of the street. Before we could catch up, he flew over the next wall, gliding out of sight.

"Link up, ladies. We don't know what we're going to find."

Ms. Zuberrie paused long enough to accept a balance of magic from Kylie and me before resuming her march. She held our link lightly, letting magic flow between us without drawing on any, but I suspected she had numerous offensive spells mentally queued up to spring upon unseen assailants.

We cut left at the next cross street. The lots shrank; the homes crowded closer together. Two-story peaked-roof Victorians gave way to sturdy single-story homes that put more stock in defensibility than style, but no one had skipped out on solstice decorations. Beautiful pentagrams of all types—iron, brass, wood, ceramic, holly branches, and one made of icicles suspended in a freezing spell—adorned front doors. Red, green, silver, and gold ribbons and banners hung from fence posts and eaves, illusion spells sparkled in windows, and everywhere I looked, lanterns and glowball hangers stood ready for the holiday's all-night celebration.

Laughter sounded to our right. Through the broken slats of the fence, I caught sight of a solstice party in full swing.

Over a dozen people crowded the backyard, everyone dressed in their finest. Judging by their formation, they were getting ready to perform a group spell. We would be doing a few of those ourselves, once we returned home. It was tradition on the winter solstice for families and friends to travel from house to house, cleansing the elements in and around each home and reinforcing common house spells, like the cold spell on the icebox and the air-and-earth spells that kept the house from being overrun with dust and dirt. For good luck, everyone took part in five group spells—one at home, and four others of their choosing. Given the amount of spell work Ms. Zuberrie did all year round enhanced by multiple gargoyles, we probably didn't have much to do, but I looked forward to helping our neighbors.

I smiled at the sight of a couple of teenagers setting up a viewing nest atop their roof for tonight's fireworks competition. Personally, I always watched from inside Focal Park, where I could sit on firm ground while admiring the city's talented fire elementals' attempts to outshine each other with their fiery sky art. This year, Marcus was competing, and he had gotten Oliver and me coveted tickets to sit in the stands, close to the action. I couldn't wait.

The rich aroma of roasted vegetables wafted on the breeze, and my stomach grumbled. Our cookie thief must have been starving to have trekked over two blocks and counting just to grab a bite to eat. Maybe the delicious scents emanating from so many yards had drawn it farther from its nest or burrow than normal. Or did it know we were following it, and it was fleeing? Injured and on the run. My hunger pangs twisted into a knot of guilt and anxiety.

Oliver coasted into view, skimming distant rooftops. His muzzle hung between his front paws, his gaze scanning the ground. A couple on a flying carpet nearly crashed into a tree, too busy gawking at Oliver to watch where they were going. With a squawk, the person in front yanked the carpet back on course, only to swing wide around Quinn, nearly flying over the opposite sidewalk in their haste to distance themselves from us. I tucked my chin into my scarf, squinting against the breeze their spastic flight generated. Beside me, Kylie chuckled.

"Quinn, you're doing a great job looking fierce," she said.

Quinn grinned, his face achieving an expressiveness impossible for a true lion. "That's nothing. How about this?" His smile changed to a snarl. Arching his neck, he lifted his wings a few inches from his back, adding unnecessary bulk to his massive feline frame.

A trio of men approaching from the far end of the street took one look at him and wordlessly turned around, their steps speeding up as they rounded the corner. The patter of their running retreat echoed back to us.

"That's perfect," Ms. Zuberrie said.

We turned the corner, and the neighborhood visibly deteriorated. Weeds grew unchecked in small fenceless yards, where property borders were defined by scorched earth and volatile spells. Yet even here, among the peeling paint and gap-toothed roofs, residents displayed solstice decorations on their homes: hand-painted pentagrams brightened doors and lintels; silver chimes dangled from eaves and in windows; and symbols of the new moon, prosperity, luck, and love cluttered shallow stoops, advertising zealous hopes for a better new year.

"Look, Oliver is circling up ahead." I pointed to the flicker of crimson between a tree trunk and the top of squat roof. I didn't add that Oliver hadn't touched down in the last two minutes. Either he had lost the trail or he had found the animal and he didn't want to spook it by landing.

We hurried forward, and Oliver met us halfway.

"The tracks lead to a small outbuilding behind the corner house, some sort of shed," Oliver reported. "Fresh prints go in, only old ones come out."

In a cluster, we crept down the sidewalk. Three humans in boots and two gargoyles with quartz paws tapping against cracked concrete weren't exactly stealthy. The dingy house came into view first, a sad structure small enough to make the tiny lot look big. I stepped around Ms. Zuberrie, straining for my first look at the shed, afraid I would spot the tail end of our injured thief fleeing once more.

"Oh crap." Kylie grabbed my arm, stopping me from stepping off the sidewalk into the dirt. "Look." She pointed toward the lot's front corner.

A bright yellow post pierced the untouched snow. My stomach sank. I stepped into the street for a better angle to read the spell-preserved sign hanging from the post. Bloodred text screamed a warning to everyone who passed: FORECLOSURE. HAZARDOUS SPELLS. KEEP OUT.

The sign wouldn't have been placed on the property lightly. Perhaps unpredictable or unstable spells had gotten lodged on the premises, or maybe the evicted former owner decided to retaliate against the bank with some nasty surprises. Either way, the injured animal was hiding on lethal land.

"This is going to complicate our rescue," I said.

Ms. Zuberrie arched a pale brow at me. "Our 'rescue'? We're after a thief."

"No matter what its motive, we can't leave a hurt animal in obvious danger." I waved a hand toward the sign.

"No, we can't. Our *capture* is going to require some caution."

"I wish I had brought my camera." Kylie patted her pockets like it might have materialized while she wasn't looking. "I've got a feeling this is going to be an article-worthy resc—capture."

A small brass plaque affixed to the bottom of the sign listed the property under the ownership of Firebrand National Bank. Firebrand hadn't bothered to wrap the grounds in a ward, only their sign. Maybe it meant the hazards weren't too terrible?

When I voiced my theory, Ms. Zuberrie shook her head.

"Firebrand is cheap. It costs them money to install full-property wards. If this were a more profitable bit of real estate, they'd have the place double wrapped in the elements. Out here, the sign is all we get."

"Someone should do something about that," Kylie said.

"Someone with a byline?" Ms. Zuberrie asked.

Kylie grinned. "A little public shaming goes a long way toward encouraging a company to make better choices."

"Darn right."

The neglected yard looked innocent enough, more pitiful than dangerous. The house was hunkered near the front of the small lot, squinting suspiciously at the world through three slit windows tucked beneath a low roof. Stunted shrubs clawed out an existence near the sidewalk, and a hint of a gravel path led between them to the battered front door. No one had stepped foot on the walkway since the last snowfall, not even our thief.

"That's where I would hide defensive spells." Ms. Zuberrie pointed to deteriorating wooden planks of mismatched lengths scattered along the front of the house in a gross approximation of a porch. Or maybe it was a collapsed awning. The edges of a spell peeked from beneath a warped board, too indistinct for me to identify.

"Yep. And look at the lintel," Kylie said. "That shadow doesn't look right."

I squinted at the door frame. Patches of snow clung to the rough wood, and I couldn't tell if the powder gave the optical illusion of a curve or if the shadow hid something sinister.

"Unoriginal, but I bet you're right," Ms. Zuberrie said.

"Oliver, you said the tracks led to the back?" I asked, hoping to avoid the house entirely.

"To a shed."

I strode past the cautionary sign for a better look at the backyard, careful to keep my boots on the sidewalk. The outbuilding Oliver had mentioned looked as if it predated the house by a century. Sun-bleached and rain-warped boards formed a vaguely rectangular structure hardly larger than my closet. Rotting shingles covered the roof, and barren vines encased the shed, holding it together. A sharp wind cut across the yard. I held my breath, half expecting the building to collapse. Rusted hinges creaking, the listing door knocked a discordant beat against the frame. Snow sifted from the roof in a glittery exhale. Then the yard stilled.

"Were you able to look inside?" I asked Oliver. The decaying exterior provided plenty of peepholes—and plenty of entry and exit points for a small creature.

"I was afraid to get too close and spook it again," Oliver said.

"Good thinking." I turned to Kylie and Ms. Zuberrie. "How do we proceed?"

"Cautiously," Ms. Zuberrie said. "That porch spell looks nasty. Whoever set it wasn't messing around. We should assume anything close to the house is as safe as a phoenix nest in a hailstorm. But I doubt anyone went through the trouble of booby-trapping the lean-to. You never know, though."

"What if we surround the shed with a soft-air ward?" Kylie asked. "If the animal runs, we gently cage it. Once we know what type of creature we're dealing with, we can get it the proper medical attention."

"That's a good plan." Ms. Zuberrie pulled her spine

straight and squared her shoulders. "Kylie, you and Quinn head around back. I'll take this side. Mika and Oliver, you'll cover the far side, so the animal doesn't make a run for the next yard. No one takes a step without first testing the ground. If you encounter a spell, leave it be and go around it. Let's maintain our link, but keep a piece of magic to yourself. We'll move faster if we can each test our own path."

"Give me a second." I closed my eyes, turning inward. Forming an individual pool of magic isolated from Kylie's and Ms. Zuberrie's took effort. By its nature, a link was intended to give one person control of all combined magic. I could more easily take command of the link from Ms. Zuberrie than I could divide out a personal stream. A year ago, I would have needed one of the other women to help me, but practice had given me better control.

After thirty long seconds, I successfully held a bundle of magic outside the link—more than enough to make a test pentagram, which I created in the air in front of me. Kylie smiled when I focused on her, her own pentagram floating above her upheld hand. Ms. Zuberrie's pentagram zigzagged back and forth in front of our feet.

"Slow and steady," she said. "And as quietly as possible, so we don't spook the creature."

We stepped in Ms. Zuberrie's footprints across the barren side yard, then split to circle the shed. Oliver stayed on my hip, positioned between me and the shed, his wing bunching the fabric of my skirt with each undulating step. My floating pentagram swept the soil in front of us. Any magic it encountered would cause one or more of the penta-gram's five elements to fluctuate and serve as an early warning.

The lines of my pentagram held steady. Maybe the sign was a decoy. By claiming this abandoned property was unsafe, Firebrand made it a less-appealing target for vandals.

I winced when my boot squished in the mud, then flinched again when the wet soil sucked at Oliver's paw. Even with snow muffling our steps, we weren't silent. The injured animal knew we were closing in on it, and I could feel its eyes on me through the gaps in the shed's boards. A tingle of unease ran down my spine. Its tracks indicated it would be small, but that didn't mean it wasn't dangerous. Especially while hurt. Even a beloved pet could lash out when in pain. And despite Ms. Zuberrie's confidence in her trained-thief theory, I suspected we were dealing with a feral creature, which would make it even more unpredictable.

I halted when I reached the front-left corner of the shed, with Quinn and Kylie visible behind it and Ms. Zuberrie in sight on my right. A cluster of tracks dotted the snow near a gap in the planks, where the ground had been dug away to create a deeper opening. To my untrained eye, they looked the same as the paw prints we spotted in Ms. Cartwright's backyard. I didn't see any blood, and I took that as a good sign.

Using crude sign language, I relayed my finding to Kylie and Ms. Zuberrie. Kylie made a circle with her hands and squeezed it, extending her arms in my direction. She wanted to herd the animal toward the opening. I gave her a thumbs-up. Ms. Zuberrie nodded and handed Kylie control of the link. Magic pulled through me as Kylie built a soft net of air around the shed. Slowly, she constricted it, pushing the spell through the back of the shed, driving the animal toward the gap.

Something clanked inside the shed. I froze, straining to hear the animal's next move, ready to call off our plan if the creature sounded distressed. Slanted rays of sun cut through gaps in the shed's roof. I caught a glimpse of brown fur and a rounded shape before it disappeared into the shadows. Squinting against the bright glare of the sun on the snow around me, I leaned closer, eyes locked on the hole dug beneath the siding.

Claws screeched on wood, and the creature burst through a gap near the roof, leaping for me. I yelped and ducked. Oliver barreled into me, shoving me to the ground. One large carnelian wing splayed over me, blocking out all but a patch of sky. A tiny beast sailed overhead. Four muddy feline paws flashed beneath the emaciated body of a speck-led-brown kitten. Tiny, half-formed wings jutted from its back. At the apex of its leap, the animal looked down. My eyes connected with two golden owl eyes rounded in terror, its flattened owl face flecked with pale brown spots and grime, its beak gaped in panic.

"A baby gryphonette," I whispered, whipping my head around to follow the kit's flight.

With its truncated wings, the gryphonette couldn't remain airborne, and it landed a few feet beyond Oliver—well beyond Kylie's air net. In a flash, it tore across the yard to the house and leapt for a high window. A normal kitten wouldn't have made the jump, but with the assistance of its frantic wing beats, the gryphonette caught the window ledge. Contorting itself, it squeezed its scrawny body through the broken windowpane and disappeared into the booby-trapped house.

9

I rolled out from under Oliver and surged to my feet, my eyes locked on the smear of blood glistening beneath the window frame.

"Are you all right?" Kylie asked, rushing to my side. Magic tugged through the link, and she ran a water, fire, and wind spell over me, cleaning muddy slush from my backside and hair and drying me in the time it took me to inhale. I shivered as magic slid along my scalp and down my neck, warming skin chilled by snow.

"I'm fine, but we need to get in there."

Despite its appearance, the name gryphonette was a misnomer. Whereas gryphons grew large enough to carry multiple human passengers, preyed on wild buffalo and sheep, and were considered tame only in comparison to wyverns, gryphonettes were prized domesticated pets more closely related to house cats. They topped out at twenty pounds and hunted small rodents, lizards, and birds—and, apparently, cheesy cookies. A gryphonette was the last creature I expected to find abandoned and alone, and my heart broke to see its fear. It should have known nothing but love from humans. This one couldn't have been more than a few weeks old. It didn't know how dangerous the world could be, and in its panicked state, it might not notice a catastrophic spell before it bungled into it.

I broke into a sprint for the house. Kylie called out, her fingers grabbing for my arm but missing.

The link swung from Kylie's control to Ms. Zuberrie's. I was two steps from the back door when a wall of air solidified in front of my face. I slammed into it and bounced back, ears ringing.

"What the—?" Arms windmilling, I caught my balance.

Ms. Zuberrie grabbed my bicep and pointed at the ground in front of us. A broken stepping-stone lay half buried in snow, coils of fire and air element churning beneath it. "*That* is a fireball spell set to engulf whoever blunders into it."

Ice shot down my spine. One more step, and I would have been immolated.

"I didn't— Thank you." I patted Ms. Zuberrie's hand with trembling fingers.

"I take it our creature isn't something evil," Kylie said. She approached slowly, testing the ground all around her with a pentagram. Quinn trailed her, vigilant for traps she might overlook. Oliver plodded behind them, wings drooping, head bowed.

"It's a gryphonette kit," Ms. Zuberrie said, holding up her hands to indicate its size. "It's in a bad way and needs help—needs *us*—but we can't help it if we rush into every trap on the grounds."

Painful heat bit my cheeks, but I didn't back down. "If we don't hurry, we might be too late to save it from getting hurt or killed." The presence of one lethal trap increased the odds of even worse spells inside.

"No one's saying we lallygag. But we work together. That fire spell isn't the only one on this back door. Let's check the sides of the house—*carefully*—and look for another way in. Whatever you do, avoid the front porch. Mika, you're with me."

Dutifully, I followed in Ms. Zuberrie's footsteps, turning left around the house. She walked slowly, expanding her pentagram and guiding it with extreme caution across the uneven, snow-dusted ground. Kylie and Quinn went right, disappearing around the corner of the house. Oliver hesitated, staring remorsefully at the broken window.

I backtracked to kneel beside him.

"Are you all right?" I asked.

Oliver swung his muzzle toward me, his lips twisted in a glum line. "This is my fault. That little kit was no threat to you. I shouldn't have been so overprotective. If I hadn't overreacted, we would have caught it before it climbed into more danger."

I shook my head. "If I had been faster, I could have grabbed it with an elemental cage, but all I did was gawk."

"It's not your fault. You were surprised, and I knocked you down, and I—"

I placed a finger against Oliver's muzzle. "It's not your fault, either. We both miscalculated. You didn't know what was coming out of that shed. If it had been a baby basilisk, your actions wouldn't have been overprotective. And I've been in enough tense situations to know to have backup spells ready, but I wasn't thinking. Just like I wasn't thinking when I nearly ran into that trap." I gestured toward the fireball spell, but I didn't break eye contact with Oliver. It was easy to cast blame, especially on ourselves. But I didn't want Oliver to beat himself up, just as he didn't want me to wallow in self-recriminations. "The best thing we can do now is figure out how to help the gryphonette where it's at. We have more information, and we'll do better next time."

Oliver searched my eyes. After a moment, he leaned into my touch, and I stroked a hand down his glossy mane. Together, we were learning to be kinder to ourselves.

"Are you tall enough to see inside this window?" Ms. Zuberrie asked.

I straightened and followed her footprints in the snow, stopping more than an arm's length from the house. The bottom of the window was eye level. A film of dust obscured the glass, and I couldn't make out more than the dark seams of the wooden ceiling.

"Can we get closer?"

Ms. Zuberrie shook her head. "The house is wrapped in a sticky mess of wards. See?"

She nudged her pentagram toward the peeling paint. The elemental star warped and twisted, reacting to the house's spell. Ms. Zuberrie guided the pentagram upward, then side to side, and the effect didn't fade.

"I suspect it's some form of fly trap–style spell. I think it's anchored in the house's support beams. I might risk slashing it apart, if not for the kit. I don't know what the broken magic will trigger inside the house." Ms. Zuberrie blew out a frustrated breath. "This property should be domed in a no-trespass ward to prevent innocent creatures like the gryphonette from getting trapped like this. Whoever used to live here rigged this place with every foul spell they could cobble together, and Firebrand knew it, otherwise they wouldn't have put up the sign. If it were any other day, I would be raising a stink from here to the courthouse, and the city guard or your boys would already be here, disman-tling the vindictive magic littering this property."

The winter solstice was the biggest holiday of the year.

The courthouse and the bank were both closed. Only a skeleton crew of guards were on duty, and backup wouldn't be called in for something as minor as a feral animal trapped in a dangerous house. The same inadequate staffing at the local guard house that had saved us from being caught when we demolished Ms. Cartwright's wards now worked against us. Even if we solicited the local guards' help, it could be hours before they made time for us. The gryphonette might not have that kind of time.

"Do you think we should wait for Marcus and Grant?" I chafed at the thought, but if Ms. Zuberrie believed caution would be more prudent, I would listen.

"I'm not ready to call it quits just yet. You, me, Kylie, and our gargoyle friends should be able to figure this out. We just need to know what we're working with." Ms. Zuberrie's eyes narrowed on the horizon, where the clock tower above the distant courthouse peeked above the rooftops. "But don't think I'm going to let this go. First thing when those offices open after the solstice, I'm reporting this public safety infraction. If we don't step up as a community, businesses will think they can treat us like we don't matter. And that's the surest way to admitting defeat and letting the blight overtake us."

I hid my smile. Ms. Zuberrie's crusade to clean up the blight took many forms. Half of them seemed to be nosy busybody activities, but I was learning to appreciate her zeal. She did a lot of good in her self-appointed role as the neighborhood protector.

"Oliver, will you help me get a better look?"

"Of course." Oliver flattened his wings and braced his legs, and I stepped gingerly onto his shoulders. Ms. Zuberrie gripped my hand, helping stabilize me as I craned to see past the grime coating the window.

"It's little more than a box," I reported. "Living space and bedroom along the front, kitchen and bathroom at the back. Only the bathroom is partitioned off."

"Do you see the gryphonette?" Oliver asked.

I shook my head. A threadbare armchair slumped in the center of the open space, its dirty skirt hiding the floor beneath it. Moldy fabric mounded in the far corner, the lumps all but indistinguishable in the limited light penetrating the high windows. The rest of the house was bare, at least from this vantage, but I couldn't see into the bathroom or under the kitchen counter.

"Too many hiding places for something that small," I said.

"Any visible traps?" Ms. Zuberrie asked.

"The front door is laced with spells. The back . . ." I dipped my knees, then stood on my tiptoes. "I think there are more spells on the back. And the far window has air element twisted into something wicked I don't recognize."

"That means all the windows are probably spelled," Ms. Zuberrie said, helping me down.

"Why didn't the kit activate any spells when it went through the broken window?" Oliver asked as we retreated to safe ground in the backyard.

"Probably because it's too small," Ms. Zuberrie said.

"Or for the same reason it didn't activate Ms. Cartwright's or our wards," I mused. "People don't usually protect against gryphonettes."

"So maybe it's safe inside?"

Oliver looked so hopeful that I wished I could lie.

"The types of spells we've seen around the property don't make me think the person who set them was using logic. Large-scale spells like the one on the house might not detect something as small as the kit, but we don't know what other nastiness was left inside."

Kylie and Quinn rounded the side of the house, looking grim.

"No openings over here," Kylie reported. "Nothing big enough for us or the kit, and plenty of traps. I would suggest we dismantle a spell on a window and go through that way, but the windows are too awkward to get to, and I don't think we could reach one without touching the side of the house. I don't want to do that. Whatever ward is embedded in these walls, it's lethal. I ran element-specific pentagrams over the siding, and every one of them reacted."

"Then we'll break in through the back door," Ms. Zuberrie said.

I squared off with the house, a rush of nerves making it hard to get a full breath.

"Give me a second to update Grant." Kylie formed a message spell and spoke into it, letting Grant know our location and our plans, summarizing the house's fortifications as "difficult spells" to bypass.

I suspected Grant's reply would be swift.

"Everyone, all in," Ms. Zuberrie said.

I relaxed my split magic, letting it all flow into the link. Kylie did the same, and I bent my legs and sank into my stance until the rush of magic leveled and my faint vertigo ebbed.

Ms. Zuberrie shooed us back two steps, then raised an ice-laced shield in front of us. Splitting spells, she created a dome of raw water element over the broken slate and anchored it with spikes of water-woven earth.

"Brace yourselves," she said.

10

I gripped Oliver's wing. Kylie cupped Ms. Zuberrie's bicep, looking prepared to yank our landlady to safety if necessary. Oliver and Quinn flanked us, and I caught a glance between them. Likely, they had their own plan to keep us safe if Ms. Zuberrie's spell backfired.

Magic built in the link, and Ms. Zuberrie formed a ball of air, pressing it down on the broken slate with the force of a footstep. The spell beneath it exploded. Ms. Zuberrie didn't flinch as the stepping-stone launched through her water dome as if it didn't exist. She let the stone fly past us, then slammed it to the ground, embedding it harmlessly in the mud several feet behind us.

Heat bathed my face. I raised a protective hand, peeking through my fingers at the white-hot flames battering Ms. Zuberrie's containment dome. One more step, and that spell would have roasted me. My stomach hollowed out, and I breathed through a vertiginous slosh of delayed fear and relief.

As if sensing my thoughts, Oliver wrapped a wing

partially around my legs. I squeezed his feathers in response, unable to tear my gaze from the fire.

Ms. Zuberrie cycled the elements, driving spikes of ice into the flames. They pierced the spell beneath the inferno, hacking it apart. The fire guttered and died. Ms. Zuberrie let her water dome collapse.

I lowered my hand. "That was drama—"

Magic snaked across the ground toward the house, a single spark of fire element blazing along a spell so delicate we had all overlooked it. Lightning fast, it split and split again, racing to ignite sinister traps on either side of us.

Panic shot through me. We didn't have time to run. I sank into my stance, prepared to seize control of the link and dome us in earth if Ms. Zuberrie faltered.

As if she had trained for this moment, my fierce landlady wrenched magic through our link, seizing everything I had to give. Black dots danced in my vision as she slammed water domes over four identical fireball spells seconds before the sparks ignited them. Muffled concussions echoed off the house siding. Mud and gravel spewed into the air, pelting the ice shield. Oliver and Quinn spun in unison, rising on their hind legs and splaying their wings, caging Ms. Zuberrie, Kylie, and me between their quartz bodies. Kylie squeaked and grabbed Ms. Zuberrie, yanking her into a crouch. I dropped beside them.

Heat washed over us, radiating from four half suns burning beneath Ms. Zuberrie's magic. All were close enough to have set the house on fire if they hadn't been contained. Likely, that had been the maker's intent. Being evicted must have spurred the former homeowner's vindictiveness, or perhaps they had already been unstable.

"Cowardly bastards," Ms. Zuberrie growled. "If I ever get my hands on the idiot who lived here or Firebrand—"

Holding four spells and attempting to form a fifth taxed Ms. Zuberrie's abilities. The newest spell—knives of ice cutting up the closest fiery trap—wavered, the precision she had exhibited earlier missing.

"Earth," I gasped. "Add earth."

"Good thinking." Ms. Zuberrie disbanded the complex ice knives and laced a water dome with earth, slowly flattening her spell. Half smothered, the fire guttered and dimmed to a softer orange flame.

"Message from Grant incoming," Quinn said.

A second later, a bundle of elements speared over his wings and dropped between us. Even with Quinn's warning, I flinched and nearly fell on my butt. Kylie activated the message.

"I'm twenty minutes out," Grant said, his voice as loud and clear as if he were standing beside me. "Send a beacon if you need me sooner. Quinn, a tracker spell tuned to me will arrive in a few seconds. Use it to find me if those 'difficult spells' prove too much for the ladies. Ms. Zuberrie, I look forward to trying your famous shoo-fly pie, so please don't hurt yourself. Happy Solstice, and be safe."

Ms. Zuberrie crushed one fire. "Take that," she crowed, adding earth to the next watery containment. The flames inside diminished to a weak sputter. With a surge of power, she extinguished the spell. The instant it was out, she shoved earth into the remaining two domes, dousing the flames. After pounding the ground around each squelched fireball with air and earth, Ms. Zuberrie ran a test pentagram over the soil. When no surprise sparks ignited, she finally sat back on her heels and blotted sweat from her forehead with the back of her hand.

Kylie was the first to stand, and she helped Ms. Zuberrie to her feet.

"That was exciting," she said.

I straightened, touching Oliver's paw to reassure him he could stand down. Both gargoyles dropped to all fours and folded their wings, and I segregated enough magic from the link to check them for injuries. Thankfully, neither was harmed. A glowing arrow floated a foot from Quinn's muzzle. When he turned his head, the arrow stayed with him, but the tip rotated to remain pointed in the same direction, toward Grant's current location.

"Grant says he's twenty minutes away, but I predict we have less than ten minutes until he arrives," Kylie said, eyeing the arrow.

"Do you want to wait?" Ms. Zuberrie asked.

"Hardly. I love the man, but he's ridiculously overprotective. The sooner we rescue the gryphonette, the sooner I can remind Grant I can take care of myself."

Ms. Zuberrie nodded approvingly. "Just because we don't work for the Federal Pentagon Defense doesn't mean we don't know how to take care of the riffraff in our neighborhood."

"Darn right."

I had a vision of Kylie's future self, and she looked a lot like Ms. Zuberrie, except with a camera hanging from a strap on one shoulder and a golden gargoyle at her side. Both women were warriors in their own right, fierce and independent. Personally, I wouldn't mind Grant and Marcus showing up right about now. They could clear malicious spells quicker than us sand rescue the gryphonette that much faster. But I also wasn't willing to wait for them to arrive.

"We can't exactly hurry through that door," I said, thinking of the spells I had glimpsed on the other side.

"Let's see what we're up against." Ms. Zuberrie scanned

the ground between us and the back door with a test penta-gram, and we all crept up to the threshold together.

Something clanged inside the house. We froze. The sound didn't repeat.

"The kit's on the move. Give me a second to cover the window," Kylie said. She split off magic from the link, then crafted a net of air and suspended it less than two inches in front of the cracked window.

"Don't let it touch the house," Ms. Zuberrie warned.

"I won't. But if the gryphonette comes back out this way, I won't miss."

Ms. Zuberrie raised another shield between us and the door and began to probe the spells around the frame. Harsh magic nipped at her pentagrams.

"That felt electric," Kylie said.

"And this feels combustible." Ms. Zuberrie retracted her magic, testing another spot.

"That feels like a knife," I said.

"More like a tomahawk set to decapitate." Ms. Zuberrie's eyes narrowed as she conducted a second sweep of the door-way. "These spells are stacked. Whoever left them is a real piece of work. Trigger one, and the rest go off in a chain reaction. If I could find the spell that activates the sequence, we could disband them all by disbanding one. But from here?" She puffed a breath, her frustration visibly clouding the cold air. "It would be guesswork. I need to see what I'm doing."

"These don't seem like the kind of spells a disgruntled evicted homeowner would make," Kylie said. "These would have taken time. Months, maybe years. Same with the walls. Those look like defensive spells, not destructive ones."

"That's exactly what they are," Ms. Zuberrie agreed.

"Whoever lived here used the spells for protection. Everything is set to react outward. Except those fireballs. Those must have been a recent addition." She glared at the craters in the earth, their blackened centers still smoking.

"Do we activate the door's spells and hunker behind a ward?" I asked.

"We can't chance it." Ms. Zuberrie fisted her hands. "These spells might be old, but they could trigger some harebrained spell left inside like those fireballs. I don't want to risk the gryphonette."

"If only we had a key," Kylie said, peering wistfully at the lock.

She was right. No one would take the time to dismantle and recreate this number of spells every time they entered or exited, which meant the spells would only go off if the lock was broken.

"Is the lock the activation point?" I asked, feeding off Kylie's logic.

Ms. Zuberrie probed around the rusted lock with a delicate band of elements. A warning whip of magic cracked back. Pain vibrated along the link. Ms. Zuberrie dropped the elements, rubbing her temples. I found myself doing the same.

Something crashed inside the house. We all jerked toward the sound, unable to see anything through the wall. It sounded as if it had come from the kitchen. A moment later, crackles and pops rang out across the room. A high mewling and chattering chirps followed, the gryphonette's distress muffled through the walls. I ground my teeth. Waiting out here, impotent to help, grated.

The house fell silent, and I glanced hopefully toward the open window, but the kit didn't appear.

"Did you test the lock itself, not around it?" I asked.

"What are you thinking?" Kylie asked.

I reached into my skirt pocket and pulled out three seed crystals. "If a key is all we need, then let's make one."

11

An ominous silence radiated from the house as we changed positions. I took point, with Ms. Zuberrie and Kylie close behind me. The two women remained linked, but I dropped out. I wanted to dedicate my full concentration to the delicate task I had set for myself. Kylie wrapped us in a five-layer ward that would have done the FPD proud, even if it was tight enough to squeeze us into each other's elbows. Any larger, and her magic—and therefore, the ward—weakened, which was why Oliver and Quinn stood across the yard, near the shed. Neither of them were happy about their location. I tried to convince Ms. Zuberrie and Kylie to wait with them, but they both insisted on being close enough to see if they needed to intervene. Considering the volatility of the spells on this house, I conceded they might be right; a few seconds of delayed reaction could be the difference between the gryphonette's and my safety and our deaths.

"Ready?" I asked. I floated a bar of connected seed crystals outside the ward, holding it level with the lock.

"Ready," Kylie said.

Sinking quartz-tuned earth element into the crystal felt as natural as breathing. Picturing a key in my mind, I squeezed the clear rod and shaved the bottom into a level line. Ever so gently, I nudged the generic form up against the lock.

"Here we go." I mentally crossed my fingers for luck.

Kylie's ward tightened, sprouting yet another layer of protection. I didn't protest. If not for her and Ms. Zuberrie at my back, I wouldn't have risked this.

Rather than push the quartz into the lock, I stretched the tip, treating the solid stone like water. It melted into the rusted lock. Resistance from a tumbler pushed back, and I firmed up the crystal. A soft snick inside the bolt had us all holding our breath.

"Easy does it," Ms. Zuberrie said.

I let out a shaky breath and trickled more magic into my quartz key. The next tumbler clicked into place, lower than the first. I tried turning the lock. It didn't budge. Blindly, I melted the quartz deeper into the rusted channel. A third tumbler snapped home. The lock rocked to the side, loose. Tweaking my magic, I solidified the quartz into the shape of the key, holding the tumblers open. With a twist of air, the lock ground open.

The door shifted on its hinges. I flinched, jostling Ms. Zuberrie and Kylie.

But the attack I anticipated never came; the spells around the door's frame failed to activate.

"That's quite an interesting skill," Ms. Zuberrie said, her tone unreadable.

"Truly, Mika." The speculation in Kylie's tone was much easier to interpret.

"Kylie, I can hear those ideas forming, and they're all bad," Ms. Zuberrie said.

"I'm only intrigued. In the name of research."

I kept my gaze locked on the sliver of an opening. I didn't expect the gryphonette to burst out with us so close to the doorway, but scared animals were unpredictable.

Rotting wood crumbled in the corner of the threshold, and the boards beyond appeared hardly more solid. Cautiously, I nudged the door with a puff of air. It swung halfway inward with a creak. When nothing burst into flames or tried to hack us to pieces, Kylie let the ward drop. We tiptoed forward.

A cracked stone countertop butted against the wall to our left, open shelves beneath and a rusty sink basin completing the bare-bones kitchen. The sunlight spilling through the open doorway did the abandoned armchair no favors. Grime coated the armrests and smeared the front, and a permanent butt imprint puckered the threadbare seat. Only the side panel retained a hint of its original shamrock green, the rest faded to a color more consistent with a year-old pickle. Stains marred the pockmarked wooden floorboards, sketching out the location of missing furniture.

"Do you see the gryphonette?" Oliver asked, creeping up softly behind us.

"Not from here," I whispered. The door blocked my view into the bathroom and the right corner of the house, plus I couldn't see under the bottom shelves in the kitchen. The chair and the lumpy pile of fabric against the far wall could have hidden a tiny scared gryphonette, too.

"Those floors won't hold Oliver or me," Quinn said, peering around Kylie.

"They might not even hold us humans," Kylie said.

"I'll go in alone," Ms. Zuberrie said.

"This place could be rigged with traps. No one goes in alone," I said.

Kylie nodded firmly. "Mika's right. I'll stay out here, keeping a net over the broken window. But you two need to watch each other's backs."

Kylie and Ms. Zuberrie disbanded their link, and Ms. Zuberrie and I formed a new one. I handed control to my landlady. She had more experience detecting and dealing with malicious spells, as she had proven. Kylie tugged a cloth napkin from her pocket and handed it to me. It wasn't until I felt the lumpy shapes within that I remembered the cookies she had nabbed from our duplicitous gift basket for Ms. Cartwright.

"These might help convince the kit we're friends," she said.

"Good thinking," Ms. Zuberrie said. "We'll shut the door behind us so it can't come out this way. Are you ready if the gryphonette bolts your direction?"

Kylie double-checked her air net and nodded.

Oliver planted himself two feet from the door, curled his tail around his back feet, and sat. "I'll be right here if you need me," he said.

"Thank you." I stroked my fingers down his glossy scales, wishing he could enter the house with me while also feeling grateful he would be safe outside.

Ms. Zuberrie formed a test pentagram and floated it through the doorway. It wavered when it got close to the frame but otherwise remained stable. With two fingers, Ms. Zuberrie pushed the center of the door. It swung fully open, thumped against the bathroom wall, and held. She swept the pentagram back and forth over the floor, the ceiling, then the kitchen shelves. Satisfied, she stepped over the threshold. The floorboards creaked beneath her boots.

I stepped inside, dropping to a crouch to peer under the shelves. Dust balls and chunks of dehydrated and blackened food hid among the shadows, but not a gryphonette. When Ms. Zuberrie took another step forward, I minced after her.

"The sink has a prank spell on it," Ms. Zuberrie whispered. "There's a false board here. Don't step on it. I don't want to know what's under it. Stand over there."

I inched sideways. Ms. Zuberrie gently hooked the door. It swung shut with a prolonged creak, enclosing us in the sinister shanty.

The musty odor of mildew and rot hung in the stagnant air. Breathing shallowly, I squinted to make out details in the relative gloom. The high windows might have made the house more defensible, but the lack of sunlight lent a depressing atmosphere to an already dismal interior.

Ms. Zuberrie kept the test pentagram in motion, sweeping it toward the bathroom door. When it crossed the threshold without wavering, she stepped forward to peer into the cramped room.

"Ugh. People are disgusting," she muttered, backing away. "No gryphonette in there, thank goodness."

Together, we tiptoed to look beyond the bathroom wall. The house groaned with each step, the ceiling echoing the sentiment with reciprocal creaks. A small cast-iron stove squatted in the corner atop a square of ash-colored bricks. The gryphonette huddled in the slender gap between the bricks and the stove. We both stopped in our tracks.

"There you are. It's all right, little one," Ms. Zuberrie coaxed. She floated her test pentagram across the room. It flickered alarmingly as a hidden spell tugged at the wood and fire spokes of the star. Ms. Zuberrie pushed the penta-gram left, around the trap. This time, the elemental star remained stable.

"An air net is our best option," Ms. Zuberrie said in a singsong voice projected to soothe the baby. "If we can cage it and get it to safety, then we can worry about our next step."

The gryphonette's eyes glimmered in the faint light, gold-rimmed irises perfectly round as they tracked the pentagram. The closer it drew, the more the gryphonette shrank into the shadows.

"Hang on," I said. "I think it's going to—"

The kit burst from beneath the stove. Scrabbling for traction, it skidded across the stained floor, shot wide around us, and slid out of sight under the armchair. Fabric popped beneath the gryphonette's claws. A spring twanged, then all fell silent.

"Shoot. It's so fast." Ms. Zuberrie thumped her fist on her thigh. "I didn't want to drop a net on it and risk hurting it or hitting a trap I haven't detected."

"What about the chair? Is it rigged with anything nasty?" I squatted, gathering my skirt close to my legs so it wouldn't drag on the filthy floor. The gryphonette's shadow moved beneath the armchair, but I couldn't see enough of the kit to determine which way it faced or if it had gotten snared in something we couldn't see.

Ms. Zuberrie let the pentagram by the stove dissipate and formed a new one closer to us. She swept the floor between us and the chair first, then spiraled the pentagram around the chair.

"It appears safe." Ms. Zuberrie twisted her fingers into her skirt, worry pinching her pale brows. "I can try our earlier tactic: surround the chair with an air net and push the gryphonette out." From her tone, she wasn't excited about the strategy.

Neither was I. The poor kit was scared enough without us dragging it into the light.

"Let me try luring it out." I drew the remaining seed crystals from my pocket, showing them to Ms. Zuberrie.

She nodded and relinquished control of the link to me. I selected a pale aventurine seed and let the others drop back into my pocket. Slicing it in half, I reshaped one portion into a lightweight grape-sized ball. I could have expanded the globe larger, but I wanted it proportional to the gryphonette. Plus, I didn't want to chance the ornament breaking and hurting the kit—again. With intentional pulses of air, I forced bubbles into the interior of the quartz. When I held the miniature ornament up to the light, the bubbles sparkled. With our combined magic and Oliver's and Quinn's enhancements, the entire process had taken mere seconds.

"Get ready with a net." I pocketed the unused half of the seed and handed control of the link back to Ms. Zuberrie.

Ever so gently, I set the aventurine toy rolling across the floor toward the chair. In the silence, the tiny crystal's friction against the wooden boards resonated as loud as a croquet ball, the hollow house amplifying the sound.

The armchair skirt fluttered. Golden eyes peeked out beneath the hem, darting from Ms. Zuberrie and me to the rolling quartz.

Ms. Zuberrie nudged the ornament, altering its path away from the chair. The gryphonette's pupils widened, tracking the crystal. Ms. Zuberrie gave the ball another nudge, spinning it in a new direction. The gryphonette released a peep and darted from shelter. Tiny kitten paws pounced on the ornament. In a flash, the kit scooped up the ball between its front paws, using its stubby wings for balance as it spun back toward the chair with its prize. Before it could retreat out of sight, it bounced off a puffy net of air Ms. Zuberrie had gently lowered over it.

The gryphonette spun in a breathless circle, testing its cage. Realizing it was caught, it hunkered its belly to the floor. Big eyes blinked at us. Twin ears, little more than delicate tufts of feathers, flattened to its head. Its pitiful mewl broke my heart.

"Easy, it's all right," I soothed.

The gryphonette's speckled brown fur hadn't finished filling out, giving it a static-charged appearance. Judging by the growth of its primary feathers, it couldn't have been more than a few weeks old. Far too young to be on its own.

I retrieved the cookies from my pocket and broke off a hunk. I started to creep forward, but I caught sight of Ms. Zuberrie's face. She stared at the kit with tears glistening in her eyes and a tremulous smile curving her lips. I recognized that look: it was love at first sight.

"Here," I whispered, handing the napkin and its cookie contents to Ms. Zuberrie.

She accepted them blindly, never taking her eyes from the gryphonette. Kneeling on the grubby floor, she extended a piece of cookie toward the kit. It cowered as far away from Ms. Zuberrie as it could get, but its eyes slid toward the cookie. She set the offering on the floor and pulled her hand back. A pulse of magic extended the net to include the cookie.

"You're going to be all right now," she said, sitting back on her heels.

Neither of us moved for a full minute, waiting for the gryphonette to take the first step. It sniffed the air. On quivering paws, it slunk toward the cookie, one foot sliding the ornament along with it. Striking fast as a snake, it snatched up the mouthful in its beak and retreated. Ms. Zuberrie let it backtrack half the distance it had covered before she brought it up short with the net.

Three more times, she repeated the morsel drop and retreat. Each time, the gryphonette grew bolder, until the last time, it didn't wait for Ms. Zuberrie to sit back before rushing forward to scarf down the cookie.

"See? We just want to be your friends," Ms. Zuberrie said. She dropped another crumb, this time leaving her hand inside the net.

The gryphonette approached slowly, ears flicking forward and back, owl head lifting and lowering in nervous circles. It plucked the cookie from the floor, eyes locked on Ms. Zuberrie's fingers. Slowly, she reached for the gryphonette. It froze, beak in the air. Ms. Zuberrie ran her fingers down its side, crooning her praise at the gryphonette's cunning and bravery. The kit held still as if mesmerized. When Ms. Zuberrie scratched the base of its neck, its eyes fluttered shut, then sprang open.

"That's it. You're safe now."

Gradually, the gryphonette relaxed into Ms. Zuberrie's touch, unleashing a raspy purr. Another cookie bribe, and it climbed onto her palm, still clinging to the green seed crystal. The tiny kit fit in her hand.

Ms. Zuberrie cautiously lifted the gryphonette. Cradling it to her chest, she kept a loose air net around it. If the gryphonette attempted an escape jump, her magic would catch it.

"Do you have a little cut there?" she asked in the same soothing tone, examining the kit's front paw. "It's shallow, Mika. Nothing to alarm your healer sensibilities." She shot me a teasing look, but her gaze barely skimmed off me before being drawn back to the gryphonette.

I resisted the urge to reach for the kit and see for myself. Not only would that alarm the baby gryphonette, but I also didn't know how to heal a flesh-and-blood animal. The bleeding seemed to have stopped, and the kit wasn't favoring its foot. We would get an animal healer to look at it, but it could wait.

The kit sank its claws into Ms. Zuberrie's coat sleeve and tipped its head up to look at her. Blinking its enormous eyes, it chirped imploringly. Ms. Zuberrie chuckled and fed the gryphonette the last of the cookies. When she met my gaze, tears glistened on her cheeks, but her expression radiated pure happiness.

Quinn, Kylie, and Oliver rushed forward when I held the door open for Ms. Zuberrie. We stepped into the sunlight, and I took a deep, cleansing breath of fresh air. Carefully, I let the door shut behind me and retrieved my improvised quartz key.

"Did you find—?" Kylie's question died when the front of Ms. Zuberrie's coat writhed.

A tiny owl face peeked out of the V of her coat. Golden eyes darted from Kylie to Quinn to Oliver, then skyward. For a second, I thought the gryphonette might attempt to bolt. Ms. Zuberrie petted its head between its tiny ears, her other hand wrapped around her ribs to support the kit's body. The gryphonette sighed, its eyes blinking sleepily.

"Everyone, meet Bandit, the newest member of our family," Ms. Zuberrie said.

Kylie, Oliver, and Quinn cooed over the adorable, filthy, perfect solstice gift. Unalarmed by the fuss, Bandit nodded off, safe and warm next to Ms. Zuberrie's heart.

THE MISTLETOE CROWN

TERRA HAVEN HOLIDAY CHRONICLES
(BOOK 2)

1

The Central City Coliseum vibrated with sound and color, all five tiers of seating filled to capacity with jovial winter solstice revelers. Snow squeaked beneath my boots as I spun in a half circle, intimidated by how much larger the stadium looked from the arena floor. My stomach took a dive toward my toes, then bounced back into place, nerves and excitement vying for dominance. I had dreamed of this moment every year for as long as I could remember, and now it was happening. Tonight, I competed in the Darling Dearest Derby with my fiancé.

I squeezed Grant's hand, grinning up at him. We wore derby-provided uniforms—matching shapeless tunics and pants dyed a shade of chartreuse typically reserved for semaphore flags. Even Grant, with his warrior physique, an early-evening dusting of scruff shadowing his firm jaw, and a summer tan still gracing his face and neck, managed to appear sickly in the contestants' garb. I could only imagine how ghoulish my pale face and blond hair looked above the lime-hued tunic.

The thought widened my smile. I enjoyed an excuse to dress up, like I had for the solstice party I threw with Mika and my landlady, Josephine, earlier today. Plus, any excuse to see Grant bedecked in refined attire wasn't to be missed. The man turned heads daily in his Federal Pentagon Defense uniform, but in cobalt pants and a tailored waistcoat, he stole my breath. This was our first year celebrating the winter solstice together, and hosting a party with Grant at my side had been surreal and wonderful in every way. But none of it topped the delicious anticipation of the challenge ahead of us or this nervous-excited feeling of battle readiness with Grant at my side. If we looked hideous while competing, well, that was part of the humor of the derby.

I shuffled my feet, then bounced on my toes. Energy radiated from the crowd with near-tangible force. I found it impossible to stand still, like Grant. Besides, moving pressed my legs into the knee-high snow, and I welcomed the cold that seeped through my thin pants.

"Winning is all about how we work together," I said, nerves making me state the obvious as I studied the line of contestants stretched to either side of us.

Nineteen other couples were primed and prepped to compete in tonight's derby. Ranging in age from late teens to early forties, the majority of our competition looked energetic and fit. Even the softest couples couldn't be dismissed, though. The derby had a way of leveling the playing field, and the youngest didn't always have an advantage.

"We shouldn't have a problem, Kylie," Grant said. "We're a great team."

"True, but the artisans aren't going to make it easy for—"

A long, clear trumpet note pierced the air, cutting me off. My stomach flipped. We were starting.

I spun to face the rear of the arena, where a massive

snow-field-painted curtain provided a backdrop for tonight's derby. The fabric split along an invisible seam. A woman atop a flying platform rocketed forth, blasting overhead close enough to blow my hair into my face. Even though I knew it was coming, I ducked. So did every other contestant except Grant.

"Welcome!" boomed the woman. She performed a sweep of the curved coliseum, then glided to a halt twenty feet above the field and halfway between our lineup and the audience.

In the light of the coliseum's numerous suspended glow-balls, her platform sparkled like cut glass. The woman atop it stood, legs braced, arms out wide, as if she were going to hug the entire audience. Her emerald-green coat cinched her torso tight as a corset before flaring on the sides and back into a pseudo skirt lined with white fur. Matching white ribbon outlined her top's deep neckline, while berry-red pants completed the solstice-themed attire. She should have looked small, suspended alone in the giant coliseum, with the vast, star-studded sky behind her, but she carried herself with such presence that she drew every eye.

"Welcome to Terra Haven's thirty-fourth annual Winter Solstice Darling Dearest Derby," she yelled, her voice spell-amplified to carry to the highest seats.

The crowd erupted into cheers. I swayed onto my heels at the surprising volume. The announcer ate up the exuberance.

"You all know who I am, right? I'm the . . ." The woman paused, leaning forward with a hand cupped to her ear.

"*Mistletoe Matron*," the entire audience shouted back.

"That's right. I'm the Mistletoe Matron, and I run this show!"

A flurry of water-threaded wood magic raced through

the stands, igniting an explosion of blossoms among potted poinsettias dotting the railing. All around the coliseum, lanterns blazed extra bright, the pops of light like camera flashes racing up the tiers. Gigantic red-and-green banners unfurled around the rim of the coliseum, the velvet surfaces painted with larger-than-life comedic scenes from past derbies: a man and woman clinging to a hemp rope, both people coated in cranberry sauce, their faces morphing to horror as their hands started to slip; a pair of men balanced one atop the other's shoulders, wrestling a giant snowman poised to deliver a frosty head-butt; a blindfolded man seated atop a carpet, his partner harnessed upside down on the carpet beneath him, her hair streaming out below her, her hands splayed as she tried to grab rings from pedestals just out of reach. I remembered the last couple from two years ago. I laughed so hard at their absurd flying that my cheeks ached for a good half hour after the derby ended.

Pinpoints of fire sparked at the center of each banner, burning silver Darling Dearest heart-and-crown logos into the fabric. Then the tide of magic reversed, sweeping down the tiers toward the arena. It built into a gust of wind that blasted across the field to stream through the matron's blond hair. The undercurrent tugged powdery snow into the air, and I shielded my eyes against the stinging assault.

"Every darling couple you see before you believes they are worthy of the Mistletoe Crown," the matron said. "But to claim their royal status, they must prove their love is strong enough to withstand any trial, their bond unbreakable by any hardship. On this field, in front of you, their peers, they seek to prove that theirs is a relationship that will last a lifetime."

She paused a beat and glanced down at us, her eyes

seeming to land directly on me. When she spoke, sympathy filled her voice.

"And I applaud your confidence, darlings. We all know that when you're with the right person, no trial is too great, and challenges only make your relationship stronger. But..." Another dramatic pause. "Love can be blind. Sometimes we don't see the flaws in the people we love...or in ourselves. Sometimes it can take an outside influence to open our eyes."

She lifted her gaze to the audience, and her voice once more boomed with enthusiasm. "That's what we're here for. To help these couples decide if they are right for each other. And we're going to do it the traditional way: through three grueling trials that will test their mettle, their wits, and their bodies! Whose relationship is strong enough to survive my devious trials? Which couples will come out the other side stronger? And which will crumble under the pressure?"

Several couples made a production of waving and pointing to themselves, miming their strength. I snorted.

The derby was notorious for accentuating flaws in relationships. It might be a game, but it also had a reputation of culling couples who wouldn't survive long term. More than one wedding had been called off after a failed derby trial.

At one point, I had assumed the derby would act as a similar litmus test for my future fiancé. That was before I met Grant. During the past year, our survival had meant depending on each other more times than I cared to count. Numerous battles with deadly creatures and hazardous magic had a way of forging an unbreakable bond. Something as frivolous as a Darling Dearest Derby should be easy for us. However, after a lifetime spent anticipating performing this tradition with my future husband, I wasn't going to let my surety in our relationship prevent me from having fun.

The Mistletoe Matron coasted from one end of the contestant lineup to the other, leaning over the edge to scrutinize us.

"We've got a good-looking group here tonight, don't you agree?" she asked. After an appropriate swell of applause, the matron gestured toward a couple near the end.

"Look at this. Young love."

A halo of light blazed into existence above a pair of teens. Beaming, the youthful contestants arched their thin arms over their heads, touching their bent hands to form a lopsided heart shape encasing their heads. Judging by the boy's acne-speckled cheeks, he must have squeaked past the derby's eighteen-and-over age requirement by mere months, and his partner didn't look much older.

"A late-in-life romance," the matron said, moving on.

The light spell shifted to hover above the oldest couple. They raised clasped hands and waved to the right, where family or friends must have been seated among the audience.

"We have Sage Roots Apothecary's own head herbalist and—*oh my*." The matron made a production of fanning herself as the glowing halo dropped over the head of a new couple, the delicate woman eclipsed by the brawny man at her side. "And her *exceptionally* muscled darling dearest."

The derby tunic strained to encase the man's shoulders and back, the seams one enthusiastic gesture away from ripping apart. He was either a blacksmith or a hippogryph trainer, and a glimpse of an anvil tattoo above the collar of his derby tunic confirmed the former. Cupping the herbalist around her waist, the blacksmith lifted her as easily as if she were a child. The audience cheered their approval.

"Oh, this is a rare treat."

Brilliant white light bathed my scalp, casting a noon shadow around my feet. My breath froze in my chest, my limbs going stiff with the knowledge that every eye in the coliseum was on us.

"Our very own Federal Pentagon Defense captain is competing today with his ladylove. You are in for a show tonight, folks."

The crowd's thunder washed over me. I hadn't considered Grant's reputation when I signed us up. Everyone would expect an FPD captain to dominate each trial. By outing him, the matron had made us a target; the audience would pay extra attention to us . . . and be extra hard on us.

Grant waved. I lifted a hand, my smile weak. Desperately, I sought out friendly faces. It wasn't hard to find Quinn. In the dazzling coliseum illumination, my gargoyle companion's citrine lion body shimmered like gold. His brother, Oliver, pranced in place beside him, the carnelian scales of the gargoyle dragon glinting as he swiveled his head back and forth to take in everything. Too large to fit in regular seats, both gargoyles watched from the end of a second-tier row in a flat area designed for four-legged attendees.

Light refracted off Quinn when he canted his head toward the woman next to him, giving her a faint glow. Even from afar, I recognized Mom's delicate features. She laughed at whatever Quinn said, patting Dad's arm on her other side to get his attention. Dad leaned across her to hear what Quinn said, and then all three were laughing.

On the other side of Dad, Mika perched on the edge of her seat. I swear I could feel sympathetic nerves radiating from her. The fire elemental of Grant's FPD squad, Mika's boyfriend, Marcus, lounged beside her, an arm around her shoulders. The rest of Grant's squad filled out the row—tall and sturdy Marciano looking cramped in the stadium's seat; his petite wife, Winnigan, talking animatedly with the people in front of them; and Seradon, not even paying attention, too busy kissing her girlfriend, Raquel.

Staying zeroed in on my family and friends rather than acknowledging the thousands of other faces staring at me, I spontaneously raised Grant's and my clasped hands. Quinn reared onto his hind legs and waved his huge lion paws enthusiastically. Mom cupped her hands over her mouth and shouted something lost beneath the noise of the crowd. Dad waved. Everyone else clapped and whistled animatedly.

Grant followed my eyes, pinpointing our fan club and giving them a mock salute.

"And a pegasus rider or two, if I'm not mistaken," the Mistletoe Matron said, continuing down the line.

The blinding light vanished, popping into place above two petite individuals farther down the line. I exhaled a shaky breath and did my best to focus on our competition. Among those the matron highlighted were a duo of female horse trainers, the head beer maker at Fifth Forge Fermentations and his stern-looking companion, and a healer with the Skyline Searchcraft airship company and her dirigible pilot partner. No couple stuck out as the obvious frontrunner. Depending on the types of trials in store for us, any couple could come out on top.

"I can practically feel the love emanating from these darling dearests," the matron said, guiding her platform back to the center of the field. "Maybe we should take it easy on them this year. What do you think?"

A wave of sound crashed over the field, the individual voices indeterminate, the crowd's sentiment unanimous: we would get no sympathy from the audience.

"No?" the matron asked with mock surprise. "You think I should be tough on them? Maybe tougher than I ever have been before?"

The audience's cheers deafened me.

Rubbing her hands together gleefully, the Mistletoe Matron projected her spell-amplified voice above the noise. "Good, because this year's artisans have put together a spectacularly diabolical set of trials."

A trumpet's bugle cut through the roar of the stadium. The single high note fell into a peppy melody picked up by a chorus of trumpets around the coliseum. My heart rate accelerated at the familiar tune. I spun toward the shadowed arch at the side of the arena, where a tunnel led under the stone stadium. A white-clad figure strode into the light. Their shapeless gown hid any of the person's distinguishing characteristics, the bell sleeves extending past their fingertips, the deep cowl shielding their face. Elemental symbols glinted in silver thread across the gown as they strode into the light, made a sharp turn to the left, and marched along the edge of the arena.

The dark tunnel exhaled another cloaked figure, a twin to the first, then another and another.

"Ladies and gentlemen, the Arena Artisans!" the matron announced.

I scrutinized the stream of disguised people. Artisan anonymity was a long-standing tradition. Anyone from a neighborhood seamstress to my boss at the *Terra Haven Chronicle* or even our city mayor could be hidden under the robes, and no one but the derby officials would know. Aside from the final two figures, both centaurs draped in silver-threaded white fabric from head to tail, I couldn't tell one person from the next.

The crowd's applause doubled when the artisans

stopped walking, faced the center of the arena, and simultaneously lifted into the air. The centaurs floated as effortlessly as the smallest human. Goose bumps shivered up my arms. The raw power of all thirty linked individuals hummed in the air. Fanning out, the artisans flew on magical air currents to take up positions on platforms inset into the basin wall.

"Our Arena Artisans design and run the trials. We couldn't do this without them, but they're not the hardest-working members of our Darling Dearest Derby." A patter of trumpet trills built in volume, crescendoing with the matron's next shouted words. "That honor belongs to . . . the Black Brigade!"

The matron's platform swiveled with her sweeping arm gesture. I twisted to peer over my shoulder. Fifteen people in form-fitting ebony jackets and pants sprinted from behind the far curtain, forming a single line like one long, sharp shadow. Twin rows of gold buttons marched from their high collars to their waists, and glossy black bars crested their shoulders, lending them a military air.

"The crew captains," the matron said.

The five tallest figures in the middle of the line bowed, including a stately female minotaur who stood a head above the others.

"And their apprentices."

The shorter Black Brigade members snapped into a coordinated bow.

The Black Brigade worked with the contestants behind the scenes, prepping them for each trial. I had seen them, or their counterparts, a dozen times, but never up close.

I was about to get my chance.

"Get ready," I warned Grant. Down the line, the other contestants—people who had obviously attended previous derbies, unlike Grant—gathered themselves in crouches. I turned to face the brigade, tightened my grip on Grant's hand, and bent my legs, my whole body tense.

"For?" Grant asked, but he sank into his battle stance, his eyes sweeping the arena for potential threats.

"Darling dearests, it's time for you to *run!*"

The matron's bellowed words shot lightning down my spine. I burst into a sprint, immediately hampered by the high snow. Grant broke into a painfully slow jog.

"Hurry up," I urged.

Shoving through the knee-high powder was out of the question. Instead, I had to lift each foot above the drifts and high-step it across the field. My arm wrenched in its socket as I attempted to haul Grant behind me, and sweat broke out along my hairline.

Right now, the audience would be assessing us, placing friendly wagers with seatmates and purchasing last-minute snacks. Over the years, I developed a good strategy for picking the derby winner based on this initial stampede. Those first to the staging area were almost never the final winners, but the slowest of the stampede *never* won the Mistletoe Crown. Right now, Grant and I were dead last. Even the oldest contestants managed a faster jog through the thick powder than us.

An unnatural tailwind sprang up behind us, blowing snow against our backs. I stumbled under the pressure. If we slowed much more, the artisans' wind would flatten us face-first into a snowbank just for the laughs.

Finally, Grant stopped resisting me and surged forward.

"Get behind me," he said.

Grateful, I dropped back a pace to jump into his footsteps. Grant drove a wedge of air in front of him. The snow parted, exposing the field's hard dirt basin. We ran three unimpeded steps before the powder quivered, then tumbled to fill in Grant's impromptu path. Grant speared a sheet of fire through the snow, melting a five-foot trail. Snow washed back in like water to fill the trough.

"It's the artisans. You can't overpower them," I huffed.

"Just testing things."

Of course.

Ten feet from the waiting Black Brigade, the deep snow abruptly gave way to a few packed inches. I floundered against the lack of resistance, then picked up my pace to catch up with Grant. Three couples staggered into the contestants' holding area after us, a wall of wind clipping their heels.

Magic snapped into place with an audible pop. The arena behind us vanished beneath a gigantic dome of opaque air and earth. Breathing hard, I staggered to a halt and dropped my hands to my shaking knees. The official derby hadn't even begun, and my legs already felt like water.

This didn't bode well.

2

———

Whenever I had envisioned the contestants' backstage preparations before each derby, I pictured feverish energy, anxious milling, and possibly some light stretching. I didn't anticipate the yelling.

"Listen up," the Black Brigade minotaur barked, loud enough to make a gryphon rider drill sergeant proud. She emphasized her order with a single clap, the sharp report cracking against my eardrums. "Look at your costumes. Look at where I'm pointing. Number one, stand there. The rest of you form into a line in numerical order. Don't dally. Don't move from your spot. Don't ask questions. And above all else, no matter how tempted you may be, no matter who you were before you entered this arena"—at this, she looked squarely at Grant—"don't argue with a member of the Black Brigade. Do what you're told, and you might just become Darling Dearest royalty."

I glanced unnecessarily at my chest, where a pink 7 stretched from my collar to my waist. A similarly large number adorned my back. Grant's tunic matched mine.

The dirigible pilot trotted to the start of the lineup. I

didn't know him, but I recognized his type: lean, with a rolling gait and a year-round deep tan. I had grown up around plenty of men like him at my parents' shipping company. His partner bounded after him with the grace of a dancer.

People jostled each other, the number two couple falling into place, then the third, fourth, and fifth. The couples with even numbers wore uniforms in an inverse color scheme, their tunics and pants vibrant pink, the numbers on their chests and backs chartreuse. Everyone looked alternately sickly or florid.

As Grant and I hustled to our place in line, the Black Brigade apprentices disappeared behind the curtain blockading the rear of the field. Not only did the canvas barrier provide a neutral backdrop for today's activities, it also hid the brigade's secrets. Anything from one-wheeled carts to bonnacons could be back there, waiting to be sprung upon us during a trial.

I sniffed the air. If it was bonnacons, they had an air net around them to dampen any smells.

"What do you think the first challenge will be?" the number six woman asked her partner.

"I hope it's nothing sticky," the other woman said, scrunching her nose.

"I bet it's something with fire," the petite pegasus rider on our left chimed in.

"Fire is allowed?" Grant asked.

"Nothing dangerous," the number eight man said.

Just to be safe, I braided my hair and secured it with a knot of air.

Grant gave the brigade crew captains a squinty appraisal. "How many people get sent to the healers during a normal derby?"

I shrugged. "In all the years I've attended, maybe two."

A lanky boy in all black skidded to a halt in front of us. A handful of woven bracelets filled one fist. With his free hand, he shoved a lock of inky hair off his forehead. He couldn't have been more than twelve, but he spoke with confidence.

"Wrists, please," he said.

Reluctantly, I held out my arms. Grant kept his crossed, his gaze assessing the bands the boy held.

"What are those?" he asked.

"Dampeners, sir."

The brigade apprentice selected skinny loops two shades brighter than my tunic and slid them over my hands. The cloth cuffs hung loose around my wrists. Less than a finger's width thick and fashioned out of silken embroidery thread woven into a flat circle, the bracelets were spelled with a skill the eye-watering color couldn't disguise.

Twin pentagrams of earth sprang to life above the boy's fingertips and brushed against the cuffs. I braced myself. The embroidery writhed, bunching at strategic knots, cinching the bracelets against my skin. My connection to the elements choked to a pinprick.

Despite myself, I lunged for magic. The elements slid across the dampeners, parting and dispersing just beyond my reach. Only a fraction of my usual power dribbled through into my grasp. I clutched the thimbleful of magic, almost afraid to let it go.

Grant grunted as the boy activated the dampeners on his wrists. A glowball hardly larger than his thumb bloomed above Grant's palm. He pushed more fire into the simple spell. The cuffs shivered on his wrists.

"If you shred your dampeners, you'll be disqualified," the brigade boy said.

"Noted." Grant let the elements disperse.

I took a deep breath and let it out slowly, panic edging my vision. I wasn't helpless. I wasn't in danger. I could still touch the elements.

Grant bent his knees, leaning close so his concerned expression filled my vision. Using one blunt fingertip, he brushed a strand of hair behind my ear, his eyes searching mine. "Nothing we can't break if we need to," he whispered.

I gave him a tight smile, acknowledging his reassurance even if I didn't feel soothed. I formed my own glowball. It flared into a sphere the exact same size as Grant's. When I tried to add more fire, the fibers of the dampener quaked against my skin. A bit more pressure, and I could snap the spell handicapping me, just as Grant said.

I'm not helpless, I mentally repeated. *This is a game. I'm here to have fun. I'm safe with Grant.*

My panic receded with my next exhalation. Squeezing Grant's hand, I silently thanked him and forced myself to release the elements. My glowball dispersed into a puff of heated air.

My magic was strong, but Grant's was stronger. He wouldn't have risen so far in the Federal Pentagon Defense if he didn't possess incredible elemental control. But right now, our abilities to work magic were equally weak, almost as negligible as a low-spectrum toddler.

Up and down the line of contestants, others tested their restricted abilities. Glowballs and ice crystals and spheres of water popped into existence above people's hands. None surpassed the size I had been able to create, but none were smaller. The dampeners had effectively equalized everyone's magical abilities.

Grant straightened and tested his limits, running through the elements. Water, air, earth, fire, and wood coalesced in tight knots of magic, each the same size, flickering in and out of existence almost too fast to follow.

A crew captain clapped her hands, causing me and the brigade boy to jump.

"Don't dawdle, Milo," she said.

The young apprentice Milo tore his gaze from Grant and darted to the number eight couple, adorning the slender pair with dampeners.

"Speak your name," the crew captain said.

I jerked to face her, surprised to find a recording spell suspended in front of my face.

"Kylie Grayson."

The spell caught my words, and the crew captain tweaked the elements within the sphere, tuning it to my voice. She made it look easy, but the modification required a level of finesse hard to replicate. It was far easier to simply record all ambient noise and tune them out when listening to the recording later.

Which made me suspicious. Why was it important for this recording sphere to capture *only* my voice?

The woman attached the specialized spell to the collar of my tunic and turned to Grant, another sphere already spinning into existence. Grant spoke his name, then lifted his chin to give the crew captain access to his collar. She no sooner had moved on to the next couple when Milo bounded to a halt between us.

My gaze locked on the clay baby in Milo's arms. Its chubby legs kicked feebly. Its stubby arms waved. Little red-clay fingers flexed and fisted. A barely there nose curved above a soft mouth. Its smooth eyelids were closed, and its round head was a perfect dome. If it were human, I would have described it as cherubic. Since it was an element-animated golem with a chartreuse 7 painted across the swell of its stomach, I regarded it with a shiver of trepidation.

Milo thrust the golem toward me. I recoiled.

"You have to take it," the boy said.

Gingerly, I cupped my hands under the golem's armpits. Milo let go. I staggered, tightening my grip on the leaden aberration.

Last year, the derby contestants had been given baby golems for their final trial. The audience's roaring laughter at the antics of those tiny terrors had shaken the coliseum. Exiting the stadium with a stitch in my side, I had praised the brilliance of whoever thought to include babies in the derby. Today, I cursed them *and* my past self. If I hadn't laughed so hard—if *everyone* hadn't laughed so hard—I wouldn't be holding a golem right now, at the start of the trials.

"This isn't good," I said.

Milo flashed an impish smile and sprinted away.

I checked the other contestants. Numbered golems infested the whole lineup. We were in for a frightful first trial.

"Should we name it?" Grant asked.

"Um." My gaze drifted to the active recording spell at Grant's throat. No one had announced the start of the trial, and the audience couldn't even see us yet, but I had a sneaking suspicion that the derby had already begun.

Grant jostled me with his elbow. "For luck?"

"It can't hurt."

I stared blankly at the fake baby.

Grant poked a finger against the golem's palm. Tiny clay fingers curled around his knuckle.

"Cute," he said. "How about Easy Win?"

"That sounds like a racehorse." I twisted the golem to

face away from me when one of its sleepy kicks connected with my stomach.

"Champion?"

"Same." Visions of last year's final trial flashed through my mind. At any moment, the magic inside this innocent-looking clay baby would activate, and it would transform into a beast designed to test our limits. "What about Calvin?"

"Are you sure you want to give it a human name?"

I nibbled my bottom lip, considering. "The only Calvin I've known was a sweet person. Maybe that'll rub off on this thing."

"First of all, you shouldn't call our baby a thing." Grant extricated the golem from my grasp and cradled the clay creature to his chest. "Don't you find him cute?"

"Um, can we agree it's creepy cute?"

Light danced in Grant's eyes. "Second, what makes you certain little Calvin is going to turn on us?"

"I've been to a derby before."

"Ah. That."

"Are you sure you've never *once* been to a derby?" I asked, still finding it hard to believe. Part of me expected him to say he'd been teasing me, and of course he had been to a Darling Dearest Derby. They were a winter solstice tradition, after all.

"I've always had other duties or obligations on the solstice." Grant twisted the golem in his hands, inspecting it.

"Even as a kid?"

"They didn't hold derbies in the town where I grew up." Grant lifted the golem so its face was beside his. "Answer honestly: Does he look more like me or you?"

"He?" I asked.

"Calvin isn't a girl's name."

"Mmm. Good point. Definitely more like you. He's got your jaw."

The corner of Grant's mouth quirked. Using his free hand, he traced his stubble-dusted lantern jaw, then Calvin's round cheeks and tiny jut of a chin.

"Hmm. True. But he has your hair," Grant said, moving his fingers to cup the golem's bald head.

The crew captain's whistle drowned out my chuckle.

"Push forward! I want to see your noses up against that ward."

The magic cloaking the field hardly qualified as a ward. It wouldn't repel so much as a bat or a stiff breeze, but it wasn't designed for defense. The ward was pure theatrics, hiding the floor of the coliseum while the Arena Artisans constructed the first trial. I jogged forward with the other contestants but stopped a foot short of the magical barricade. No part of the elemental dome would harm me if I touched it, but a healthy dose of suspicion made me cautious anyway.

Grant fell in beside me, one warm hand resting against my lower back. His gaze swiveled up and down the line, monitoring our competition and the Black Brigade. When Calvin squirmed and reached blindly for the ward, Grant absently bounced him as if he were a real baby.

I groaned. Grant had infected my thoughts. Already, I was mentally referring to this lump of spelled clay as a *he*.

The Mistletoe Matron's voice floated overhead, muffled by the massive ward, as she regaled the audience with tales of last year's Mistletoe Queen and King. The royalty dais would be lit up, the reigning champions decked out in ruby-red capes trimmed with live mistletoe, each beaming under bronze filigree crowns loaded with clusters of white mistletoe flowers. Last year, the reigning champions had brought their newborn twins, the cheerful laughter of the infants melting the hearts of everyone in the coliseum. The year before, the queen and king had re-enacted the aerial stunt that had netted them their crowns.

Normally, I enjoyed this part of the show, happy to relive last year's memories while the matron built anticipation for the night's games. Now, though, I just wanted to get on with the derby. The longer we waited, the more nervous energy built up pressure in my muscles. I bounced on my toes and shook out my hands. The artisans never used the same tricks twice, so I had to be prepared for anything.

Grant bent to whisper in my ear. "Do you think anyone else has infiltrated a thunderbird-plagued island together?"

"That would be incredibly unlikely." I dropped to my heels and twisted to check his expression. "What does that have to do with anything?"

He shrugged. "You look nervous, but you shouldn't be. We have nothing to worry about from this group."

"We don't." It came out flat.

"We won't be crass about it, though. We'll make it look like a real competition. It'll be a good show, and everyone will feel like they had a chance."

My eyebrows furrowed. "Are you serious?"

"Serious as an FPD captain." Keeping a deadpan expression, Grant flexed his left pectoral muscle, then his right. The fabric of his tunic jumped.

"I know you haven't been to a derby, but you told me you knew about them," I said, fighting to keep my voice low and calm.

"I talked with my team. They filled me in."

My fingers curled into the fabric of Grant's tunic. "Tell me what they told you."

Grant shrugged. "A derby is three physical tests, usually

speed, endurance, and coordination. They're supposed to strain a couple's relationship, but we've been through far worse than anything this theater troupe can dream up."

He paused when I made a strangled sound. I motioned for him to continue.

"The arena changes. Nothing like Lunacy Labyrinth, but it'll probably challenge us."

I prompted him to continue again.

"That's it," Grant said.

"That's it?"

The first tinges of panic nipped at my stomach. I couldn't tell if Grant's squad had downplayed the derby because it seemed trivial compared to the hazards they faced daily or if they had intentionally misled Grant as a joke.

"No one mentioned the absurdity?" I asked.

"Well, it's a contest, and we're all dressed like we're color-blind, so I figure it will be a bit silly."

I gaped at Grant.

He was a warrior. He ran an FPD squad. He subdued creatures too lethal and magic too twisted for the city guard. He was diligent, deliberate, and thorough. He should have known every detail about the derby before he stepped onto the field.

I hadn't factored in his ego, though.

Oh, sparks and splinters. Grant thought this would be *easy.*

3

"Count down with me!" the Mistletoe Matron's voice boomed as she coasted overhead. "Five . . . Four . . ."

The crowd took up the count, the sea of voices distorted by the elemental layers between us. Magic swelled inside the Arena Artisans' ward. I broke off my dumbstruck stare with Grant, whipping around to face the shrouded field.

"Three . . . Two . . . One!" The Mistletoe Matron clapped her hands.

The ward dropped.

Silence splashed over the coliseum, ringing in my ears. The field lay empty, the thick snow gone, an unbroken expanse of ice in its place. I frowned. Nothing marred the surface. No magic swirled beneath the frozen field. No animals or obstacles stood atop the glossy veneer. It was just a boring, unimaginative ice rink.

A murmur ran through the audience, escalating into an ugly rumble.

"It doesn't look like much, I know," the matron said,

addressing the palatable disappointment. "But trust me: Your patience will be rewarded."

Her throaty chuckle sent chills down my spine. I leaned forward, then from side to side, looking for hidden pitfalls embedded in the ice. Squatting, I brushed the edge of the pale-blue surface with my fingertips.

"Anything?" Grant whispered.

I shook my head and straightened. Whatever traps awaited us remained dormant while the matron outlined the derby rules.

"To beat this trial, our darlings have two simple tasks. The first is a race to the finish line."

Finally, magic crackled. Twin streams of ice shot from the ground on the far side of the field. Splitting and dividing as it grew, the ice wove itself into an eight-foot-tall arch of floral mistletoe. A crystalline heart-and-crown derby logo sprouted at the apex.

I eyed the distance between us and the finish line. Even if it was a humdrum challenge, scrambling to beat the others across two hundred yards of ice wouldn't be easy.

"The couples' times will be recorded as they pass through that arch," the matron said. "And if we were trying to make this easy on our darlings, we'd leave it at that. But speed isn't everything. . . . Not when you have children in tow."

The audience surged to the edge of their seats for a closer look at our lineup. Fingers pointed and people exclaimed as they spotted the golems among us.

Opening her arms wide, the Mistletoe Matron shouted, "Darlings, raise those babies high."

Clutching Calvin by his back, Grant lifted him overhead. The golem kicked his legs and twisted his head, as if aware of the surge of excitement bouncing around the coliseum.

I peered around Grant to check the other mock babies. They squirmed and fidgeted like Calvin, restless but not threatening. Yet. One woman held her golem upside down by a leg, and it didn't react any differently than the rest.

"Each of these babies weighs exactly ten pounds. For now. The parents among us can attest that babies are leaky, though." The matron made an exaggerated face. "Which is why our darlings' scores will be a combined tally of how quickly they reach the finish line *and* how heavy their baby is when they get there. Sadly, the darlings with the five lowest scores will not continue to the second trial."

Twisting Calvin in his grip, Grant examined the golem's spell.

"See any magical flaws?" I asked, picturing a premeditated gap in the golem's casing that would cause a leak, maybe something we would need to keep patched while we slid toward the finish line.

"No."

So much for that theory.

"Since this is a Darling Dearest Derby," the matron continued, "and our darlings are here to prove their love to one and all, they must cross the finish line together. Or rather, as a family."

I shared a speculative look with Grant. This challenge couldn't be as simple as cradling a fragile golem while balancing across a slick surface. Something hidden within the ice was going to do its best to separate me from Grant.

I wasn't going to let it.

"Without further ado, let's get this derby started." At a gesture from the Mistletoe Matron, a booming drum roll kicked off. "On your marks, darlings."

Golden light burst into existence at the edge of the ice. I

stepped forward, setting my toes atop the glowing line. Grant cupped my sweaty hand, his palm dry and warm.

"The derby is a series of metaphors about relationships, right?" he asked. "Ice represents balance. All we have to do is keep each other upright, and we'll be across the finish line in no time."

"That's, ah, a rather simplistic view," I said.

Up and down the line, everyone crouched, ready to leap into action. Everyone except the petite number eight couple next to us.

"Simon, do you have enough magic to create some padding for my rear if I fall?" the woman whispered to her partner.

Simon flexed his fingers, crafting a pulse of air. He cast a dubious look at his partner's backside. "Maybe one cheek?"

She chuckled.

"Seriously, which one is your favorite, hon? Left or right?"

"I'll take left, you take right," she said.

Grant's exhale sounded awfully close to a snort.

"Seeeet . . ." the matron sang.

My stomach dropped, then rebounded, sending tingles of anticipation to my fingertips. Grant squeezed my hand. The bottom-up illumination of the start line cast shadows across his cheeks, sharpening the intensity of his eyes. His gaze didn't waver from the ice arch. Calvin, tucked under Grant's armpit, remained blissfully still.

"Go!"

I planted a boot on the ice. It squeaked and slid half an inch. Grant stepped up with both feet, sinking into a deep-kneed stance as his momentum carried him forward.

Our linked hands pulled me off balance. Before I tipped too far, I shoved off the firm ground and skated toward

Grant. He caught me, and we performed a wobbly dance. I took a hesitant step. My back foot shot out from beneath me, and only Grant's solid hold on my bicep kept me from crashing onto a knee. I modified my next step, tottering forward. Grant fell in beside me.

"That's it. Tiny steps. You're doing great."

A few contestants had already fallen, but most mirrored us, hunched over, mincing away from the start line, arms flailing for balance.

"There's got to be more to it than this." I scanned the ice, then the artisans.

No one in the stands had paid to watch a bunch of people shuffle across a patch of ice. A handful of slips and falls were amusing, but we were too far apart to topple each other. The matron had given no incentives to encourage couples to sabotage one another, either. All the elements that made the derby entertaining and hilarious were missing.

"Stay focused, Kylie. We need to build up some speed. Look at the librarians."

I followed Grant's subtle point to the number eighteen contestants. The oldest couple crouched close together, feet moving in synchronous sweeps as if they wore skates. Since their boots didn't provide the same grip as a blade, they hadn't gained much momentum, but it was more than the rest of us. A closer look at the man confirmed Grant's assessment, too: I recognized him as one of the archivists at the city library. His partner, though, had a wiry strength that spoke of a physical profession.

I gave an experimental push with a foot, mimicking ice skating. Grant matched me, and we slid several inches in the same direction. His greater momentum carried him farther, and our clasped hands forced me to bend off-kilter.

I wobbled and grabbed for Grant's tunic with my free hand.

"Again," he encouraged.

This time, he modified his stride to match mine, and we coasted a heady seven inches forward.

"Right," Grant instructed, setting the rhythm. "Left."

When I glanced up from my feet, we were at the front of the pack. Three other couples had pulled ahead with us. We had a lot of ground to cover to reach the arch, and I felt uncomfortably exposed.

"I'm telling you, it's not going to be this simple." My boot grazed Grant's, and I scrambled to keep my footing. "Ease up. It never goes well for the people out in front, not this early in a trial."

"That's it, push with the right . . . aaand the left," Grant said, as if I hadn't spoken.

"Did you hear me?"

"Of course I did, but you don't have anything to worry about. Besides, fear will only slow you down."

"I'm. Not. Afraid," I gritted out. "You don't understand how this works. I do. Rushing will hurt us."

"The whole point is to rush. Kylie, you and I have experience in genuinely dangerous situations. This is a patch of ice. Let's not pretend it's harder than it is."

"So help me, Grant Theodore Monaghan—"

"Oh, darlings," the Mistletoe Matron sang. "Did I forget to mention that my crafty Arena Artisans have laced the ice with irrwurz spells?"

A snarl of wood and water magic ignited beneath the frozen arch. It swelled into a wave, then dove into the field. Pulsing green fractures snapped through the ice. Elements flared and flashed too rapidly to track, the leading edge barreling down on us. Grant and I wobbled in different directions, trying to anticipate the magic's path.

Curses pelted the air on my right. Someone's yell cut off with a squeak and the thud of flesh hitting ice.

"Left, Roy, *left.* Your *other* left," a woman shrieked.

A spear of green magic split three feet in front of us, branching asymmetrically. It swung wide around Grant, but the other jagged line spiked toward me. Wood and earth boiled under my boot.

"Jiggling jingle bells!" I flung myself right. My feet went left, and I came down hard on my side. Skittering on palms and heels, I scrambled away from the pulsing magic, managing only a few inches of slippery separation.

The leading edge of green magic raced onward, but I couldn't tear my eyes from the spell frothing into existence next to my heel. As if traced by an invisible hand, a beautiful irrwurz fern leaf etched itself into the ice just below the surface. Earth, wood, and water magic spiraled through the frond from stem to tip and back, spinning like a dervish. As the spell built, it siphoned power from the magic snaking across the ice, absorbing the green tint along with the elements. For a second, the fiendish spell flared bright, then the color faded, leaving the irrwurz frond little more than a ghostly sketch of frost on the underside of the ice.

I scooted another awkward inch backward.

"Sparks and ash!" Simon cursed. The number eight man toppled to his butt, his thigh landing solidly on an irrwurz spell. Magic burst from the ice. Green-tinted elemental vines spiraled around Simon's thighs and torso, spun him like a top, and shoved him back to the beginning. His high scream faded comically as he slid helplessly toward the start. The irrwurz spell fizzled and vanished, its powers drained.

"Simon, baby! Are you all right?" his partner called. Clutching their golem to her chest, she tottered after Simon. She managed two steps before slipping, triggering a different spell. The irrwurz magic seized her, whirled her, and sent her along the same trajectory as her partner. Simon held out his arms to catch her and their golem when they slid off the ice at the start line.

Spells that discombobulated and misdirected were often referred to as irrwurz spells. Their natural namesake were toxic ferns known to simultaneously stimulate and muddle a person's thoughts. Those who came in contact with irrwurz plants and the potent oil coating their fronds had been known to wander, lost, for days. The artisans had tweaked these specialty irrwurz spells to send every dizzy victim back to the beginning.

Simon and his partner weren't the only contestants struck by irrwurz spells. On either side of us, people slid helplessly across the ice, not skidding to a stop until they hit shallow snow. A humorous mix of shock and disbelief transfixed their faces.

Now *this* felt like a derby.

"See?" I said, tapping Grant's boot. "I told you it would be harder than it looked." The luster of my self-righteousness faded marginally when I had to crane my neck to meet Grant's eyes from my prone position. Naturally, he had kept his footing.

"What was that curse you yelled?" he asked.

"Jingle bells?"

"Of the jiggling variety, apparently."

My cheeks heated. "Just trying to maintain a solstice theme."

"Ah."

Pretending not to see Grant's smile, I rolled to all fours.

My hip stung, but it wasn't as bad as I expected. Hitting the ice had been more like landing on a hard, thick rug rather than the granite I expected.

"The ice is kind of soft," I said, rubbing my hands together. My palms should have stung from being pressed to the frozen surface, but no frost burn manifested.

Grant formed the world's cutest test pentagram and sank it into the ice beside his boot. "It's got an excess of air."

"Must be a buffer. No one wants to see broken bones." Thankfully. I might have a bruise on my hip tomorrow, but I and everyone else would be able to walk out of here. "I don't think number eight will have to worry about her rear."

I crouched, then slowly straightened. Grant's hand shot out and caught me when my feet attempted to slide into the splits. A serene glossy field stretched once more between us and the finish line. Without the jagged green pathways highlighting their locations, the irrwurz spells blended in perfectly with the ice.

"Get behind me." Grant tugged my hand toward his waist. "I'll pull you along."

"Can you see the irrwurz spells?"

"I don't need to. I made a mental map of their locations."

"Really? All the way to the finish line?" Disbelief made my voice sharp.

"More or less."

I planted my hands on my hips. "If I'm behind you and you trigger a spell, you'll take me out, too. We should go side by side and keep a gap between us. That way we'll be less likely to both get caught in a trap."

"Or we'll double our chances of one of us getting sent back to the start and slowing us down." Grant's tone implied which of us would blunder into a spell, and it wouldn't be him. "Lining up makes the most sense. Come on. We're in the lead. Let's not lose this advantage."

Alarmed, I assessed the field. The librarian and his partner had been flung back to the beginning. Our nearest competition staggered five feet behind us.

"We should wait," I said, thinking of the target the matron had painted on Grant's back. "It won't hurt to take our time."

"That doesn't make any sense. The goal is the fastest time. The only way to get it is by being in the lead when we cross the finish line." Grant gave my hand an impatient tug.

"Oh, is that how the derby works?" My teeth should have ached from the amount of sugar I put into my question.

"It's been my experience that's the way *all* races work."

"They'll punish us if we're out front too early," I said.

"That's a chance we'll have to take."

I considered arguing more. If I distracted him long enough, other couples would pass us, and the whole conversation would be moot. But I didn't like how manipulative that felt. Instead, I compromised, taking Grant's hand but not getting in line behind him. "Let's go."

I thought I heard Grant's teeth squeak, but it could have been his boot on the ice.

"Left, then right," he said, squeezing my hand tight.

We limped into motion.

"Irrwurz," Grant said, shimmying left.

I spotted the faint frond impression a second later. Experimentally, I sank a coin-sized test pentagram into the spell. Magic burst from the frost-etched fern leaf. Green tentacles of wood-strengthened air whipped in a two-foot-high frenzy, seeking prey. I shied aside, almost jerking Grant into the spell in my haste. He grunted and shoved forward, dropping to his knees to glide around the seething magic.

His weight and momentum towed me past the wild elements. We collided, and I fell on my butt. Grant seized my legs, rolling me onto my back and yanking my feet out of reach of the writhing irrwurz spell.

"What did you do that for?" he demanded.

Breathless, I blinked up at the stars and wondered if my embarrassed blush could be seen from the stands.

"Just testing things."

Grant's nostrils flared. Those were the same words he said to me when he tried to clear a path through the artisans' snow dunes earlier, and I had repeated them in an identical placating tone. Or I tried. My discomfiture added an unintentional tartness.

"Satisfied?" he asked.

He loomed over me, casting a shadow across my face and his.

"I believe the information will prove useful." I didn't meet his eyes. I must have looked like a beetle tipped on its shell, arms and legs waving in the air.

With a gentle tug, Grant slid me up against his thighs, not releasing my bent legs. I reached for his arm and rolled toward him.

Calvin swiveled his head, locking his vacant gaze on me.

I shrieked and shoved against Grant. He grunted, releasing my legs but catching my hand. We separated half a foot, then slapped back together.

"Kylie, what—?"

"His eyes are open."

Grant checked Calvin. "Yep."

"'Yep'? That's it?"

Grant shrugged. Calvin's head twisted unnaturally past his shoulder to look up at Grant. Grant gave the golem a pat on the head. "Good golem."

Calvin twisted his head all the way around his body until he locked on to me again. A shiver that had nothing to do with the ice squirmed down my spine.

"We're falling behind," Grant reminded me.

He all but hopped to his feet, as stable as if the ice were sand. I fell twice before gaining my footing. When I finally straightened, Grant directed my hands to his waist.

"This time, let me take the lead. Just stay behind me and I'll pull you."

I worked my jaw back and forth, feeling like a chastised child. I didn't sign up for the derby to be towed around. I came here to compete. Which was why it was frustrating to admit Grant might have a point. He had proved himself more agile and coordinated. I was the one hindering our progress.

Taking my silence as assent, Grant shoved off with one foot. I dutifully clung to him.

The blacksmith skated past, his fragile partner clinging to him the same way I was to Grant. In comparison to her strapping partner, the woman looked tiny and helpless. Useless.

Just like I felt.

4

Pride smoldering, I locked my elbows and sank into my stance, attempting to assist Grant by timing my kicks with his. Calvin squirmed, his tiny clay heels grazing my forearm. I shifted my grip on Grant so the golem and I wouldn't touch.

"Try to keep still. It's hard to balance with you moving so much," Grant said.

I pretended not to hear him. Beneath the roar of the crowd and the shouts and curses of fellow contestants, it might have been believable if Grant didn't have years of practice pitching his voice above the cacophony of battle. Tucking my chin to my chest, I focused on syncing my feet with Grant's. In my peripheral vision, two couples collided. They toppled each other over, and a flurry of irrwurz spells swallowed them in seething magic, flinging them out of sight.

"Oh no you don't," Grant said, eyeing the teens gaining ground far to the right. They pulled into the lead, cutting a diagonal path across the ice. Grant picked up his pace, and I scrambled to keep up.

"Turnabout! Anchor me, anchor me!"

I startled, twisting toward the frantic yell on our heels. An irrwurz spell shot from the ice six feet off our flank, greedy vines clutching at the pilot with the large number *1* on his uniform. His graceful partner grabbed his arm and swept a leg to the side, sinking into a deep crouch. With her other hand, she planted their golem, pivoting them around the fake baby.

The pilot cleared the irrwurz spell, but an exuberant band of air magic slapped his heel.

"Tailwind!" he crowed.

Like they had practiced it a dozen times, the woman tossed the golem into the pilot's arms and rose to a half crouch, hands braced against her partner's hips, coasting in front of him as his momentum shot them toward the finish line.

"Brilliant, Morgan!"

The pilot's grin morphed to a wide-eyed grimace when he realized their new trajectory put them on a collision course with us.

"Ahoy, on your starboard!" he shouted.

I tightened my grip on Grant. With their greater momentum, the other couple would overtake us before we could pick up enough speed to move out of their path, and the ice made it impossible to change course quickly.

"Flaming figgy balls," Grant cursed, having come to the same conclusion.

He spun lines of ice, anchoring them one after the next in front of his boots. If he had full access to his magic, Grant's elemental barricades would have stopped us in our tracks. Handicapped as he was, though, he couldn't create a blockade thicker than a pencil. His boots tore through the fragile barriers as quickly as he anchored them, but they served their purpose—we slowed. The coordinated couple passed in front of us, close enough to touch.

Their agility carried them another five feet before the pilot lost his balance and knocked his companion over. Morgan fell with a huff of laughter, grabbing the pilot's ankle. He toppled next, and they both lay on the ice, laughing as they caught their breath.

I glanced away, not liking the jealousy squirming through my gut. The pilot didn't seem like someone who took himself—or silly games like the derby—too seriously. He could probably thread a clean landing amid a crowded windy shipyard or sail his airship through a storm, but that was likely the extent of genuine peril in his life. Before I met Grant, the pilot was exactly the kind of man I thought I would end up with. A man like my dad.

Instead, I had chosen a more serious partner, one hardened by a lifetime of danger. Grant had smile lines, but the crease between his eyebrows would always be deeper. He intimidated with ease, and he was proud of it.

Which made it all the more special when he showed me his softer, funnier side. I had anticipated enjoying some laughs with him during the derby, but I had grossly underestimated his competitiveness.

In the distance, the teens suddenly split. The woman's foot clipped an irrwurz spell. The frenzy of magic missed her, but she had to bend in half to catch her balance. The golem clutched in her hand swung in a ponderous arc. Its clay leg hit the ice and popped clean off.

I gasped. The crowd echoed me. Helpless laughter welled up my throat as the severed limb skimmed across the ice. It activated three irrwurz spells, got caught in the last, and pinged back to the start. The audience roared with one throat, a ravenous predator scenting blood and voicing its approval. If possible, the cheering after the initial excitement grew more frenzied.

Grant tucked Calvin closer to his chest.

"You're all heartless," he said, but I heard the smile in his voice.

"Now you're starting to understand the derby. Also, uh... 'figgy balls'?" I asked.

"Not solstice-y enough?" Grant peeked at me over his shoulder.

A smile quirked my lips, unbidden. "Nope. You nailed it."

Maybe there was hope for my stern fiancé to get into the derby spirit after all.

AT THE HALFWAY MARK, WE WERE IN THE LEAD. IT MADE MY skin itch. The blacksmith and waif trailed a close second, along with couples number twelve, twenty, and three. We had been in the front of the pack for too long. The artisans wouldn't let this continue.

"I just got a chill," the Mistletoe Matron said, right on cue. "Did you feel that? There's a cold wind coming from the west. Arena Artisans, what devious trick do you have up your collective absurdly long sleeves?"

Flashes of fire magic sparked above the artisan to my right. It winked out, then appeared above the next artisan, then the next. Bright streaks of gold and red lights raced along the rim of the field, touching each artisan before veering into the stands. The dancing lights bounced up the seats, eliciting gasps and excited applause as they climbed from tier to tier. I curled my fingers into Grant's waistband.

"What's happening?" he asked.

"We should drop back."

"Maybe we should push faster. What do you think, Calvin?" Grant held the golem up so it could peer over his chartreuse shoulder.

The golem blinked at me and smiled, cherubic cheeks rounding to showcase twin dimples. I tore my gaze from the enchanted lump of soil, refusing to acknowledge its charm.

A silvery cloud of dense magic bubbled into existence at the top of the coliseum, swallowing the racing fire magic when it arced skyward from the highest tier. Lightning crackled within the elemental cloud, visible in flashes of muted gold and white. Drums pounded a slow beat, building in tempo, each percussion echoing louder and louder.

Grant slowed and stopped, his back muscles tense. Around us, the other contestants came to wobbly stops. Like me, they watched the cloud with expressions of dread and anticipation. Grant was the only person who didn't fixate on the magical display, his head swiveling to keep track of the entire arena. The rest of us knew the next threat would come from whatever was forming within that elemental maelstrom.

Lightning illuminated the middle of the cloud, revealing a sinister shadow with two legs, long claws, and sharp wings. The drumbeats pounded faster, harder, louder, drowning out even the crowd's noise. A deeper rhythm pulsed beneath it, a rapid heartbeat that could have been my own. I recognized the creature within the cloud. The last time I had encountered one, I nearly died.

"Was that a—?" Grant asked, but the crescendo of drumbeats drowned out his question.

The cloud split. A wyvern burst into the night sky. The two-legged dragon stretched over thirty sinuous feet, with a long spiked neck and tail, talons designed to disembowel oxen, and a jaw big enough to bite a human in half.

The deadly predator beat its wings in a holding pattern, dipping its snout toward the crowd. The mass of helpless people cheered and waved, jumping excitedly in their seats. I unclenched my fingers from Grant's pants and let the elements siphon from my grasp. The vibrations threatening to rip through the dampeners on my wrists subsided.

True wyverns, those of flesh and blood, not elements and illusions, did not possess scales in that shade of fuchsia. Nor did they have lime spots dotting comically chubby sides. The ruby-red crown-and-heart Darling Dearest logo branding the wyvern's stomach like a bizarre glossy birthmark negated the last of my alarm. When the pink wyvern grinned down at the audience, its teeth were flat, like a human's. Laughter rang from the stadium.

"It's Wanda the Whirlwind Wyvern!" the matron announced. "Say hello!"

In one voice, the crowd shouted, "Hello!" Wanda dove for them.

"Hold on to your hats and your popcorn. Wanda has some tricky wings," the matron warned.

The wyvern flapped, and cyclones of air spun from the tips of her wings.

"Ah," I said. A big pink wyvern with green polka dots was an exciting visual, but it didn't add to the trial's complexity. Those blasts of air, though, would be the challenge.

The whirlwinds spiraled across an invisible boundary above the stands, the elemental ceiling protecting the crowd from all but a firm breeze that lifted a few hats and fluttered scarves. I doubted we would be so lucky.

"At what point does she stop changing the rules on us?" Grant grumped.

"She hasn't," I said, confused.

"The irrwurz spells added after the fact? And now that abomination?"

Wanda took a second sweep of the stands, huge mutant teeth on full display.

"Wait." I tugged Grant's waistband until he twisted toward me. "Did you really think all we had to do was cross the ice?"

"That was the task set out for us."

I pressed my lips together, eyes wide. Just how much had his squad left out of their explanations? No wonder Grant thought the derby would be easy!

"The derby runs on one rule: keep the fans entertained." I gestured toward the audience.

People stood in their seats—*on* their seats—hands stretched toward Wanda. Even Quinn reared on his hind legs, his paws waving at the air beneath Wanda's long tail.

"The rest of it can change at the matron's whim."

Grant grunted. He eyed the ice remaining between us and the arch. Several couples had begun to inch toward the finish line again. If I were in the stands, I would have been yelling at them to remain still.

"Then we have even more reason to hurry," Grant said, his back tensing. "On three. One, two—"

"No, wait—"

"Three." Grant surged forward.

I let go, wobbling in place.

"Come on." Grant cast a scowl over his shoulder and motioned for me to catch up. "Hurry."

"We should wait."

"Look around. We've got the advantage."

We were out in front, right where we shouldn't be.

"We should find a safe spot and hunker down," I said, gesturing a bit behind us, toward a patch of ice already cleared of irrwurz spells.

"We need to push forward. Come on." Following his head-on approach, Grant tossed test pentagrams into the ice ahead of his feet. He barely made it two strides before a pentagram activated an irrwurz spell, and he was forced to slow.

Was it possible to feel smug and frustrated at the same time? Grant was using the method I discovered to nullify irrwurz spells before he bungled into the nearly invisible traps, but he wasn't listening to me. He thought he could muscle through to the finish line. I knew better.

The distance between us widened as Grant pulled ahead.

"Wanda is a kind and accommodating wyvern," the Mistletoe Matron said. "She's here to help. So shout it out. Who do you think needs the most 'help'?"

The audience erupted into discordant yells. Leaning over her platform, the matron cupped a hand to her ear.

"Am I hearing number eleven?"

The blacksmith and his pocket-sized partner. *Good choice,* I silently praised the crowd.

The hullabaloo swelled. I couldn't tell one voice from another or even make out individual words. Neither, I suspected, could the matron. But that wasn't the point.

"Oh, number seven? We couldn't do that to our noble FPD captain, could we?"

The audience somehow grew louder. A thrill of dread arrowed through me, and I did my best to ignore the tiny vindictive voice that agreed with the hungry crowd. Grant was going to get a lesson in humility. Maybe then he would stop being so bullish and start listening to me.

"Artisans, if you would be so kind? Numbers seven, twenty, and eleven require Wanda's help."

The illusionary wyvern speared into the sky, her fuchsia body cartoonish against the star-studded backdrop. Turning nose to tail, she plummeted toward the field. Her first wing flap took out both number twenty participants, knocking them to their butts and sliding them sideways across the ice. They tangled with an irrwurz spell and were launched toward the start line.

"Brace yourself," I said.

"Push forward," Grant countered.

I sank into a deep crouch, fingers splayed against the ice. A whirlwind sent the blacksmith and waif careening toward us. Wanda came faster, barreling across the sky, her goofy grin pointed straight at us. Her head sailed past, then her neck. In a flash, her wings whipped down.

The cyclone slammed Grant first. It lifted him three inches into the air, and when he landed, his heels shot out from under him. He crashed to his rear with an audible thud. Our eyes met, then Wanda's whirlwind bowled into me. I toppled to my knees.

"Sparks and splinters!" The uncreative curse tore from me as I dug the tips of my boots into the ice, flailing for control.

I craned my head around in time to see Grant unleashed from an irrwurz spell he hadn't had time to nullify. Flat on his back, Calvin clutched to his chest, he whooshed away from me. The golem grinned and waved his arms. Grant scowled at the arena at large.

I ducked my chin to my chest to hide my laughter. Served him right. If he had listened to me—

Elements frothed from the ice and yanked my knee out from under me. I crashed to my side as disorienting irrwurz magic latched on to my hips. With a shriek, I spun like a malformed top. The festive coliseum transformed into a blur of colors. Gravity intensified, scrunching my body into a ball. Then a boot of air kicked me out of the spin, and I careened across the ice, my vision a dizzy glaze.

Gradually, I slowed. A warm hand caught my shoulder, halting the last of my momentum. I stared up at Grant from my limp sprawl. He lifted a single eyebrow.

"That was a truly wicked smile you had when I fell on my ass," he said.

"I don't know what you're talking about." Pretending my cheeks weren't burning, I eased to my hands and knees.

The field was a mess. All the front-runner couples were at the back of the pack now. Multiple people weren't even in the same vicinity as their partners. Dust swirled in a waist-high tornado on the right; someone's golem was leaking badly, and Wanda wasn't helping. The wyvern swept back over the ice, her wing beats timed for ultimate disruption. I lifted a hand to shield my eyes against a blast of dry air, waiting until it passed to regain my feet. We hadn't been thrown to the start line, but it was near enough.

"How's Calvin?"

Grant rolled the golem, revealing a scratched leg and arm, both shedding trickles of sand. "All limbs attached."

Calvin pumped his arms, tiny fists grasping at the air. Sand spilled faster with his movements, and Grant tucked the mock baby against his chest to hold him still.

We faced the ice together. Only one other couple was farther from the finish line than us. Even those out in front encountering fresh irrwurz spells weren't being flung as far back as we had been.

"Still have a mental map of all the spells?" I asked with petty sweetness.

"No need. Everyone else is so far ahead they'll activate them all before we get a chance." Grant slid his gaze to mine, his expression far too polite. "Unless you want to stop wasting time with I-told-you-so's and get back in the game."

I valiantly reined in my urge to stick my tongue out at him. Instead, I thrust out a hand. Grant grabbed it and tried to guide my fingers to his waist. I twisted free.

"No. I'm done with being towed. Now we do it my way."

"Why, when my way worked? At least it did right up until you let go."

My jaw dropped open. "You're blaming me for getting tossed back here?"

"I'm not interested in assigning blame. I'm trying to be logical. My strategy worked. Splitting up made us vulnerable."

"Then why did you do it? Why didn't you listen to me and wait?" My fists clenched, and I forced them smooth against my thighs.

"The goal is that arch." Grant cut a hand toward the finish line and the entire pack of contestants edging closer to it while we argued. "We're not going to reach it by standing still."

"Mmm, yes, and rushing to the lead really benefited us."

Grant drew a deep breath and let it out slowly. "All I'm saying is that together, we're stronger."

"Together? Like side by side? Like partners? Like *I'm* suggesting?" The last came out too loud, but it was better than releasing the frustrated scream climbing the back of my throat. "Come on. We're wasting time."

I shoved off my right foot, then flailed with both arms when I almost face-planted. Sheer stubbornness—and some fast footwork—kept me upright. Grant grumbled something I couldn't hear under his breath before catching up with me. When he didn't reach for my hand, I told myself it was just as well.

We skated in silence, tossing puny test pentagrams into our path and letting them disperse when they didn't activate hidden irrwurz spells. Far faster than I anticipated, we passed the halfway mark and caught up with the bulk of the contestants. Then Wanda made another pass.

"Drop and form an anchor," Grant instructed. He demonstrated, crouching and locking a finger's width of solidified air behind his boot, sinking the tip of it into the ice.

I repeated his spell, attaching it to my right boot. As far as anchors went, it looked like it wouldn't hold a feather in a stiff breeze, but neither of us could form anything larger. The minuscule bit of magic I held already taxed the dampeners' limits.

Wanda's cyclone spun a jagged path across the ice, skimming us. Wind buffeted my tunic, flattening the thin fabric against my chest and thighs. Ice squeaked beneath my knees. I curled my fingers uselessly into the glass-smooth surface. Grant's anchor broke, and I lashed out a hand to catch him. He slid in a slow circle around the fulcrum of my arm, halting when his boot hit mine and shattered my spell. The wind died.

Cumbersomely, we rose. Both of us looked at our clasped hands.

"You're doing it all wrong," a woman barked, making me jump. "Lift your heels, Roy. *Lift!* And what are you doing with your arms? Push as if you mean it. Put some effort into it."

"I can't breathe, Jan."

"Don't be so dramatic. I can feel you gasping. It's practically making me seasick."

I pressed against Grant as the bickering couple passed within arm's reach. Or rather, within hip's reach. Roy lay on his back, his partner, Jan, riding his lower stomach like he was a human raft on the ice. Roy swam his arms across the frozen surface, using them like horizontal oars. Jan leaned over her crossed legs to sweep her hands along the ice near his shoulders, ostensibly to assist in propelling them, though I couldn't tell if her efforts made any difference. Their golem lay on Roy's chest, wiggling its fists in the air and kicking Jan in the stomach.

"Lift your legs higher, Roy. Your fat feet are slowing us down."

Roy scrunched his knees into Jan's back, his face florid with exertion. They swept past, picking up momentum.

I shared a wide-eyed look with Grant.

"That's . . . creative," he said.

"Surprisingly fast, too."

Jan and Roy huffed into the lead, gliding along while the rest of us struggled to balance on slick boots.

Grant lifted an eyebrow in question.

I shook my head. Even if I thought it was a sound strategy for navigating the irrwurz spells ahead, I wouldn't sacrifice Grant in a similar manner. He wasn't a tool to get me across the finish line. He was my partner.

"Let's both stay on our fat feet," I said.

Grant's shoulders shook with silent laughter as we pushed off in sync. He didn't let go of my hand.

The irrwurz spells thickened the closer we skated to the finish arch, funneling us toward the chaos of the other contestants. Repeatedly, the people out in front fell prey to hidden spells, capsizing and bowling into contestants behind them. Nevertheless, my earlier caution morphed to urgency. Now was the time to surge toward the front if we were going to score in the top fifteen, but every time we gained ground, something forced us to slow: a test pentagram igniting a fresh irrwurz spell, another contestant falling in our path, and once, a loose golem slamming into my boot, knocking me to my butt.

"Merry berries," Grant cursed, snapping my attention from a cluster of people falling like dominoes into each other far to our left. He jerked his hand from mine and seized me around the waist, yanking me against his side.

"Jump," he barked in my ear.

A blur of chartreuse flashed in my periphery, headed straight for me. I shoved off the ice, my launch weakened when my boots slipped. Grant pivoted, and I tucked my knees to my chest. The number three woman slid beneath my heels, her fingers grazing Grant's ankle as she tried to stop herself.

"Ha!" I crowed, triumphant, when she failed to bring us down.

"Wyvern incoming." Grant didn't sound strained as he held me. In fact, he was so calm that the meaning of his words didn't register until the gust of Wanda's whirlwind smacked us.

Too late, I dropped my feet, an ice anchor on the tip of my thoughts. Grant slipped, then we were airborne. Gravity slammed us down. My elbow hammered Grant's stomach; my head bounced off his shoulder. I rolled aside, gasping for air.

"Are you all right?" I asked, twisting to check Grant.

He squinted at the stars. I desperately wanted to know what he was thinking right at that moment, but I was too scared to ask, afraid he would admit he regretted agreeing to participate in the derby with me.

After the longest second of my life, he sucked in a breath through his nose and sat up.

"I'm fine."

Calvin flailed both arms, punching Grant in the chin. He grunted and shifted the golem in his grip. Sand trickled from Calvin's leg to form a small pile on Grant's lap.

"I told you not to try to straddle the spell, Erin. If you had listened to me, we would still be in the lead," the number five man shouted to his partner, who was slipping and sliding her way back to him.

"I wouldn't have needed to attempt the splits if you would have followed the path *I* said we should take."

"Your path was too long."

"And this is fast?" Erin flailed her arms to make her point and ended up falling to all fours.

"Get it together, Erin. And hurry!"

"Don't rush me, Daryl!"

I cringed and peeked at Grant through my lashes, hearing echoes of my own words in Erin and Daryl's argument. Grant gave me an unreadable look, then offered me a hand up. I accepted his help. Neither of us spoke as we shoved off again.

The crowd's nonsensical cacophony coalesced into a bloodthirsty chant for number fourteen. A break in the contestants revealed Roy and Jan, still using their painful-looking human-raft method, barreling toward the finish line—right up until Wanda heeded the crowd's call. The wyvern bore down on the isolated pair, twin whirlwinds driving against them. Roy tried to control their slide, his legs and arms windmilling haphazardly across the spelled ice. Jan yelled, face red, her commands lost in the wind. A flurry of irrwurz spells surged to life, catching hold of Roy. Jan clung resolutely to her partner as they whipped from one dizzying spell to the next. Somewhere between the fourth and fifth spell, their golem flew free and rocketed across the field, not stopping until it bumped up against an artisan's platform. Jan's wail pierced the crowd's roar, instigating a second round of cheering from the frenzied fans.

"This is a close race," the Mistletoe Matron said, her running commentary drawing my attention. "Darlings ten, three, six, and seventeen are neck and neck, but the threes are most desperately in need of a winning time."

The number three contestants were the young couple whose golem had lost a limb early on. Half of the poor mock baby's stomach had eroded, and its body more closely resembled a puzzle piece than a real baby now.

"If they can keep their footing, they might make first, but will it be enough to save them? Oh, and then there's this surprise . . ."

A piercing crow cut through the stadium's din, the broken, high-pitched scream sending a chill down my spine even as my hands instinctively slapped over my eyes. The sound had been drilled into us as children, a cry of deathly danger to be avoided at all costs.

Through the slits of my fingers, I watched Grant whip toward the source, a complex spell falling in tatters around his face when he couldn't grab enough magic to make it work. Around the stadium, black wards sprang up, shielding entire rows of seats. My stomach sank, fear a sharp tingle in my fingertips.

A cockatrice was loose in the coliseum.

5

———

"It's another damn illusion," Grant growled, shooting a furious glare toward the Mistletoe Matron. He gently cupped my wrists, drawing my hands from my face. "Listen."

I stared into his eyes, afraid to look anywhere else. Cockatrices fell into the same horrendous family as basilisks. Half rooster, half lizard, they petrified their prey with twisted earth magic. All it took was a shared glance, and a person would be frozen in place, their organs hardened. Without the ability to draw a breath, they suffocated, fully aware and helpless.

My heart thundered in my ears. My memory superimposed a dark warehouse over the bright ice field, basilisks hidden in the shadows. I reached for Grant, curling my fingers around his biceps.

"Take a breath, Kylie. You're safe."

I gulped in air. Grant's warm gaze didn't waver from mine, his brown eyes calm. Goose bumps crested my scalp and raced down my body when a cockatrice shrieked behind Grant.

"Hear that?" he asked.

The terrifying blend of a rooster's crow and a dragon's roar peaked, ending in a high-pitched cackle. The eerie laughter did nothing to soothe me, but it did cut through my panic.

Cockatrices didn't giggle.

"Oh, *dear*," the Mistletoe Matron exclaimed, her exaggerated concern hitting just the right note of humor and contrition. "It appears the artisans have outdone themselves. Drop those wards, my beloved audience. This is all part of the derby, and you're missing quite the show!"

My dark memory receded, and I blinked the derby into focus.

Pandemonium churned across the ice, hopscotching from the lead contestants toward us. Babies were flung, little clay forms pinging across the ice, igniting irrwurz spells. Couples collided, and cockatrices crowed and cackled from every direction.

"What—?" I started.

A golem careened across the ice, slamming into my foot. It ricocheted away, lost in a cluster of contestants, but something about it was odd.

"Was that golem *eating something*?" I asked, adjusting my grip on Grant's arm so I could peer around him.

"When this is over, I'm having a chat with those artisans," he said, scowling once more at the Mistletoe Matron. "Or her. This is too mu—"

A terrible cackle-crow cut him off, as loud as if it came from the air between us. Grant palmed Calvin's stomach and swung him out in front of us at arm's length. The golem opened his mouth, unleashing another chill-inducing cockatrice scream. Sand sprayed from his mouth. My shock morphed to horror as a cherry-red beak poked out past the golem's lips like a malformed tongue. The rest of the rooster-like head followed as a cockatrice emerged from *inside* the golem, pushing itself out of his mouth. A strangled scream clawed up my throat.

Suddenly, the flurry of flying golems made sense.

"Demented. The Arena Artisans are demented," Grant said, and I nodded rapidly in agreement.

The cockatrice flung its head back, bashing Calvin's nose and releasing a full-throated crow. Sand trickled from Calvin's face. His eyes collided with mine, and I swore I read confusion in the golem's gaze—as if Calvin were aware his body was slowly birthing a deadly animal *through his mouth*. If the artisans were kind, they would have made the cockatrice pure illusion. Instead, wood-hardened earth limned the air-and-fire illusion, and the cockatrice scraped clay from Calvin's insides as it materialized. Sand spilled in a waterfall over Grant's stiff wrist, pinging against our boots.

A cockatrice was no larger than sturdy chicken, but so was Calvin. At this rate, the golem would be gutted before the monster finished clawing its way free.

Calvin wasn't alive. Despite us having given him a name, he was still a lump of clay that happened to be shaped like a baby. He—*it*—couldn't feel pain. Nevertheless, a pang of empathy hollowed out my stomach.

Steeling myself, I yanked the golem from Grant's grip and slammed his clay chest against my shoulder. The cocka-trice cackled in my ear, and I shivered uncontrollably. Gripping Calvin tight, I slapped my free hand against his back. The golem convulsed.

I lifted Calvin, shuddering to find the cockatrice dangling halfway out of his mouth. Red-gold chest feathers swelled with the cockatrice's inhale, smothering Calvin's chin and neck. The clay baby looked like a snake in reverse, trying to regurgitate a creature far too large for his jaws.

The image would haunt my nightmares.

"Kylie, what are—?"

"Hang on." I smashed Calvin to my shoulder once more and pounded his back hard enough to hurt my hand.

Grant took my words literally, seizing my hips to stabilize me when my energetic efforts would have toppled me. A final slap to Calvin's back, and the cockatrice slid free. A torrent of sand sprayed down my tunic. The golem stilled.

With a triumphant crow that set the hairs on the nape of my neck on end, the cockatrice flew gracelessly on stunted chicken wings, landing less than five feet away. Gnarled bird feet clawed at the ice.

I swallowed hard. The artisans had spared no horrific detail, giving the illusion a verisimilitude that chilled my blood. The cockatrice's bright red crest flared in warning, the rust-colored feathers along its neck and wings shiny with water-repellent oil. Red stripes ran down its gray wyvern-like thighs and tail, a silent warning of the animal's danger. Of course, typically, if you saw the stripes, it was already too late for you.

I glanced up to find Grant staring at me with wide eyes, his eyebrows twin arches of shock. After a second, his mouth clicked shut.

"What was that move?" he asked.

"It's something I've seen mothers do."

"When their babies vomit death chickens?"

I shrugged. "It seemed more like Calvin had a spot of indigestion."

"Indigestion?" Grant's eyebrows dropped. "Calvin *definitely* takes after your side of the family."

The cockatrice launched from the ice with a rooster's battle cry, vanishing into a puff of colorful sparkles.

Before I could enjoy a sigh of relief, a clear bell rang through the coliseum. The crowd's cheers swelled to new heights. Clasped hands raised, a triumphant couple in chartreuse stood on solid ground just beyond the arch. The first contestants had finished the trial.

I grabbed Grant's hand, tucking Calvin tight to my hip. Every second we spent on the ice now would be counted against us. We needed to hurry.

With no clear path through the chaos of contestants, we were forced to skate conservatively. While we nullified two irrwurz spells in our way, the finish-line bell sounded three more times. It rang twice while we dodged a couple quarreling over who should chase down their cockatrice-infested golem. I lost count of the bell rings while we clung to the ice through three additional whirlwind passes of Wanda. Finally, the delicate arches loomed over us, and we staggered across the finish line.

Against my hip, Calvin became deadweight. Stepping through the arch deactivated his spell, halting all sand loss and robbing the clay creature of his personality. His tiny arms no longer wiggled. His legs didn't kick.

I ignored an unexpected jab of sadness in favor of counting the couples in the post-trial holding area. Thirteen numerically paired people milled in the roped-off area.

We had come in fourteenth.

My heart sank. We had real-life experience working together in genuinely dangerous situations. Grant was a warrior by trade, and I wasn't a stranger to physical battles. Yet we had barely scraped across the finish line with a time good enough to get us through to the next trial.

"Do you think it'll be enough?" Grant asked.

Confused, I glanced at him. He gestured to Calvin, and I remembered the second factor of this challenge: the golem's weight.

To my tired arms, he felt heavier than when we started, but that was impossible. I tried to assess the other golems. Two were missing feet, but the rest were merely scratched or dinged. Like Calvin, most of their sand loss had been internal.

"I don't know."

For the first time in my life, it occurred to me I might not win a Mistletoe Crown.

I might not even make it past the first trial.

I trailed after Grant to the weighing station. The Black Brigade minotaur solemnly took Calvin and placed him on the scale's metal plate. The beam tipped, and she made careful adjustments to the counterweights to even it out.

"Eight pounds, six ounces," she announced, and a young brigade member at her elbow jotted the number down on a piece of paper. The minotaur handed Calvin back, and Grant tucked the lump of clay under his arm.

The audience's screams swelled, and the bell rang again. Our brigade handler, Milo, appeared and shepherded us toward the pack of finished contestants milling near the field wall as a new couple wobbled off the ice.

The pilot and his partner had beaten us. I wasn't surprised, and that somehow made me feel guilty. Seeing the blacksmith and his waif of a partner relaxing among the finished contestants stirred more guilt. They had used Grant's bullheaded towing strategy for the entire trial, and it had worked. It wasn't proof that I had slowed us down by insisting on skating independently, but I couldn't help but wonder if we would be better ranked if I had meekly followed Grant's orders.

My lips twisted at the thought. *Grant wouldn't have wanted that,* I consoled myself. I was headstrong, confident, and capable. Grant had fallen in love with me *because* of those traits.

But maybe, just this once, he would have preferred a more biddable partner.

I made a mental face at that thought, but I couldn't shake the whisper of doubt that came along with it.

On the ice, five couples fought toward the finish line. They slid. They fell. They got tossed around by a few remaining spells. But for the most part, they powered forward. Only the number twenty woman appeared to be having disproportionate problems. She activated irrwurz spell after irrwurz spell, and I couldn't tell if she was a klutz or intentionally sabotaging herself. Four of the remaining couples charged through the arches practically on top of each other. The number twenty woman slid toward the start line for the umpteenth time. After a bleak survey of the empty field, with her partner standing to one side of the finish arches, waiting for her, she flopped onto her back on the ice and gave up.

"This is going to be close," Grant said.

A scoreboard burst into the sky, the complex display of fire writing containing columns showing contestant numbers, race times, golem weights, and most important, our rankings.

I ran my gaze down the contestants' column until I reached number seven. Grant and I were ranked eleventh. Calvin's weight had bumped us ahead of three people who finished before us.

While I watched, we dropped to twelfth, then thirteen. Two couples with slower scores had heavier babies.

When the score finally settled, we were back in fourteenth place.

My chest felt tight, disappointment over our terrible score wrapped in relief that we had scraped through to the second round.

Grant touched my elbow. "They only cut the bottom five, right?"

I nodded glumly.

"We're about as far from being in the lead as we can get. Shouldn't you be happy?"

I squinted at him. Sarcasm was an underused weapon in Grant's arsenal, but he knew how to strike a blow with it. Or maybe he was being genuine, and it was my sour mood making me hear gloating that wasn't there.

"It'll have to be good enough," I groused.

The problem was we were supposed to be better than this.

The crowd sang rambunctious solstice songs as the Black Brigade herded us to the staging area at the far side of the arena. We walked close to the inner wall, skirting the giant opaque ward that cloaked the field as soon as the last person cleared the ice. The five lowest-scoring couples split away from the pack, exiting through a side tunnel to change and join the crowd for the remainder of the derby. The rest of us lined up against the canvas curtain in numerical order once again.

I let the other contestants' conversations wash over me, grimly replaying moments from the first trial. Grant and I had wasted too much time arguing. We had worked counter to each other rather than as a team. Our passing score could be credited as much to luck as any effort we made. Maybe it had *all* been luck.

That didn't sit well with me.

I wondered if Grant was similarly troubled, because neither of us spoke while four of the brigade crew captains wove among the contestants, testing wrist dampeners and patching golem spells. The fifth captain, the woman who had attached the recording spells to our outfits, moved methodically down the line, trailed by two younger brigade members elementally linked with her. With too many people in the way, I couldn't see what she was doing until she was upon us.

"Chins up, please," she instructed Grant and me.

Magic whispered against my skin as she plucked the recording sphere from my tunic collar. A twist of magic freed Grant's recording spell, too. Cradling each in a web of air, she spun a new spell. At its base, it appeared to be a larger recording sphere, but unfamiliar twists of air and fire laced the edges, and flashes of wood peppered the interior. As a journalist, I had made hundreds of recording spheres, but I had never thought of layering earth between the air layers like—

Grant's grip on my shoulder pulled me up short of sticking my nose into the spell. Embarrassed, I straightened. The giant sphere cracked open, extending tendrils of air magic to activate the recording spheres Grant and I had worn. Instead of Grant's voice and mine spilling into the air, replaying every word we uttered during the first trial, all sound siphoned into the new spell.

Perplexed, I watched the bits of vibratory air currents that were our voices merge and weave before vanishing into the crew captain's larger spell. If I didn't know better, I would have said she just made gibberish out of our recordings.

"Golem." She pointed to the air between us. Her two assistants jumped into place, arms outstretched.

Grant ceremoniously placed Calvin into their hands. I jumped when the golem's lips parted in a soundless O. Grant tensed, too. Envisioning another cockatrice emerging, I readied myself to grab Calvin.

A smile flirted with the corners of the crew captain's mouth, our jumpiness amusing her.

"Hold it still," she said, then fed her mystery spell down the golem's throat. Fibers of earth and fire ignited inside Calvin's mouth as the spell animating the golem reacted to the new, intruding magic.

Grant backed me up a step. The crew captain's smile widened, but she didn't look up from her work. For a second, the mutant recording spell protruded from Calvin's mouth like an elemental pacifier. Then the center collapsed as the golem appeared to breathe in the crew captain's spell. Calvin's mouth closed, and he became inert once more.

"Next," the woman said, already moving toward the couple to our left.

Nonplussed, I accepted Calvin, holding him high to examine him. Grant touched his thumb to the golem's chin and applied gentle pressure. Calvin's mouth remained clamped shut, his body statue still.

"Did you recognize that spell?" I asked.

Grant shook his head.

That wasn't worrying at all.

Milo jostled my elbow, startling me. The slender boy held a pile of leather straps in his hand. I studied them, looking for hidden spells.

"You've got the golem, so we'll suit you up," he said.

"Um. All right."

Milo performed a sleight of hand, and the pile divided into two sections. The first went over his shoulder. The second he gripped at strategic points to reveal a harness with three holes: one for each of my legs and another for my torso.

Dropping to a crouch, Milo said, "Step into this."

Reluctantly, I placed my feet in the leg holes, my mind racing. What would the matron have us doing next that would require a harness?

Milo slid the straps up my legs, helping me smooth the folds of my pants before he cinched the leg loops tight. With an impersonal touch, he lifted the hem of my tunic top to secure the waist belt, then he slid two straps over my shoulders. I brushed his hands aside to latch the front strap across my breastbone myself. With deft tugs, Milo pulled the slack out of the harness.

Heat flushed my cheeks. I felt like a snake had me in its coils. I hadn't worn a harness like this since I was a child and my parents would tether me to a dirigible when we were airborne for my own safety.

"Will we be flying?" I asked.

Instead of answering, Milo lifted the remaining straps from his shoulder, revealing a contraption that vaguely resembled a gryphonette harness.

"Place the golem against your chest."

I shot a glance at Grant, and he shrugged. Hesitantly, I pressed Calvin's back to my chest. Milo laid a long strap against Calvin's stomach. Lines fed off it, and with Grant's help, he looped a harness together that secured the golem's legs and torso to my chest. Additional straps across my shoulders and waist distributed the clay's weight more comfortably and ensured the fake baby wouldn't slip out without serious help.

"Arms out," Milo said.

I dutifully made a T with my arms. Calvin stayed in place. The extra weight pulled at my balance, but it wasn't anything I couldn't adjust to.

"Good," Milo said, circling me and tightening various straps. A tingle of magic coursed through the leather lines when Milo activated a spell embedded in the harnesses, and sturdy weaves of wood and earth swelled to reinforce the brass O rings and buckles. I fidgeted with the shoulder straps, trying not to think too hard about what would require such secure harnesses.

"Here, put these on." Milo thrust a pair of flying goggles at me.

My nerves skittered higher, then settled as I pulled the goggles into place. The leather padding around my eyes was stiffer than I was used to, and the strap had a long tail when I tightened it to my head, but the sensation of goggles was familiar. I had grown up as much on airships as I had on land. Maybe I would have a natural advantage in the next challenge.

When Milo vanished behind the curtain, Grant double-checked every buckle and strap of the harness, then tucked the spare tail of the goggle's strap so it wouldn't flop against my head. His ministrations were gentle, but he still didn't speak. I racked my brain for a way to break the stilted silence between us. This was supposed to be a fun event. When I signed us up for the derby, I had envisioned us forming amusing memories and coming out the other side feeling closer to each other—and in possession of a pair of mistletoe crowns.

Neither seemed probable now.

Before I could summon the right words, Milo returned. I

expected him to hold up a harness for Grant, but he darted to the couple next to us.

I leaned around Grant, verifying only one person in every couple was receiving a harness.

"Any ideas?" Grant asked. He smoothed the back of my tunic, removing a wrinkle that had pressed uncomfortably into my spine.

I turned and searched his eyes, unable to read his expression and hating it. I wanted to talk about us, about how we had behaved and spoken to each other in the last trial, but the words stuck in my throat.

"It looks like we'll be separated," I finally said, shying away from acknowledging the awkwardness between us. "But other than that, it could be anything."

Flashes of past derbies cycled through my thoughts, and I drummed my fingers against my thigh. Heights almost always played a part in the trials. Thankfully, being far above the ground didn't faze me. It was the fact that I was the only one harnessed that amped up my anxiety.

"Two years ago, they attached contestants to a wheel ten feet above the ground," I said. "The contestants had to catch dyed eggs their partners tossed them, then throw them into bins, all while the wheel spun them in a dizzying circle. The year before, one person in each couple dangled from ropes attached to a tall beam, and they had to swing themselves to reach rings suspended in the air. The rings, of course, kept switching locations, because they were linked to energetic snow minks running around the field. The rings only stood still when their partner on the ground caught a mink."

Grant studied my expression, not speaking for several seconds. "Snow minks?"

"Like snowmen, but minks. And animated by the arti-sans." I could hear the crowd winding down on the latest solstice song. Judging by the readiness of the contestants I could see, it would be the last.

"So what you're saying is the next challenge could be anything."

"Yep."

Trumpets blared, and the matron's voice cut through the last notes of the song. Calvin woke up. His little legs kicked feebly, and he yawned, tiny fists stretching into the air. I contorted my body to check the golem. The scrapes on his arms and legs weren't shedding sand. Yet.

Impulsively, I kissed the golem's bald plate. His cool scalp smelled like freshly turned earth.

"For luck," I said, catching Grant side-eying me. "Here. You should do the same."

I stood on my tiptoes, pushing the golem toward Grant.

"After what just came out of him?"

"It's not his fault a cockatrice was living inside him. Aren't you glad it came out the end it did?"

Grant's eyes widened marginally as he processed that mental image.

"It's derby tradition," I said. "No one who has kissed a golem has lost yet."

"Is that so?"

I nodded, silently urging Grant to play along with my teasing.

Holding my gaze, Grant stooped to brush a kiss against Calvin's forehead. The golem wriggled happily. A flutter of hope tickled my stomach, dispelling some of my earlier pessimism.

Grant straightened enough to be eye level with me. My heart flipped in my chest at the glint of humor in his gorgeous eyes. I held his gaze, not blinking, reminded of why I wanted to compete in this derby with this man. I loved him, and I wanted the world to know it.

"Exactly how many people have kissed golems in these things?" he asked.

"Two so far."

Grant's eyes narrowed. "Should I be worried by how easily you convince me to do insane things?" he whispered.

"I think it bodes well for your future happiness," I whispered back.

"Fortune save me, I think you're right."

6

———

When the artisans dropped the ward, a snowy field covered the arena floor. Delicate hills and valleys of powder glistened in the stadium lights, each pristine mound a trap in the waiting. The air above the field was empty, the sky star-studded and clear. I tugged at the harness leg loops, squinting at the empty air suspiciously. Why strap us into flying gear if we weren't going to be airborne?

Magic ran beneath the snow, a rush of elements tingling the edges of my awareness. Glowing golden rings burst from the snowy dunes, sending sprays of powder into the air. The shining hoops levitated to varying heights, none higher than six feet, and they twisted and pivoted so no opening faced the same direction. Half the rings bled from gold to red, then two-thirds of the remaining golden rings morphed to green, leaving fewer than five golden rings floating above the snow.

"Gold must be special," Grant murmured.

I nodded. Aside from the color differences, the rings were also different sizes, some as large as wagon wheels, others as small as the circle of my arms. But if a pattern existed, it couldn't be seen from this angle.

"That's right, darlings. We've got a classic ring toss on our hands," the Mistletoe Matron said. "But what are we supposed to toss? Surely not our darlings."

The crowd thought that would be a fine idea. I tried to picture lifting Grant, let alone throwing him through a ring. The dampeners on my wrists would make it impossible. Unless the harness had something to do with it . . .

"Hmm, I like your enthusiasm. Maybe next year," the matron said, tapping her chin speculatively. "Artisans?"

A dozen fist-sized wicker balls burst from beneath the snow. Colored bright red, green, and gold to match the hoops, the balls reacted to gravity like normal, dropping to land atop the snowy field and half disappearing in the soft powder.

"The goal of this trial is simple," the matron said, reaching down with a scoop of air to collect a red ball. "Each team needs to get as many balls through the rings as possible in the allotted time. Points are awarded for each ball that goes through a hoop. Red rings are worth one point, green rings are worth two points, and gold rings are worth three points. For unnecessary complexity"—she mock-glared at the Arena Artisans—"each ring that the darlings get a matching ball through, they get double the ring's points." With a pop of air, she tossed the red ball through the red hoop, and a fiery 2 lit up above the ring.

What she didn't say was that the score complexity would make it harder for the contestants and the crowd to keep track of who was winning. It also added another level to our possible playing strategy: Contestants could aim for matching rings to get the most points or focus on sheer quantity.

"Now, watching our darlings flounder through snow might be enjoyable, but we've got something better in mind." With a sweep of her arm, she drew every eye to the curtain, where Milo and the other Black Brigade members had quietly disappeared.

Trumpets sang the brigade's tune. A flood of ebony-clad people rushed from the back, telltale rolls of fabric beneath their arms. My eyes locked on Milo. He sprinted to an invisible marker halfway between us and the number eight couple. When the rest of the brigade lined up near their respective contestants, he thrust twin flying carpet rolls into the air above his head. Down the line, the other brigade members did the same.

"For the second trial, our couples will try their hands at the ancient art of puppetry, with one fun twist." The matron flipped a wrist toward us.

The Black Brigade took a coordinated step forward. Milo snapped his wrists. Twin beige carpets unfurled, levitation spells activated so they floated at chest height. They were far narrower than standard flying carpets, hardly as wide as Grant's shoulders. Loose spells dangled from their sides and rear, and a single wrought-iron ring protruded from the base of each carpet.

"One darling in each couple will lay atop the carpet. Using the spells provided, they will guide their loved one like their own personal marionette." The matron paused to let her words sink in.

My eyes cut from the carpet to my harness and the golem strapped to me. I would be the puppet; Grant, the puppet master. Something deep in my gut tightened, and I couldn't decide if it was apprehension or adrenaline.

"That's right, my dear audience, today we're giving these couples a chance to feel what it's like to be their loved one and an eye-opening chance to understand their partners better." The matron's grin sharpened. "And it should be endlessly entertaining for us!"

Grant's soft chuckle broke my wide-eyed stare of disbelief.

"Have you ever done anything like this?" I hissed.

Eyes twinkling, he shook his head. With far too much eagerness, he climbed aboard the flying carpet Milo pushed in front of him. When he lay down on his stomach, the slender platform sank three inches before the levitation spell in the fabric compensated for his weight. As if he had done it a dozen times before, Grant deftly hooked his feet through the spells at the base of the carpet. I didn't recognize their design, and I studied them suspiciously, figuring they had something to do with turning me into a puppet.

"This carpet has more than marionette, levitation, and propulsion spells in it," he said, scooting forward so his head protruded past the lip of the carpet. Twin spells to those on his ankles now encased his wrists. Knots of magic dangled from the spells, phantom strings that would soon be connected to me.

"Like what?" I asked, bracing myself for the next surprise of this trial.

"Some sort of illusion, I think."

"You're right, sir," Milo said. "Just wait. It's going to look hilarious."

I pictured an illusion camouflaging my body, making it look as if Grant controlled a clumsy dragon. Or, knowing the derby sense of humor, I would look like a giant green bunny or a pink squirrel. Examining the carpet didn't give me any clues, though. Whoever had designed the spells had done a superb job of layering them, and I couldn't make out more than the top propulsion spell.

"Hold steady," Milo said. He unhooked a metal rod from his waist, pulling the shiny length from a specially designed pocket. Rings were welded to each end of the rod, and clasps hung from each ring.

Ducking low, Milo attached the rod to the flying carpet's ring. Grant sent a trickle of air into the levitation spell, and the carpet climbed higher. When he floated over a foot above my head, I shuffled under the carpet, and Milo attached the other end of the rod to the back of my harness.

A bubble of nerves frizzed through me. Rolling my head back, I stared at the underside of the carpet. The rod would prevent Grant from coming down on top of my head. It would also hold me stiff beneath the carpet.

Grant leaned forward, tipping his chin so he could peer at me past the rim of the carpet.

"This is the most bizarre thing I've ever done," he said.

"Me, too." I leaned forward, testing the harness and my own balance. The rod brought me up short even as Calvin's added weight pulled me toward the ground.

"Arms out," Milo said. He looped a dangling spell over my right wrist, then my left. A pulse of earth activated the spells.

Magic laced my forearm in a firm but gentle press of air and earth. I flexed my fingers. My hands were my own to control, as were my wrists. But when I tried to lift my forearms, the spell held them in place.

"This is going to be interesting," I muttered.

Grant, watching, nodded. Experimentally, he bent his right arm. Magic pressed into my forearm, bending mine to match. I looked as if I was trying to shake Milo's hand.

I lifted one foot, then the other, as Milo slid twin spells around my ankles and activated them. Magic wound up my shins, as comfortable as tall socks. Milo stepped back.

"Raise up six inches," he said.

Grant pulsed air into the levitation spell. I gasped as the ground receded and the harness constricted around my hips and thighs. My body tipped forward, canting at a ten-degree angle, suspended by the single hook beneath the carpet.

Grant didn't move—therefore, I didn't move—while Milo made his final inspection of my harness. Satisfied I was safely trussed up, the brigade boy swung around to outfit the couple beside us.

"Wave to your parents and Quinn," Grant said.

"I can't." With my arms constrained by the spells and dangling at my sides, my attempt to flap my hand in a proximity of a wave looked like I was trying to dust nonexistent dirt from my thigh.

"Allow me." Grant lifted his right arm and waved for both of us.

I chuckled. Since Grant was lying down, when his arms dangled on either side of the carpet, my arms hung at my sides. When he raised his hands toward his head, mine lifted as if I were reaching for a wall in front of me. Tethered in this manner, I couldn't wave like a normal person. Grant's arm movements made it look as if I waved at the ground. I bent my wrist back so my palm at least pointed in the general direction of our friends and my parents.

Quinn was easy to spot again, and even from across the field, I could read the excitement in the lines of his body. He said something to Oliver, and they both pointed at us. Everyone else's expressions were too far away to see, but their exaggerated waves made me grin.

Grant let my arm drop. Magic squeezed my calves, and my feet kicked. My vision jostled as I bounced in the harness. So long as I didn't fight the spells, the movement didn't strain—or even engage—my muscles.

"This is so strange," I whispered.

Grant lifted both my legs simultaneously, resting my calves against my thighs. I squeaked as my center of gravity shifted, and I tipped forward. Instinctively, I tried to catch myself with my hands, but the elemental sleeves held my arms loose at my sides. The harness creaked. I rocked to a stop with my heels above my butt, my body canted at a forty-five-degree angle.

"What are you doing?" I asked, staring at the trampled snow beneath us.

"Just testing things."

My left leg dropped, rotating me toward being vertical again. I craned my head back, giving Grant the squinty-eyed look that comment deserved. He grinned at me and stretched his arms to the side, mimicking a bird in flight. My arms floated up to a T, pulled effortlessly into place by the spell connecting us. He brought his hands up to touch the top of his head. My arms formed a circle in front of my chest.

"You look like a dancer," Grant said, holding the pose.

With a flick of his magic, the carpet spun in a slow circle. I pirouetted beneath it. The coliseum twirled around us. People leaned forward in their seats, pointing and laughing as the line of contestants got situated. The pilot hung beneath his partner, looking as if he were doing push-ups against the air as she used her hands to center herself on the carpet above him. A nearby couple shot six feet into the air, the dangling man flopping helplessly in his harness as the carpet skittered forward and backward in jerky motions. Beside us, the number six women practiced swinging their arms, calling out adjustments to each other—a far more practical exercise than Grant's pirouette, though I suspected he was using this turn to scope out the competition, too.

Then all I could see was the canvas behind us and the Black Brigade members rushing in and out of the staging area in a controlled frenzy.

A bit farther around, and the lineup on our left came into view. I swallowed my laughter when the blacksmith sent his suspended doll partner into a wild flail when he rolled too far and almost fell off his carpet.

Jan's piercing voice cut across the five couples between us as she badgered Roy. The former human raft lay atop their carpet, and his limbs twitched in response to Jan's orders, flopping her around and eliciting more screams from the woman. If I were in the audience, I would be keeping an eye on them. Roy was being far too patient. No one would begrudge him if he took a little revenge on his not-so-sweet darling dearest while he was in control of her.

Grant let my arms drop when we faced the exuberant audience once more. I studied the snowy field, mapping out ball locations and their corresponding colored hoops. Anticipation made me want to twitch, but with my arms confined by the puppeting spells, the best I could do was flutter my fingers.

A shrill whistle to my right snapped my head around. Milo ran out in front of us and clicked his heels together, forming a line with the rest of the young brigade members. The five crew captains jogged along the contestants, checking spells and straightening carpets that had floated astray. With soft touches, they locked down the carpets' propulsion and levitation spells so no one could move until the trial started.

I twisted slowly beneath the carpet, waiting. If not for the straps pinching my thighs and the buzz of adrenaline quivering in my stomach, this would have been almost peaceful.

While we prepared for the trial, the Mistletoe Matron had floated among the audience, chatting with people on various tiers. Now, with a final wave to her adoring fans, she powered her platform back over the field. If the sweep of wind through her coat's train and her streaming blond hair wasn't enough to pull every eye in the arena, the flourish of golden sparkles dancing around her signaled it was time to pay attention again.

Reinstating her amplification spell, the matron held her arms wide.

"Are you ready for the most brilliant part of this trial?" she asked.

A chaotic swell of noise answered her.

"Arena Artisans, transform our darlings!"

Magic whispered through the carpet above my head. A collective gasp issued from the stands, followed by a burst of laughter. I glanced up. The night sky floated above me, the edges blurred, the stars stretched and warped.

"Grant?"

"Still here." His voice issued from nothing.

I peered at my fellow contestants. Fourteen men and women hung on either side of me like flesh-and-blood marionettes, seemingly suspended from empty air. The illusions weren't perfect. A smear of distorted scenery appeared to float above each puppeted person. True invisibility spells were nearly impossible to create, but these worked just fine, especially when viewed from afar. Hiding the puppet masters only emphasized the awkward akimbo poses of those of us left hanging below the invisible carpets.

The teen woman started dancing, her feet kicking spastically, her arms conducting a nonexistent orchestra. She glared at her invisible partner, her expression at odds with the happy jig her body performed. Laughter rang through the stadium, and I chuckled along with the audience.

I almost wished I could be in the stands to watch this trial.

"You'll notice the golems are back in play," the matron said. "Along with ring toss points, our darlings will once again be judged on the weight of their golems at the end of the trial. So, darlings, remember: Your baby should end this trial with as many limbs as it started with."

A smattering of nervous chuckles sounded on either side of me.

"She's going to change the rules in the middle of the trial again, isn't she?" Grant asked.

I nodded. Nothing about a ring toss competition should endanger the golems. Nibbling my bottom lip, I examined the snowdrifts once more, searching for clues about what dangers lurked in their depths. I wasn't the only contestant to groan when the wicker balls plunged into the snow, disappearing. The artisans weren't going to make it easy on us.

"Also, I must regretfully remind everyone that the five darlings with the lowest scores at the end of this challenge won't be continuing on to the final trial." The Mistletoe Matron cast a doleful look at our lineup. Her sympathy would have been more believable if her expression didn't immediately transform into sinister delight. "Are we ready?" she shouted.

The crowd roared.

She let the sound build until her amplification spell could barely compete. "On your marks. Get set . . . *Go!*"

The carpet lurched forward. I rocked on the cable beneath it, arms hanging at my sides, feet dangling, feeling distressingly stiff. I flexed my ankles, kicking my feet against empty air. The irony of being in Grant's control wasn't lost on me. Last trial, I had resisted his every bullheaded attempt to take charge, and here I was at his complete mercy. If he were a lesser man, he would rub it in.

Grant didn't say a word, though. He might have originally thought the derby would be an easy win, but now he was taking it seriously.

I tried to relax into the harness, symbolically relaxing into Grant's control. His competitive ego aside, Grant was a good partner. He and I were good together. We wouldn't be together if we weren't. We wouldn't be *alive* if we weren't.

We just had to prove it this time.

7

Our initial snap of speed drained to a pace hardly faster than a brisk walk. I didn't need the confirmation of Grant's curse to suspect the brigade had throttled the propulsion spell, since no one else was going any faster. Like the dampeners on our wrists, the carpets' capped speed evened out the playing field.

We glided across the start line a nose in front of the contestants on either side of us and a full carpet length ahead of the last couple. Sprays of snow erupted across the field. I flinched, my nerves strung tight. Colorful wicker balls shot three feet into the air, falling to pepper the powdery snow.

The line of contestants devolved as everyone veered toward their chosen targets. Number six and number five both spun toward a gold ball ten feet in front of them. Number eight cut left, leaving the field open in front of us.

"Green ball, green ring," Grant said.

My left arm gestured toward a crest of green wicker I could barely see from my vantage point, then swung to point toward the nearest green hoop several yards to the left.

"Got it."

Soft powder walloped my shins. My boots dragged through a deep snowdrift, slowing me—slowing *us*. The carpet lurched, the levitation spell decaying under the pressure. Belatedly, I drew my knees toward my chest, lifting my legs clear of the snow. My shins remained vertical. My abdominal muscles quivered. At this angle, my feet felt as if they weighed fifty pounds apiece. Calvin's heels drumming against my flexed thighs didn't help.

"Lift my feet," I gasped, straining to maintain the awkward crunch.

Soft magic swung the heels of my boots toward my butt. I let my knees fall with a relieved grunt. My shins rested horizontally on the puppet spell connecting me to Grant, my toes coasting above the snowdrifts. Calvin's weight tipped me forward, and I rocked as the carpet accelerated to its full, if modest, speed.

Slowly, so, so slowly, we approached the green ball. Fortunately, no one else looked to have selected the same target. The numbers five and six marionettes were engaged in a protracted snowball fight to our right, one that involved a lot of flailing legs kicking snow in each others' general directions. After one well-placed kick, the gold ball sailed through the air. Both human puppets went stiff and pirouetted to face the ball. They floated in rigid unison until number six's feet dragged in the snow, slowing her. Number five rushed past, arms thrust straight ahead, as if he was braced to hit a wall.

Farther away, the pilot submerged in snow up to his armpits. His arms flailed, sending sprays of powder in every direction. The red ball he was trying to grab rolled across the top of the snow and sank out of sight. His partner must have tried to fly after it, because the pilot face-planted into the soft powder when his body suddenly tipped forward. I snorted, hoping I didn't suffer the same fate but unable to deny the humor of it. When he rose into the air, I expected his golem to be shedding sand, but the little mock baby gleefully waved its arms and legs. The dusting of snow stuck to the clay gave it a bizarre, festive look.

The harness dug into my breastbone, reminding me I had more to do than spectate. The carpet slowed and stopped, but the green ball rested two feet behind me.

"It's like working with molasses," Grant grumped, reversing us.

I tugged a trickle of magic past the dampeners on my wrist, the entirety of what I was allowed to hold barely enough to form a palm-sized scoop of air. When the ball came back into view, I dove the magic toward it. Unaware of my intention, Grant twisted the carpet to align us. My magic flew wide, punching uselessly into the snow two feet to the right of the ball.

"Hold still," I said. "I'll grab it."

The carpet ground to a halt. Reforming the air scoop, I slid it under the ball. Or I tried to. The weak cup couldn't penetrate more than an inch into the soft powder. I managed to scrape out a small divot, and the ball shifted into the hole. Switching to pincers, I shaped the air like two fingers and hefted the wicker. It lifted two inches above the snow before my dampeners quaked. The ball slid from my weak elemental grip.

"I don't have enough magic," I said.

"Going lower."

Grant dropped my shins, and I braced my feet. Snow crunched and gave way as I sank. A shiver ran through the snowdrift, and the ball rolled farther away.

"Lower!" I called.

The carpet descended. My feet hit solid ground, and I bent my knees as the carpet pushed my shoulders down. Cold powder cocooned my lower body, the chill chasing goose bumps down my legs. Calvin kicked his feet, knocking snow into the ball. It quivered, rolling another half turn away from me.

Bending at the waist, poised midway between sitting and standing, I angled toward the ball, intentionally dunking the golem in the snowdrift. His arms and legs continued their mindless thrusts, but his antics no longer jostled the green ball.

"Get ready," Grant said.

My dangling arms formed a circle in front of me, and I pictured Grant resting his palms on the carpet above me as he leaned farther over the lip to see what he was doing. My right arm retracted to my body, swung up to the side, then swiped diagonally across the snow. I grazed the ball, and it bounced and rolled down the snowy slope, out of reach.

"Hang on." I grabbed air again and punched the far side of the ball. The lightweight wicker jumped up the snowy incline. I strained my hand toward it, but the puppet spell held my arm in place.

"Good job," Grant said. "We're going to take this nice and easy."

My arm floated with painful slowness toward the ball. I splayed my fingers. A carefully timed puff of air, and the ball jumped into my palm.

"I've got it!" I crowed.

The harness jerked me out of the snow, and we shot toward the green ring. It hung suspended less than four feet above the snow, the glowing hoop tilted ten degrees off vertical. It was almost as if the artisans had designed the ring to be an easy target, all the better to make the contestants look foolish when they couldn't hit it.

The carpet slammed to a halt. I yelped as the harness cinched around my chest and legs. When my arms jerked toward my head, my fingers spasming around the ball, and I almost lost my grip. Calvin's head knocked painfully into my breastbone.

"What happened?" I asked, staring up at the distorted stars as if I could examine the carpet's spells. I spotted the faint shimmer of elements around the green ring even as Grant spoke.

"The ring has a no-fly proximity ward. We can't get any closer."

My forearms pressed to my chest, then away as Grant resettled himself on the carpet.

"We have to throw from here. Ready?" he asked.

My empty hand dropped. The other lifted out to the side and bent at a right angle. My palm pointed at the ground.

"Set—"

"Wait!" I kinked my wrist back, trying to aim my hand toward the target.

"Throw."

Grant whipped my arm faster than I expected. The ball slipped from my grip and splatted into the ground near my dangling feet.

I burst into laughter.

"What was that?" Grant asked, miffed.

I shook my head, laughing too hard to speak. I should have been more charitable. Grant was contending with a whole different body. On top of that, his ability to judge angles and distances was thrown off by his prone position and my location beneath him. But this was *Grant*. He exuded athleticism. He relied on his supreme coordination every day to keep himself alive. And he had just helped me throw a ball with all the grace and dexterity of a petulant toddler.

Still giggling, I waited for Grant to lower the carpet. Instead, he thrust both my arms forward and lifted my shins until my calves rested against the backs of my thighs. I tilted forward. Calvin's added weight tipped me farther, until I hung nearly horizontal.

Grant lifted my arms out to the sides, like I was flying, then brought them slowly together in front of me above the snow. I timed my magic assist, popping the ball into the air as my hand passed over it, snagging it.

"Well done," I said, digging my fingers into the wicker sphere as my body swung vertical.

"Let's try this again," Grant said, and I bit my lip to suppress another fit of laughter at the stiffness of his tone.

My arm moved through the same motions as before. I pictured Grant. Lying down, when he lifted his arm out to the side and bent his elbow, his hand would be raised near his ear. If he were standing, it would be the perfect position from which to throw a ball. But the marionette spell didn't mirror our bodies. My arm lifted to the side like his, but when he bent my elbow, my hand remained at shoulder height, my palm pointing toward the ground.

"Wait, look," I urged. "Underhanded. We need to throw underhanded."

My forearm moved slowly, pivoting at my elbow. My hand swung down. If I released the ball, it would fly behind me.

The crowd's cheers dipped into a harmonious groan, and I scanned the competition, spotting the source of their disappointment: the pilot had flung a gold ball, and judging by its tumbling trajectory, it had just missed passing through a gold ring.

A burst of laughter swelled from the left side of the coliseum. Across the field, a woman hung stiff as a board as she was dragged face-first through a tall snowdrift, her arms locked to her sides. Her head and shoulders drove the fine powder into a wedge on either side of her body. For one brief moment, she arched into the air, cresting the surface of the snow like a salmon swimming upstream. Then she plunged into the next snowbank. Another contestant's mistimed ball toss beaned her in the head when she emerged near a red ring. Fury radiated from her, and even though I couldn't hear her curses, I could read her lips. Her golem had its eyes screwed tight, its fists clenched, and its mouth open on a silent wail. The sight sent a shiver down my spine. I checked Calvin, but I couldn't see much more than the curve of his scalp.

My arm dropped to my side, then swung back and forth, imitating an underhanded throw. I tuned out the rest of the field and focused on the green hoop.

"Ready, Kylie?"

"Let's try a practice throw."

My arm swung. I sighted down my hand.

"More to the right."

The carpet rotated. My arm swung once. Twice. I let the ball fly. It sailed through the green ring.

A loud bell rang, announcing our achievement. That was two points for a green hoop, and an extra two for using a matching ball. We were the first to score and already off to a great start. I let out a whoop of excitement, the sound lost beneath the stadium's applause. Since most of my body wasn't mine to control, my attempted victory dance was reduced to a happy head wiggle.

The snow rumbled. Tiny furrows raced beneath the surface, scattering across the field. I froze.

Oh, crap. We were the first to score.

"What's coming? Can you see?" I shouted, feeling vulnerable and stiff.

My arms folded to my chest. My calves tucked against my thighs. The ground fell away. Something small and bright purple burst from the snow, spinning wildly. It slammed into a woman's thigh and exploded into a mist of purple chalk. She swung clear of the cloud, looking no worse for the wear.

"Your *other* left!" screamed a demonic voice.

The crowd hushed at the bellowed, nonsensical declaration. Every head whipped toward the source. A teal cloud of chalk surrounded a man dangling like a giant T. The golem harnessed to him had taken a direct hit, and teal dust coated it from crown to toes. Its mouth moved, and the horrific voice issued forth again.

"You're almost ther—arrggh!" the golem gargled. Clay powder puffed from its mouth.

"Oh no," I whispered.

An explosion of chalk pellets burst from the snow beneath me. Rapid fire, two spun into my bicep and side. I barely felt the impacts before the world was drowned in canary yellow and mandarin orange chalk. The fine powder coated my goggles, blinding me.

"Together, we're stronger!"

I flinched. The bizarre bellow sounded like it originated right in front of me. The deafening volume, though, meant the people in the coliseum's top tier had probably heard it. No contestant could have cobbled together enough magic to make an amplification spell that strong, which left only one other option—

Shaking my head, I dislodged chalk from the goggle glass. Hasty swipes of air cleared the rest of my vision.

"Is *that* how a derby works?" asked the voice of a monster.

My jaw dropped open. Those were my words and my voice, but with Grant's overlaying it. And it had come straight from Calvin's mouth. Sand sprinkled my thighs, expelled with the golem's words.

The recording spells. The crew captain had somehow combined Grant's with mine, mixing our voices but keeping our individual words. That first statement, the one about working together, Grant had said that. The impact of the chalk ball must have been the trigger, releasing a small dose of the collected words.

"Calvin's got your mannerisms," Grant said.

His words broke through my shock. I stuck my tongue out in his general direction. The air tasted of chalk, and I made a face.

"He's got your volume, Captain."

Grant laughed. "That he does."

Wind gusted across the snowy field, pulling the chalk from the air and rearranging the snowdrifts. The wicker balls vanished and popped up in new locations while the rings lifted, twisted, and darted to settle into new positions.

I rocked in the harness as we started flying toward a new target, this time a red ball. Before we made it halfway, the bell rang again. The rings whipped into a dizzying dance. Snow sprayed all around us as chalk beads launched skyward. Grant yanked the carpet in a circle but not fast enough. Pink and teal powder exploded against my thigh and hip. Calvin yip-grunted.

"Babies vomit death chickens," he shouted inanely.

"Shh, shh, it's all right," I soothed, trying not to breathe in the colorful haze. "It's just a little dust. You're made of dust. You're fine."

"What?" Grant asked.

"Just trying to keep the baby calm. You want to be calm, don't you, you little clay terror," I soothed in a gentle tone.

"Very . . . maternal of you."

I couldn't tell, but it sounded like Grant was laughing at me.

We floated into clear air. Grant dove toward a red ball, my arms extended. I splayed my fingers and prepared a puff of air to guide the ball into my hand. A trio of bells rang nearly on top of each other. I fired off my pitiful air magic, desperately clawing for the wicker ball before it disappeared.

My feet dropped; my arms hugged Calvin. The edges of my vision darkened as blood rushed to my toes. I lost track of the red ball as the world spun. Disappointment shot through me.

"I almost had it," I protested.

"You were too vulnerable."

"Put your back into it, Roy!" shrieked a golem in a goosebump inducing mix of Jan's and Roy's voices.

My legs flopped forward as Grant jerked the carpet backward. A chalk pellet sailed past Calvin's face, missing him by inches.

Chaos spiraled across the arena. Pops of colorful dust dappled the air like poorly constructed ghost illusions. Human puppets jerked and flapped in their harnesses, their choppy movements made all the more spasmodic in contrast to the graceful chalk projectiles. Above it all, green, red, and gold rings spun and twisted like a solstice light show before descending into the raucous field.

Grant wasn't the only puppet master prioritizing his

partner's well-being. About half the field practiced active defense to avoid chalk beads, manipulating their harnessed partners like flea-nipped ballerinas, much to the delight of the crowd.

The other half focused on scoring points at the expense of their partners—and their golems. The arena rang with shouts somehow both shrill and hoarse as chalk strikes unleashed recorded words from the golems' mouths. With each caterwauled declaration, red clay spewed from the struck golems. The poor men and women strapped to those golems wore grim expressions beneath dense coats of colorful chalk.

I looked away, searching for our next target, a smile on my face. My partner put my safety first. In all the adventures we'd undertaken together in the last year, Grant always had. He always would. It was his nature to protect. No other objective would ever outweigh my personal well-being.

I glanced down at Calvin. *And the well-being of our children,* I silently amended. Warmth suffused my chest, affection for a fictional future child transferring itself onto this lump of clay.

All too soon, a bell rang. The world jigged sideways, and my arms came up to hug Calvin. Chalk nailed my elbow, enveloping the golem and me in a yellow cloud.

"You're blaming me," Calvin shouted.

"That's not true, little boy, and you know it," I said, my placating tone ruined when the carpet canted, knocking my breath out in a rush.

"I'm. Not. Afraid."

Laughter burst out of me. "Of course you're not. We'll be fine in a moment. Just breathe through the chalk."

"That's it. Tiny steps," Calvin said, his words parroted marginally softer.

"I think it's working, Grant."

"What is?"

"My maternal instincts."

Wind gusted across the field, cleansing the air and erasing body prints and chalk dust from the snowdrifts. Grant powered our carpet toward a gold ball.

"Pat the baby," I said, curious if I had found a secret loophole in the golem's spell.

"What?"

"Bend an arm toward my chest."

My left bent. I worked my wrist to pat Calvin's shoulder. The golem grumbled incomprehensibly. I couldn't tell if my choppy soothing was doing the trick or if Calvin was quieting because no new projectiles were bombarding him, but I kept up my awkward pats.

My right arm flared out to the side, then forward. The carpet dipped. I tipped toward the gold ball, my toes kissing the snow behind me. I struggled to keep up a rhythmic patting while forming a puff of air.

"Almost there. A foot. Six inches," I said, guiding Grant.

The carpet halted above the ball. My arm hung too far to the right. Slowly, it rotated closer. I used my negligible magic, and the ball jumped into my hand.

"Got it!" I hollered.

Grant wasted no time spinning toward the nearest gold ring and dropping my feet so I hung perpendicular to the invisible carpet.

"Are we lined up?" he asked, swinging my arm back and forth.

"Um, left fifteen degrees. Higher on the swing . . . A bit more . . . Good!" I released the ball. It sailed through the golden hoop. I grinned, mentally adding another six points to our score as the bell rang.

A second bell sounded, then another and another before the rings lifted out of reach. Everyone was getting the hang of it. We had to get faster if we were going to keep up.

Chalk pummeled my back, three concussive hits of pink.

"Flaming figgy balls!" Calvin burst out. Sand sprayed the snowdrift, its red tint giving the golem's expulsion an alarming macabre flair. The sight distressed me far more than I wanted to admit.

"Shhh, you're being dramatic," I said, patting him frantically and reminding myself that the golem didn't experience pain.

"Demented. The Aren—" Calvin stiffened, his loud proclamation cut off.

Alarmed, I tried to check his face.

My legs and arms dropped.

"Wait, Grant, I need to—"

The carpet jerked to a halt, then reversed course, flying steady in a straight line away from the stands. I braced myself for the next chalk impact, but it never came.

"Grant, what—"

The sound of trumpets filtered through my confusion. All the other contestants floated with similar mannequin stiffness, only their heads swiveling. We beelined along straight paths toward the start. One by one, the glowing rings winked out, and the wicker balls vanished. A steady breeze swept the edge of the field, collecting wayward pockets of colorful dust before it drifted into the stands.

"Carpet's not in my control," Grant confirmed.

"I guess the trial's over," I said, disappointed. We'd gotten only two balls through their rings. Would that be enough to score in the top ten?

"Oh, that was fun, wasn't it?" the Mistletoe Matron asked the audience.

Cheers answered her.

"Would you like more?"

The stadium noise doubled in volume. A wave of fresh snow undulated across the arena floor, rolling over the chalk-splattered mounds. In its wake, pristine snowdrifts sparkled in the warm glowball illumination, as if the frantic trial had never taken place.

"I wouldn't mind a bit more of that myself," the matron said, and the crowd broke into a chant of "*more, more, more.*"

The start line slid beneath my toes, and the carpet jerked to a halt in the staging area. I waited, but the spells holding me didn't loosen. Mind spinning, I scoured the field, trying to anticipate the next obstacle the artisans would throw at us.

"My nanna had a saying I always liked," the matron said, waiting until the crowd's chants subsided to continue. "You probably know this one: What's good for the goose is good for the gander. So what say we swap our darlings' positions?"

A rush of excitement shot energy through my limbs. Grant would have to relinquish all control to *me*?

This was going to be *glorious*.

Lying on my stomach atop the carpet, I squirmed forward until my head hung over the edge. The marionette spells looped around my forearms and shins slid and resettled, not yet activated. A mist of purple and orange chalk sifted from my braid, so I gave my head an experimental shake, dislodging an entire colorful cloud. Milo shot me an exasperated glare from where he stood beneath the carpet, helping Grant get ready.

Somehow, the same harness I had worn accommodated my fiancé's larger frame, and it had transferred smears of teal, pink, and lavender chalk onto Grant's pants and tunic. Milo had his share of chalk dusting his hands and arms, too, the sharp colors all the more garish against his dark uniform. Calvin added his own grime. The inert golem hung with his back to Grant's chest, the bright lime number 7 on his clay belly obscured by splashes of pink, yellow, and orange dust. When I handed Calvin to Grant, I had revealed an amusing oval patch of clean chartreuse along my chest—the only undusted part of my entire body.

Milo clipped the suspension rod to the back of Grant's harness, then to the bottom of the carpet. He gave the ring in the carpet an experimental tug, vibrating the carpet beneath my stomach.

"Lift six inches," Milo said.

I tapped the levitation spell with as much air element as the dampeners allowed. The carpet's spell seized my trickle of magic. We lurched straight up two feet. Grant grunted as the harness constricted around him, the jerky ascent bouncing him. I winced in sympathy. My inner thighs still felt the phantom pinch of the harness's leg loops.

"Oops. Sorry." Gently, I decreased our altitude. Narrowing my magic down to such a fine stream took a moment's concentration; it wasn't difficult, but it wasn't something I did often.

Milo circled Grant, testing the lines of the harness, then looping the elemental cuffs over Grant's forearms and shins. Finally, he stepped back. Magic unfurled from him, activating the marionette spells. Soft bands of air and earth tightened around my shins and forearms.

"Test it," Milo said.

I lifted my arms out to the sides. I expected resistance from the spells and from the weight of Grant's limbs. Instead, our arms floated up with element-assisted ease. A quick wiggle of my legs—and, therefore, Grant's legs—assured Milo everything was working appropriately, and he darted off.

I flapped my arms again, marveling at how easy it was. Having all my upper-body weight flattened into the wood-hard carpet wasn't entirely comfortable, but the trial wouldn't last long enough to make it an issue. Kicking my legs felt more natural, and I hung my head farther over the edge to watch Grant's feet dance as if they were an extension of my body.

"Enjoying yourself?" Grant asked.

I couldn't contain my wicked grin. "Let me think." I brought our right arms up, then used my fingers to tap my chin.

Grant's hand remained still, so it looked as if he were attempting to hide his mouth.

I splayed my legs, then brought them together, matching the move with my arms. Grant did midair jumping jacks.

"Oh, yes, this is fun," I said, laughing helplessly when I caught Grant's droll expression. I bent his arms to give the impression of him flexing. Though technically none of his muscles were engaged, the tunic couldn't hide the bulge of his biceps. Straightening his arms in front of him, I practiced clapping. Easy enough. Swinging his arms took more effort, only because it rocked me on the carpet. One move too exuberant, and I felt like I would tip off the narrow surface. Kicking my feet helped. Chalk shook from Calvin, dusting a rainbow of powder across Grant's thighs.

"Is this necessary?" Grant asked.

"Hmm?" I chopped the air next to his hip with one arm, keeping his other arm lifted to maintain my balance. Grant's feet kicked like he was trying to run, getting nowhere. When Grant didn't say anything, I finally met his eyes.

He gave me his captain's glare, one eyebrow arched, his mouth a flat line. Upside down, the practiced intensity lost some of its ferocity, especially when paired with his spastic movements.

"Just testing things," I said, biting the inside of my lip to contain my grin.

A Black Brigade crew captain jogged past, locking down

the carpet's propulsion and levitation spells. Up and down the lineup, other crew captains did the same for every contestant. A flood of adrenaline sobered me. We were about to start.

I lifted my gaze to Quinn and the rest of our fan club. My gargoyle friend had acquired a red bow around his neck, and I suspected it was Mom's scarf tied into a festive adornment. When a rhythmic clapping built throughout the coliseum, he pranced in time. I smiled. Judging by his obvious delight, I suspected he was a derby convert. I couldn't wait to enjoy next year's derby with him.

Everyone else looked like they were having a good time, too. Mika no longer looked nervous for me. She clapped along with everyone else, but her head was tipped toward Dad, and they seemed to be holding a conversation in the midst of the cacophony. Oliver had wriggled into the foot space in front of the rest of Grant's squad, and he was chatting animatedly with Seradon and Winnigan.

The Mistletoe Matron sliced the air with her hands, and the fans quieted. Quinn stilled, his gaze locked on the field. If he had been any animal other than a gargoyle, his body would have quivered with excitement. Oliver wriggled backward to Quinn's side, taking a similarly still stance beside his brother as the matron got the show back in motion.

"And now for the best part," the Mistletoe Matron proclaimed.

Air and fire magic struck the illusion spell embedded in the carpet. Nothing appeared to happen from my perspective, but the audience cheered. I glanced around. All the flying carpet pilots had vanished beneath blurry invisibility illusions. A faint shimmer of elements surrounded me, too, but the spell didn't obstruct my view. I could still see the field and, when I peered over the edge of the carpet, Grant. Stretching an arm forward, I tried to touch the illusion's boundary. I encountered nothing, which made sense. Grant, with his longer arms and legs, hadn't broken through the spell.

"Focus up, Grayson," Grant said.

I jerked my attention to the field as the crowd started a three-second countdown. Glowing rings dotted the airspace above glistening snowdrifts. When the crowd hit *one*, a smattering of green, gold, and red wicker balls popped to the surface. I set my sights on the closest red ball and shoved air into the propulsion spell.

The carpet jerked into motion. Grant rocked beneath me, his weight adding a stutter to the carpet's fluid acceleration. My vision bounced. We crossed the start line at the back of the pack, and I fumbled to adjust the carpet's direction while keeping pressure on the propulsion spell.

The first tall snowdrift loomed in front of us. I bent Grant's legs, lifting his heels toward his butt, but he was still too long. Dividing the scrap of magic available to me, I shunted some into the levitation spell. We climbed, but too slowly. Grant's knees dragged through snow, leaving twin divots at the top of the white dune. The carpet's speed bogged down, then redoubled, and I flailed for balance. Grant pawed the air, his mirrored movements shaking the carpet and nearly bouncing me from the smooth surface.

"How did you make this look so easy?" I asked, righting myself and letting my arms—and Grant's—drop.

Whatever Grant said was lost beneath the sound of the first bell ringing. Disappointment jabbed me. I needed to do better, fast.

Chalk pellets snaked beneath the snow's surface, leaving

raised tracks like gopher tunnels—if gophers moved at airship speeds. I spun the carpet away from the incoming projectiles. I might have failed to get us to a ball first, but I would make up for it by keeping Grant and Calvin clean and unscathed.

The snow exploded. Dozens of tiny colorful pellets arced in every which direction. I slapped at the carpet's spells, twisting us. Something flickered in my peripheral vision, and a cloud of yellow chalk engulfed Grant.

"Crap!" It had taken less than three seconds to break my silent promise to myself.

I shunted the carpet right, then left, trying to take into account the slower sway of Grant suspended beneath me. A chalk bead speared toward his stomach. I slashed downward with an arm, forgetting my job as the pilot for a second. The projectile grazed Grant's elbow. In a blink, half of Grant's face and upper body were coated pink.

Calvin flailed his tiny fists. "I told you it would be harder than it looked," the golem screeched. Sand vomited from his mouth.

I winced. My haughty words from the first trial grated, and not just because Calvin had yelled them loud enough for the entire coliseum to hear.

Determined to spare Grant from additional chalk slugs, I hit the levitation spell hard. We shot up three feet, then slammed to a stop. Unprepared for the sudden halt, I bounced hard on my chest, wincing from the impact. I tried the spell again, but nothing happened.

The brigade had capped our height as well as our speed. Of course.

My momentary distraction cost Grant and Calvin. Three chalk beads hammered into them, enveloping them both in a rainbow of orange and purple.

"Jiggling jingle bells," Calvin exclaimed.

I groaned. Had I been proud of that ridiculous curse?

"Sorry!" I shouted to Grant, spinning the carpet and flying us into clear air. For good measure, I tucked his feet into his backside and curled his arms around Calvin.

"You're doing great," Grant said, shaking chalk from his hair. He started to say something else, but Calvin outshouted him.

"This isn't good!"

"I won't break," Grant said, timing his words between Calvin's.

"Your way isn't better," the golem declared.

"Just get me to a ball."

"You don't know how this works," Calvin yelled.

Each shouted criticism sent a punch of guilt through me. They were all my earlier words, and none of them were kind or supportive.

"I'll do my best," I promised Grant, feeling inadequate. "Red ball, there." I pointed, and Grant's arm mirrored me. Red was the least-valuable target, but it was the closest.

The propulsion spell was less sensitive than the levitation, but the steering was twice as finicky as both. Flying took all my concentration.

"Five feet," Grant called. "Three. Slower. Drop down."

I followed his instructions, juggling spells. Calvin had stopped shouting, which meant he wasn't currently leaking sand. It also meant the chalk likely hadn't hit him directly. Several other golems continued to spew emotionally charged statements and sand.

The snow's undulating surface skewed my depth perception. I eased magic into the levitation spell but still accidentally dunked Grant to his nostrils in a snowdrift when the carpet responded too fast. Then I knocked the ball out of reach when I failed to account for Grant's longer arms, hitting the ball with his forearm rather than his hand. A sense of urgency pressed against the back of my mind. Any second, someone would score, and the field would erupt. We needed points if we were going to stay in the game. I couldn't let Grant down.

Finally, *finally*, I got Grant lined up. He grabbed the ball, shouting in triumph. I spun the carpet in a half circle and pushed the propulsion to its top speed.

"Wait! The no-fly—"

Grant's warning registered a second too late. The proximity ward around the ring flashed into view when the edge of the invisibility illusion slammed into it. I went airborne. With a squeak, I grabbed the carpet to prevent being thrown off the front. Tied to my movements by the marionette spells, Grant's arms jerked toward his face. The ball smashed into his cheek.

"Sorry!" I called *again*. Thankfully, we didn't have recording spells attached to us now, or all Calvin would say in the next trial was *sorry*.

If we made it to the third trial.

Tossing the ball was yet another process Grant had made seem easy. By the time the red ball sailed through the hoop, sweat ran down my temples. I imagined I looked like melting sorbet, but I didn't care. We finally scored, even if it was only two points.

The bell chimed, echoed by a second. Chalk burst from the snow, pelting Grant and Calvin. I powered the carpet through a spastic dance, curling Grant's arms and legs to make him smaller. The man made a frustratingly large target no matter how I moved him, and four more chalk pellets smashed into him despite my best efforts.

"So help me, Grant Theodore Monaghan!" Calvin shouted.

I cringed. Even with the golem's spell merging Grant's voice with mine, my earlier words still sounded more like something his fed-up mother would say, not his fiancée.

"Shh, I'm right here," Grant soothed.

My eyebrows lifted. I leaned over the lip of the carpet for a better look at him. "What are you doing?"

"Unleashing my paternal instincts." Grant's arms dangled stiff at his sides, his legs curled behind him. Chalk of every color coated him, and Calvin's flailing kicks had to be drumming bruises into his abdomen, but Grant wore a soft smile when he tipped his head back to look in my general direction.

"Good golem!" Calvin bellowed, spitting sand.

Grant's teeth flashed white against his purple-and-orange-dusted lips.

"Who's a good golem? Certainly not you," he said in the same lilting tone I might use with a cute dog. "Kylie, lift my arm so I can pat him like you did. I think that helped."

My stomach flipped, humor and tenderness warring for dominance. I bent my arm, watching to ensure the connecting spell positioned Grant's hand close to Calvin. Grant's large palm engulfed a third of the golem, his pats sending puffs of chalk into the air. Grant coughed, but the golem's kicks subsided.

"You shouldn't call our baby a thing," Calvin grumbled.

"Wise words," Grant said, laughter in his voice.

The field reset, and we were off again. I set our sights on a green ball this time, one conveniently close to a green ring. Silently, I lamented my ineptitude. Grant had made navigating the carpet while controlling me seem easy, but every time I adjusted the steering, my arm dropped and Calvin's grumbles got louder. When I remembered to help Grant soothe Calvin, I forgot to use the levitation, and his legs dragged through snow. When I lifted his heels and raised the carpet, our speed flagged.

I flinched when the number fourteen man cut across our path. The last time I had seen Roy, he had been imitating a boat being ridden across the ice. His partner appeared to be treating him with similar tenderness in this challenge. Chalk coated his entire body, so thick it formed shadows in the folds of his clothing and matted his hair to his scalp. His golem flailed like a bizarre colorful parasite against his chest, a waterfall of sand draining from its mouth.

"Don't just lie there, Roy. Push!" shouted their golem.

"Where is it, Roy?" Jan's sharp voice pierced the air above Roy. "I can't think with that racket. Can't you quiet it?"

"Left!" Roy yelled above their golem's, "Splinters take you!"

Roy's thick arm swiped dangerously close to Grant when he changed direction, aiming for the green ball.

Pressure pushed against my forearm, Grant's instinctive reflexes straining the spells connecting us. I whipped the carpet away from Roy and Jan, tucking Grant's arms to his chest to avoid a collision. A fan of air brushed my face, and I glanced up in time to see Jan's heels spin past so close they penetrated the invisibility spells wrapping us both.

"Hey!" I shouted, but their golem drowned me out.

"Dig in your heels, you big oaf! Flaming splinters up your—" The diatribe devolved into curses so inventive, I blushed.

Shoving our carpet around the unpleasant couple, I set my sights on a different green ball. Frustration made my movements jerky, but I wasn't going to try to battle with Jan for the closer ball, not when she was willing to use her partner like a literal battering ram.

"I know you heard what that other golem said." Grant's serious voice filtered up to me, muffled because his head was tipped toward Calvin. "But that's not appropriate language for a child."

All the irritation knotting my body was released in a huff of laughter. Grant glanced up, *almost* directly at me, and winked. My heart flipped in my chest. He could have been angry with the other couple or frustrated with my clumsiness. Instead, he saw the humor in the situation. Despite the odd angles I had jerked his legs into and the rigidity in his arms, he appeared relaxed.

He trusted me. With his heart. With his body. With his safety.

We were partners.

That didn't assuage my earlier guilt. Hearing my words from the first trial—my defensiveness, my superior attitude, my insecurities—mouthed through the voice of our mock baby made my insides curdle. I wasn't as bad as Jan, but I still owed Grant an apology.

THE SECOND TRIAL BARELY ENDED BEFORE THE THIRD STARTED. The Arena Artisans didn't bother cloaking the field in a dome. They didn't do much more than run gusts of air through the snow, flattening the drifts and hiding the splatters of colorful chalk. After a rushed detangling from our connective spells and Grant from the harness, during which time Calvin and the other golems were weighed, the scores were announced. Grant and I scraped through to the final trial in tenth position.

Out on the field, ten glowing circles appeared, dotting the snow seemingly randomly. A number flared inside each circle.

"Out you go," the brigade minotaur announced. "Find your number and stand in the circle. Try to be quick about it, too."

In a tired mass, the remaining chalk-dusted contestants trudged onto the field, shoving through knee-deep snow. Grant and I split from the others, angling toward our circle on the far side of the arena. I tucked Calvin's inert body to my hip. The minotaur had dusted all the chalk from the golem before weighing him, but a fine layer of pink and yellow transferred from my tunic to his clay body as I walked.

Shame and embarrassment warred within me when I stared at the fiery scoreboard. I had been so certain at the start of this derby that I had it figured out. I had watched countless trials and studied how couples overcame the oddest of obstacles. I had assumed I would guide us to victory. Instead, I had been the handicap that nearly got us sent to the stands.

"Do you regret doing this?" I asked after making sure no one was close enough to overhear our conversation.

"The derby? Not at all." Grant dipped his head to study my expression. "Do you?"

"I . . ." I blinked back tears I didn't know were going to form. Shaking my head, I tried again. "This is nothing like I imagined."

"Harder than you thought it would be?"

I chuffed. "Yes, definitely. But it's more than that." I

watched snow kick up in front of my feet for several steps before forcing myself to meet Grant's inquisitive stare.

"Ever since I was a child, my favorite story of my dad's was how he and Mom competed in a Darling Dearest Derby. Everything about it sounded fun and daring. He makes me laugh every time he recounts guiding Mom through a mirror maze with her blindfolded and him deaf. He and Mom were committed to each other before the derby, but Dad claims he lost his heart to Mom when she fought her way through a chocolate pudding kraken to rescue him from an ice pit. He says he had never seen a more beautiful sight than Mom, fierce as a gryphon, drenched in pudding."

I liked the mental picture of my elegant mom covered in chocolate pudding. As a child, it had been hilarious. As a teen, I felt a kinship with the carefree, younger version of my levelheaded mom. Their derby tale gave me a treasured glimpse of who she was before she had the responsibilities of a child and a business.

"Dad still makes Mom chocolate pudding every anniversary." I adjusted Calvin against my hip, irrationally bothered by his lifelessness. Grant didn't say anything, giving me space to collect my thoughts.

"The other thing Dad always says is that the derby knitted their love tighter." I peeked at Grant through my lashes. "I've been going to derbies my whole life, and I've pictured this moment with my fiancé a thousand times. Never once in those fantasies did I argue with him or blame him for problems outside of his control or arrogantly tell him 'I told you so.' Twice." Heat flushed my cheeks, but I forced myself to maintain eye contact.

Grant gripped my elbow, supporting me when I tripped in the snow. His eyes searched mine.

"Your dad told me some of that," he said. "He also said he and your mom almost didn't make it past the first trial."

"True."

"Do you think he would have cut ties with your mom if they failed their first challenge?"

I snorted. "Dad would have said it strengthened their relationship."

Grant smiled.

"But I'm sure he didn't boss Mom around like I did you."

"No, you're right. They probably spoke to each other like two prim aunts at a mayoral luncheon."

"What?"

"Kylie, where did you learn to be so opinionated, stubborn, and driven? It wasn't from me."

I gaped at him. "It could have been. You're not exactly meek or pliable."

"Never said I was." Grant gave me a roguish grin that made my heart flip. "Is it possible that your dad didn't tell you every detail about his derby? That maybe he left out the yelling and cursing and irritated bits to make a better story for his daughter?"

I frowned and looked away. "Maybe."

"Talk about stubborn," Grant muttered.

"Hey!"

"Kylie, your parents aren't flawless."

"I know that." But I had listened to their derby story retold so many times over my life that it had morphed into a fable, one with my young, perfect parents at the center.

"No relationship is flawless, either."

"I know," I repeated, leaning into Grant. Heat radiated from him, soaking into me.

"Neither are we. You might have said 'I told you so,' but I'm the one who didn't listen to you in the first place."

"True," I said.

Grant flashed a smile at my easy agreement and shook his head. "I know you're a headstrong woman with a big heart and a faulty sense of personal safety—"

"Careful," I murmured.

"And I'm bossy and competitive, with control issues, but—"

"You forgot stubborn," I said.

"Careful," he echoed me.

"And protective," I added. "Under all that muscle, you're just a big softy."

He arched an eyebrow and drew me to a halt inside our designated glowing circle.

"What I'm trying to say, Kylie, is I knew who we were before we entered this derby. Nothing about these challenges is going to make our relationship stronger, because our bond was already forged in fire. Nothing is going to make it weaker, because neither of us would tolerate that. I love you. With all my heart, I love you. I cannot fall more in love with you, because you already hold every piece of my heart."

My pulse thundered in my ears as I stared into Grant's eyes. A fine dusting of yellow chalk highlighted his thick eyebrows. More splashed his cheeks and jaw. He looked both absurd and handsome, and somehow more rugged than usual. If we had a hundred years together, I would never tire of this man. He was a riveting mix of serious warrior and compassionate champion, as comfortable barking orders as he was with expressing his affection. And when he gave me glimpses like this of his secret romantic soul, he made me feel like I could fly without the help of magic.

"I adore you with every element of my being, Grant

Theodore Monaghan," I whispered. "There's no one else I would have wanted to do this with."

I lifted to my tiptoes, my awareness of the coliseum and screaming audience fading, the importance of the final trial a distant second to the flare of Grant's pupils as he saw my intent. All sounds faded away at the answering quirk of his lips as he lowered his head to meet me halfway.

9

Grant tasted of chalk and salt, his firm lips warmer than mine. I nipped his lower lip, and his fingers tightened on my back.

Calvin shifted in my arms, snapping our location into focus. I dropped to my heels with a sheepish grin. Hoping the chalk would hide the flush of embarrassment climbing my cheeks, I pretended to examine Calvin. The golem appeared inert, his eyes closed. He hadn't so much as wiggled since the end of the last trial.

Except I could have sworn he just moved.

"Aaaand we're all in position," the Mistletoe Matron said, watching the last couple stumble into their circle.

The artisans had spaced us around the snow-covered field, a good twenty feet separating every couple. So far, all I could tell about the next challenge was that it wouldn't have a shared start line.

"Listen up," the matron said. "This one is going to be quick, some might even say explosive."

"That doesn't sound good," Grant whispered in my ear.

"Our darlings—and their babies—will have ten minutes to build a snow tower in their designated circle."

With thick, fluffy snow all around us, and a circle four feet in diameter, the challenge didn't seem difficult—

Our ring of light shrank in half. So did everyone else's.

Of course.

Grant's left foot projected past the tighter boundary. He sidled closer, wrapping an arm around me to squeeze into the confined space.

"Oops." The matron pretended to be surprised. "I guess the artisans made a mistake. Glad they caught it in time. But won't a smaller circle make things more difficult for our darlings?"

As one, the artisans shrugged. Laughter rang from the audience. Building a snow tower with such a narrow base would be a challenge, but I doubted it would be the only one in this trial.

The matron continued, "When the final trumpets sound, points will be awarded for structure height *and* golem weight, so for all that's sacred, darlings five and fourteen, keep the rest of your babies' limbs attached."

While the audience laughed, I caught Grant's dubious expression.

"What do you think?" he asked, his gaze shifting to study the cloaked artisans. "Will we be dodging hatching phoenix eggs? Maybe an illusionary snow serpent who sheds scales of fire?"

"Now you're thinking like a derby fan. Or like an artisan. Maybe you should volunteer to wear a cloak next year."

"Can't. I'll be right there with you." He pointed to the Mistletoe Royalty in the front row.

"Good point. Maybe the year after."

My gaze drifted from the happily clapping queen to the

flower-studded filigree band she proudly wore. For a second, I could feel the phantom weight of the Mistletoe Crown on my forehead. We had bested ten couples so far and made it to the final trial. We still had a chance.

I twisted in Grant's embrace to face him, amused by the amount of chalk that puffed into the air from the friction of our tunics. Cupping his cheek with my free hand, I pulled him down for a quick kiss.

"I can't wait," I said, though my words came out more distracted than I intended. Had Calvin just moved again?

I gave the golem a squeeze, then a shake. Neither elicited a reaction. Frowning, I lifted Calvin higher, rolling the baby-shaped clay in my hands, double-checking his spell.

"... the circle. Kylie? Are you paying attention?"

I blinked up at Grant, replaying his words. "Um, yeah, let me . . ." I stepped out of the glowing circle. "Give me a second . . ."

"A second?" Grant's eyebrows drove together, his gaze jumping to the audience, then to me.

"I think I—"

"... *Two, one!*" shouted the entire coliseum.

Grant burst into motion, sweeping his arms to collect snow. The impulse to do the same rode hard at the back of my thoughts, but I continued to examine Calvin, mentally testing my logic.

The derby, at its heart, was an entertaining way of declaring, *This is my person. We belong together.* By participating, I demonstrated to my family, friends, and community how much I loved Grant.

What better way to display my love than with a kiss?

"What are you doing?" Grant asked, frantically patting the snow he'd gathered into a mound within our designated circle. His frown flicked from me to Calvin, but he didn't rise from his kneeling position and his hands didn't stop moving. "What's wrong? Is it Calvin?"

I dropped to my knees in front of him, intentionally in his way. Snow squeaked beneath my weight, compacting. Ice chilled my shins.

"Kylie, what are you—?"

"Here." I thrust Calvin toward him. With the start of the trial, the golem had opened his eyes and begun to wriggle, but so far, he didn't speak up.

Grant swept Calvin into a one-armed grip against his side. I tipped forward, off balance, and caught myself with a hand against Grant's chest. It was like bracing against a warm gargoyle; my weight didn't shift him. I cupped the back of his neck with my other hand, trying to draw Grant to me. He didn't budge.

"Kylie, are you feeling all right?" He braced a hand against my hip, locking me in place.

I huffed a frustrated breath. "Never better. Kiss me."

Grant's frown deepened. "We're falling behind—"

"Grant, *kiss* me."

One thick brow arched as Grant heard his captain's voice mimicked in my tone. His mouth opened on what was likely another protest. I fluttered my eyelashes. Releasing the back of his neck, I used both hands to cup his cheeks, framing his jaw with my chilled fingers.

"Kiss me," I said again, softer, my voice nearly lost beneath the cheering echoing through the coliseum. All around us, couples built their towers as fast as they could, shouting encouragements and commands at each other. I tuned it out, focusing on the firm line of Grant's lips, the seriousness of his eyes searching mine. My smile widened when he leaned toward me. A comical blend of suspicion and confusion flitted across his features, and by the time he finally kissed me, I was grinning too wide to purse my lips.

When he would have pulled back, I tightened my grip on his jaw and sank into the kiss. I felt the moment he confirmed my theory: A jolt went through his frame. His soft exhale of surprise heated my lips.

I released Grant's face, and we separated enough to peer at Calvin.

"Did he just gain weight?" Grant whispered.

"Look at the water." I squinted at the golem's spell, certain the elemental threads had thickened, adding water weight to the clay baby. "I think it's another loophole in the spell. Expressions of love make the golem gain weight."

"We should confirm." Grant pounced, bracing his free arm behind my back and bending me over it.

I gasped in surprise, then his mouth was on mine. He kissed me with a thoroughness that set my ears aflame. It wasn't a public kiss, certainly not one meant to be witnessed by thousands of people, let alone by my parents. But I wasn't the first to pull away.

Grant smiled down at me, subtly hefting Calvin. "Definitely a loophole. Wish I knew which artisan to thank." His gaze shifted beyond me. "But unless we get building, it won't be enough."

I took in the frenetic contestants around us. Several had snow towers taller than their heads. Our little mound wasn't higher than the tops of my boots.

"Right. Let's build."

Grant kept Calvin tucked against his side, using his free arm to scoop snow. I pounded the powder into a column, spreading the base to the inner edge of our glowing circle.

A rumble ran through the field, sending a fine quiver through the fluffy powder. Round shapes pushed from beneath the snow on our left and right, creating domes under the powder. A dozen more popped up around the field, until every couple's circle had at least three ominous mounds within sprinting distance.

"Something is going to pop out of those to destroy our towers, right?" Grant asked. Like me, he had paused his snow-collection efforts to ready himself for whatever came next.

"That's definitely the plan," I said.

Knee-high bushes sprang free of the snow, sending plumes of white powder into the air. Sharp-tipped glossy green leaves adorned the bushes, along with thick clusters of small red berries.

"Holly?" Grant and I said at the same time.

"Oh! The Arena Artisans have added a bit of winter solstice adornment to our field," the matron exclaimed. "But wait. I've never seen a holly bush do that before."

Each bush closed up like a crocus flower, its limbs and leaves folding upward into a tight cone. I circled to put my back to Grant's, our calves pressing against our snow pillar. Swiveling my head, I bounced my focus between two of the nearest holly bushes.

"Get ready," Grant said.

For what? I wanted to ask, but I got my answer before I could voice the question.

The invisible drawstrings cinching the holly bushes burst. Their branches flung open. Bright berries shot in every direction. I flung my arms up to protect my face, simultaneously constructing a shield of air. The dampeners shuddered on my wrists, and the shield that should have covered me from head to toe barely protected my forearms.

Red berries pelted me. Upon impact, they exploded, releasing tiny concussions of air, like the pops of soap bubbles. Chalk puffed from my tunic. As far as attacks went, it wasn't much worse than a bit of rain.

Calvin howled.

I spun around. Grant bent his body around the golem, holding him tight. Across the field, screams loosed from other golems, drowning out the Mistletoe Matron's commentary. The flurry of berries subsided, and I darted around our snow column to Grant.

"What happened?"

Grant lifted Calvin to show me his leg. A divot the size of my fingernail dented his shin. My heart twisted with an unexpected blend of sympathy and outrage. First the artisans spelled a cockatrice to claw its way from Calvin, then they caused his own voice to scrape sand from his throat. Now, the artisans were intentionally inflicting wounds on our baby. It was too much. The golem didn't deserve . . .

The golem.

My anger slapped up against logic and dissipated. I marveled at how possessive I felt for the little lump of clay. Judging from Grant's scowl, he felt the same, and I took the opportunity to plant a kiss on Grant's cheek. He released a slow breath, his expression softening. Calvin calmed, too, his ear-piercing cries softening to grumbles.

"That was from a berry?" I asked now that I didn't have to shout over Calvin. "I barely felt them."

"They weren't designed to harm us. But look." Grant bent to point out several berry-sized divots cut into our snow tower.

The short, sturdy stature of our mound had worked to our advantage. Several taller, narrow towers toppled under the berry barrage, bringing us even in height to couples who had previously been several feet ahead of us. While Grant repaired the holes with handfuls of fresh powder, I got to work scooping snow on top of our column, keeping an eye on the holly bushes. They hadn't disappeared after their volley. Instead, an alarming number of white flowers sprouted among the leaves. In seconds, the petals dropped, revealing new green berries that rapidly ripened to red.

Grant squinted past my shoulder. "The plants are growing."

He was right. The bushes had started out shorter than my knees, but now, as their limbs slowly curled upward, the tips of the branches were as tall as my waist. The bright berries looked larger, too.

"They're going to attack again," I warned.

"Here." Grant plunked Calvin atop our now-three-foot-tall tower, then guided me to kneel across from him, with the golem between us. "We can protect him and the snow at the same time."

I leaned my thighs against the packed snow and curled my torso over Calvin. Grant did the same, wrapping his arms around Calvin. I stacked my arms on top of his.

The holly bushes exploded. Berries pummeled us. I focused my scrap of air magic into a shield above Calvin's head. Grant protected an exposed side.

Puffs of air lifted chalk from our clothing, shrouding us in a teal-and-purple cloud. When the assault subsided, Grant and I shared a kiss above our quiet golem.

"That worked well," Grant said.

The transference of chalk from our clothing to the snow tower made it look as if we had grated a rainbow over it, but for the most part, it was whole. Where our bodies had shielded the packed snow, it remained smooth, but divots as thick as my thumb and twice as deep pockmarked the unprotected sides of our stunted tower.

"Grab Calvin." Grant held up two handfuls of snow, and

as soon as I hefted the golem, he dumped it on top of our tower. I started repairing divots.

The shout of a golem drew my attention. Most couples had done a better job protecting their towers the second time around, but ours was the only silent baby. Jan and Roy's clay golem bellowed out a foul curse that cut through the noise of the others and set the crowd roaring.

"Once again, I apologize for the coarse language on the field," the Mistletoe Matron said, amusement thick in her voice. "Please remember, parents: Your children are *always* listening, and they'll usually wait until you have company to repeat the worst of your words."

Her comment elicited more laughter.

"Grant, the holly is flowering again." The nearest bushes were taller than me now, and their branches creaked as they stretched higher. Petals dropped from the flowers, revealing green berries the size of grapes.

"This is diabolical," I whispered more to myself than Grant.

Leaving Calvin propped up against the base of the tower, I rushed to a section of untouched snow. Using my arms like shovels, I swept snow toward our circle. Grant worked double-time to pound the soft powder into the pillar, adding twists of ice magic between handfuls to reinforce the structure. All too soon, he shouted a warning, and I scrambled back to our circle. We crouched over a marginally taller tower, shielding Calvin as oversized holly berries bombarded us.

Grant touched his forehead to mine, uniting our heads in a protective V over the golem.

"You're absolutely radiant," he said, his words audible over the crowd's ruckus only because we were so close.

"You're not looking so bad yourself, Captain." Exertion

added a flush to his cheeks, and his eyes sparkled. *Happy*, he looked happy, and the sight made my heart sing. I tipped my chin up for a kiss.

A berry hit our tower near Calvin's toes, spraying all three of us with icy snow.

"Ease up!" the golem shouted, his little clay feet cutting gouges into the packed snow.

Grant and I flinched away from Calvin's flailing fists.

"Just testing things," Calvin yelled.

Grant's eyes widened, and a giggle climbed my throat. He leaned around the golem, and I met him halfway, our kiss made awkward but no less wonderful by our combined laughter.

"I'm a bit disappointed we can't do this again next year," Grant said after our affection quieted Calvin.

A berry hit my temple, the soft impact spraying chalk into my eyes. Wiping involuntary tears from my lashes with the inside of my tunic sleeve, I said, "Not me. Once is enough." I had no regrets, but I looked forward to enjoying next year's derby from the stands.

Grinning, Grant grabbed Calvin, and we dove back into building a tower.

The holly berry bombs grew to the size of apples, then grapefruits, then to the crushing circumference of pumpkins. Grant and I slapped snow to our tower during the respites, applying patches and adding height where we could. During bombardments, we hugged the column and Calvin between us. Our frequent kisses slowed us down, but I didn't care. Our actions reflected our values. No matter what the world threw at us, Grant and I would face it together, as a team. We would protect what we built as best we could, defend our child with fierce intensity, and honor our love for each other every chance we got.

When the final bell rang, walls of air gently pushed us away from our tower. I stumbled and fell on my butt, landing on a pillow of snow. Grant offered me a hand, pulling me easily to my feet.

"Calvin?" I asked, dusting off my pants.

Grant lifted the lifeless golem. The clay creature's eyes were closed, his limbs unnaturally stiff. Sorrow ghosted through me. Calvin wasn't real. His personality was a figment of the elements woven into him. His voice hadn't even been his own, just a discordant echo of Grant's and mine. Yet, as silly as it was, I had grown attached to the little spelled beast.

Grant took my hand, his thumb rubbing gently across my knuckles. "He was fun, in his own terrifying way."

"Mmm," I agreed.

"Are you ready for the real thing?"

The Black Brigade swarmed the field, and the Mistletoe Matron shouted something that ignited the crowd. Milo plucked Calvin from Grant's hand before running off. I couldn't tear my gaze from Grant.

Kids were always a future plan; I just hadn't considered about *how far* in the future. Before tonight, I might have said I would be ready in another five or ten years.

"Are you?" I asked, inexplicably out of breath. My thoughts reeled, my life goals rearranging themselves, shuffling and re-sorting what I had believed was set in concrete.

"Whenever you are." Grant squeezed my hand, the promise of his words reflected in his eyes.

My heart swelled. "It might be sooner than I thought," I confessed.

A slow smile drew the corners of Grant's mouth up, and love shone in his eyes. "That works for me," he whispered against my lips.

I melted into him, suffused with love and not caring who saw it.

I could already picture telling this story to our children. They would fall in love with Calvin, laugh at their parents' ridiculous antics, and never tire of hearing how the Darling Dearest Derby was the moment their dad and I decided we were ready to welcome them into our lives.

I grinned up at Grant. I couldn't wait for the incredible adventures ahead of us.

It didn't even matter that we came in third.

THE MIDNIGHT SLEIGH

TERRA HAVEN HOLIDAY CHRONICLES
(BOOK 3)

A firework burned against the starry sky, the brilliant, orange-limned red petals of a poinsettia flower unfurling larger than a house in the air above Focal Park. The spell spun, turning the petals into a fiery pinwheel. The faster it twirled, the brighter it flared, until it burst into a shower of sparks.

"Oooh," I said, right along with the rest of the crowd packed into the wooden bleachers.

"That was beautiful," Oliver exclaimed.

My gargoyle companion pranced in place, his excited steps jiggling the plank beneath me. The temporary seating had been designed for two-legged bodies, not sinuous four-legged Chinese dragons, but he made it work. With his hind legs on the footrest of the seats behind me and his front paws braced on the bench beside me, we were almost the same height. The people behind us good-naturedly made room for his wings, which didn't curl as neatly into the cramped space as the rest of his carnelian quartz body. It helped that we sat in the less-crowded bottom row of the bleachers. Most people preferred the upper decks, but the fireworks looked the same from down here as they did from the precarious seats at the top.

"How many points do you think that was worth, Mika?" Oliver asked.

"I want to say ten, but that's what I would have given the last firework, too, and this one was better."

Attending the fireworks competition was one of my favorite winter solstice traditions. Across the country, every town hosted their own late-night displays, drawing communities together under shared blankets and warming spells to watch the spectacles. As a kid in my small hometown, I had snuggled between my parents, eyes glued to the sky until exhaustion inevitably overcame me. When I was older, we made a game of judging the fireworks for ourselves, and afterward we handed out homemade cookies to our favorite performers—all of whom I had known by name. When I moved to Terra Haven, I had been awed by the larger, more extravagant fireworks displays. Sharing the experience this year with Oliver made it twice as wonderful as normal.

We both looked to the judges. Three women and two men sat in a roped-off section at the top of the opposite bleachers, a huge white cloth behind them. Where I grew up, the poinsettia would have been a winning firework, but Terra Haven had a much larger talent pool, and competition was fierce. After a moment's deliberation, the judges' score flashed across the canvas in green flames: 7.5 out of 10.

"I thought that deserved more," Oliver said.

"Me, too, but wait until you see the more experienced competitors."

"Like Marcus?"

My grin widened. "Like Marcus."

Marcus Velasquez, my boyfriend and the fire elemental of the city's Federal Pentagon Defense squad, was the reason Oliver and I were sitting in the coveted riverside bleacher seats. Normally, I watched the fireworks from Focal Park's far hill, where I could spread out a blanket and enjoy the show for free. The slope didn't always provide the best angle to see the fireworks in their full glory, though. From here, I could see the individual contestants, including Marcus.

The contestants' stage held pride of place on the expansive sandy shore of the Lincoln River, facing the enormous park. The twin bleachers rose on either side of the stage, with over one hundred feet of trampled sand and snow between them. Earlier in the day, the open space had been used for festival performances, but now, lines of fire crisscrossed the ground, forming a flaming pentagram. Deep fire pits anchored each point, and the heat from the flames fed the warming spells wrapping both bleachers and the stage.

Even if I hadn't spent most of the time between fireworks watching Marcus, my boyfriend wouldn't have been hard to spot. At over six feet tall, he tended to stand out. Plus, he carried himself with a charismatic blend of confidence and bridled strength. It was a magic all on its own, one that drew people to him and simultaneously ensured no one crowded his personal space. At the moment, he was laughing with the young woman who had just scored, and if I didn't miss my guess, giving her pointers on how to do better in the next round.

Not for the first time this solstice, I marveled at my good fortune. Although the day had gotten off to a shaky start, everything had worked out well. My best friend, Kylie, and our landlady, Ms. Zuberrie, put together a feast fit for royalty, and all our friends and neighbors had joined us for an afternoon of games and solstice revelry, with everyone taking turns cooing over Ms. Zuberrie's new baby gryphonette. Marcus arrived early and stayed by my side throughout the party, attentive and affectionate. If that had been the extent of our celebrations, the day still would have been the best winter solstice of my life.

However, after helping several neighbors with their house spells, Marcus, Oliver, and I raced to the Central City Coliseum to watch Kylie and Grant compete in the Darling Dearest Derby. As much as I admired Kylie's bravery, I still thought she was crazy for doing anything in front of that many people, especially something so humiliating. But it *had* been hilarious. I couldn't wait to hear Kylie recount the event for Ms. Zuberrie, who had stayed behind to entertain old friends in our festive, spell-warmed backyard.

The derby ended shortly before ten p.m., leaving just enough time for Marcus, Oliver, and me to enjoy a leisurely stroll through downtown before the fireworks competition began. The entire length of Main Street had been transformed into a fair, all of it lit with strings of glowballs and decorated with festive holly garlands, intricate pentagrams, glistening ornaments, and endless ribbons and banners in traditional silver, gold, green, and red. We lingered in a cramped alley with outstanding acoustics to enjoy an impromptu violin concert while savoring steaming blueberry-stuffed pastries, perused vendor stalls full of handmade crafts, and participated in a group game of elemental hopscotch—something none of us were skilled at but we all enjoyed immensely.

Before we headed into Focal Park, Marcus gifted me with a floral crown made with white roses and froths of miniature ivory carnations. When he set it on my head and looked at me with his smoldering lapis lazuli eyes, I felt like the most beautiful woman in the world.

Just when I thought the night couldn't get any more perfect, Marcus noticed Oliver's wistful expression and draped a matching crown around Oliver's neck like a winter wreath. Against Oliver's carnelian scales, the pale flowers glowed, but not as brightly as Oliver's radiant smile. As we strolled into the park, my gargoyle had preened for passersby, and I repeatedly caught Oliver gently touching the flowers, as if to assure himself they were still there.

"The woman who made the jumping fish is going next," Oliver said, peering toward the stage. "I bet she does something stunning."

Marcus's gaze snagged on mine, and my stomach performed a happy somersault. He smiled, then looked away to watch the next contestant.

Flame bloomed against the clear night sky, the fiery outline of a horse fit for a giant obscuring the stars. The equine's light cast a warm glow across the undersides of dozens of dirigibles hovering at the outskirts of Focal Park, where the wealthier—and less height-adverse—enjoyed the show. Kylie was up there, aboard one of her parents' airships with her mom, dad, and fiancé, Grant Monaghan.

Quinn, Kylie's gargoyle companion and Oliver's brother, was also aboard their airship, which meant that even if I closed my eyes, I could still point directly to Kylie's dirigible. Like all gargoyles within my limited range, Quinn's presence glowed like a golden beacon in my head. Similarly, I could pinpoint two other gargoyles inside Focal Park and another aboard an airship to the east. Oliver's beacon glowed the brightest in my head, nearly overwhelming the others, since he sat so close.

The fiery horse reared, pawed at the Milky Way, and

then galloped in place, its mane and tail fluttering green-and-blue fire before it faded away. The crowd applauded, and Oliver added his approving whistle to the noise.

"It looked alive," Oliver said, his eyes wide with wonder.

"That's got to be a ten," I said.

The crowd held its breath while we waited for the score to flash across the white canvas. 9.5. The bleachers shook as the people around us erupted into cheers. I stomped my feet, adding to the racket.

"Marcus is next," I said, leaning toward Oliver so he could hear me.

Oliver nodded, his eyes locked on Marcus. One quartz paw lifted to cup the base of his wreath, white rose petals cradled in his red claws. I added my gloved hand atop his, and we shared a quick, excited smile. Our simplistic ritual helped soothe my sympathetic nerves every time Marcus was up. Performing wasn't in my makeup. Simply standing on that stage in front of all these people would have made me sweat through my wool coat. Crafting elaborate spells for the entire town of Terra Haven to see and judge was something straight out of a nightmare. If I were in Marcus's place, I would have been too nervous to control the elements.

My boyfriend, however, looked as comfortable here as he had strolling through the fair. Fresh applause swelled in the stands when he stepped forward. His earlier fireworks had already made him a crowd favorite.

My heart pounded faster when Marcus's eyes found mine and he winked. The women in the stands around me yelled with newfound enthusiasm, and I caught a flash of Marcus's amusement before he tipped his head skyward.

A hush fell over the stands. Fire snaked through the sky, a long, deep red ribbon that circled nearly back on itself.

Slowly at first, then faster, the flames expanded, growing ridges and depth. Four legs appeared, then a square dragon head complete with burning-ember eyes. Eagle wings of ruby fire spread from its back. The dragon opened its mouth and unleashed a stream of fire, then dove in a tight circle toward the stands. The crowd shrieked in theatrical delight. Well above our heads, the blazing beast disappeared into a fold of air, its long tail flicking sparks before it vanished.

The crowds' reaction was deafening, and I had to lean close to hear Oliver's excited squeal.

"That was *me*!"

"That was *you*!" I yelled back.

The judges' score was fast to appear: 10. I clapped my hands and stomped my feet, adding my yells to the others, unable to hear my own voice above the cacophony.

A volley of message spells whipped through the air, dropping toward the stands. Heads turned. The applause dimmed. I craned to see what the fuss was about when I heard the first jangle of a silver bell. The note rang across the bowl of Focal Park, silencing everyone. A chorus of bells clamored in the distance, drowned out by the ringing of silver bells set around the rim of Focal Park. The overlapping chimes barreled toward us faster than a steam engine, growing louder, broadcasting their warning to one and all.

Excitement had me on my feet with the rest of the crowd before the first bell rang atop the bleachers.

"What is it?" Oliver asked.

"The Midnight Sleigh. Here, come with me." I jumped off the bleachers' short riser to the ground. I landed outside the warming spell, my breath puffing visibly in the freezing air. Heat guttered from the nearest fire pit, but it couldn't compete with the icy breeze. After the warmth of the stands, the wind's cool caress felt good against my flushed cheeks, but I wouldn't want to linger unprotected for long.

Oliver flowed over the bleachers after me, and I turned to point south. Before I could explain, the head judge spoke into a powerful amplification spell, her words echoing across the park.

"The Midnight Sleigh draws near. Blessings upon you and yours in the new year." A hearty cheer lifted across the park, barely audible beneath the silver bells ringing atop the bleachers. In a firmer tone, she added, "If you're not under a warming spell, find one now. Airships, drop anchor or make way. The competition will conclude after the skies are clear once more."

"What is the Midnight Sleigh?" Oliver asked. He reared onto his hind legs and planted his wings for balance, standing as tall as me. A frigid gust swept across Focal Park, making my eyes water. I stepped closer to Oliver, using his solid wing to shield myself from the building winds.

"The Midnight Sleigh is a long-standing tradition of the Nuche people," I said, naming the indigenous tribe that had settled in this valley long before Terra Haven was formed. "When the first frost hardens the ground far to the south, the polar bell-wings begin to hatch."

"What are polar bell-wings?"

"Beautiful moths of monstrous size," a male voice said before I could respond.

I spun to find Marcus behind us. My heart did a little flip at the sight of him. The glow of the fire pits and the flaming pentagram gleamed in his navy-blue eyes and warmed the natural bronze of his skin. Wind tousled his short black hair, and dark stubble shadowed his broad jaw. Another man might have looked unkempt. Marcus looked delicious.

Scooping me into his embrace, he planted a welcoming

kiss on my lips that warmed me to my toes. When he pulled back, I smiled at my fanciful thought, realizing Marcus had enveloped us in a cocoon of fire-laced air. It was his magic, not his love, warming me. Or maybe it was both.

"Are polar bell-wings bigger than me?" Oliver asked, waiting impatiently for us to focus on him again.

"You could ride on one of their wings," Marcus said.

Oliver looked suitably impressed.

"The Nuche shamans monitor the bell-wings' hatchings," I said, taking up my explanation. "Or it's a bit more complicated than that. They protect the young bell-wings, I think, to make sure as many as possible survive."

Marcus nodded. "It's an involved process for them. The polar bell-wings are critical to the natural cycles of the region. They bring snow to the mountains, which feeds our streams in the spring and waters our crops all summer. The Nuche people have been instrumental in ensuring this valley thrives. Without their efforts, we wouldn't enjoy such reliable harvests in the fall, and our winters would be dangerously unpredictable."

"Right, but tonight is the culmination of their caretaking," I said. "Every winter solstice, the shamans fly the Midnight Sleigh across the valley, guiding the polar bell-wings to their mountainous mating grounds. We get to glimpse their beauty without getting caught in their frigid spells. For all their majesty, the polar moths are deadly. With every flap, the scales that coat their wings convert the moisture in the air into snow and ice. It's absolutely enchanting to watch—from afar."

I scanned the horizon for my first sight of the sleigh. The silver bells had quieted in the stands and throughout the rest of Focal Park, but their warning tones rang through neighborhoods farther north. The clear, pleasant tones both beckoned Terra Haven citizens to witness the bell-wings' passing and served as an alert for everyone to find appropriate shelter. Already, the air had cooled noticeably, and the bell-wings weren't even in sight. When they flew over, the temperature would drop fast, and those unprepared would suffer.

I snuggled closer to Marcus. When the bell-wings crested the horizon, we would need to move within the heated spell around the bleachers with the rest of the crowd, but for now, I enjoyed having Marcus and Oliver to myself.

"I've heard the matings are a sight to behold, too," Marcus said. He held me against his body with one arm around my waist, and his voice rumbled pleasantly against my spine. "A pair of mating bell-wings can instigate a small blizzard. The whole eclipse of moths will keep the mountains buried in storms for weeks. The Nuche people survive by building enormous bonfires, and the moths remain in the area, feasting on the fire element in the air. Which is also why we had to call a halt to the fireworks. We don't want the bell-wings to get distracted as they fly over. Or that's partially why we stopped."

"What's the other reason?" Oliver asked.

"Because no one would be watching us." I heard the smile in Marcus's voice. He shifted, and I glanced over my shoulder to find him studying the sky above us. Quieter, he said, "Though for a *Midnight* Sleigh, they're running early."

Caught up in the excitement, I hadn't given it a thought, but he was right. Normally the fireworks competition paused right before the final round for the sleigh's passing. This year, we were still three rounds away.

"The show isn't running late?"

Marcus shook his head, a frown drawing his eyebrows together.

"There! I see something," Oliver shouted, pointing with a claw.

He wasn't the only one. A fervor of noise rose around Focal Park as people caught their first glimpse of the sleigh. I strained to pick out what Oliver and the others were seeing, finally spotting a flash of white wings. From afar, the team of white-tailed perytons pulling the sleigh looked like a single, feathered millipede instead of eight individual winged deer. A box of fire flowed behind the perytons, the magnificent flame-bedecked sleigh appearing no larger than my thumb from this distance.

The first polar bell-wing looked like a sliver of the moon coasting in the sleigh's wake. As if frost-limned, the moth's wings refracted the sky's ambient starlight, giving the mammoth insect a luminous, crystalline glow. When it flapped, all three sets of wings swept beneath the moth's body, curving into its namesake shape. The bell-wing bobbed behind the sleigh, gaining height with its downward thrust, revealing another polar moth behind it, and another even smaller shimmering on the horizon.

Freezing air cut through Marcus's spell, chilling my calves above my boots. Marcus compensated, adding another layer of fire to the spell wrapping us.

"Are they really big enough for me to ride?" Oliver asked, wonder glowing in his eyes.

"In size, yes, but they're still moths with papery wings, and you're still a solid-quartz gargoyle," I said, though I was amused by the image of Oliver riding a bell-wing like his own personal airship. "You'll see when they get closer. Or, if you want, you can fly up to get a better look. Just be sure to stay clear of their downdrafts. I've seen good-sized airships knocked around by the power of their wings."

"They're flying too fast," Marcus murmured.

"What?"

I squinted at the sleigh, suddenly aware of the tension in Marcus's frame. The driver flicked a long whip. It cracked above the flying deer, the sound swallowed by the vast sky. The perytons surged against their harnesses, wings flapping hard—far harder than they should be for their long flight.

"Damn," Marcus said. "I think something is wrong with the Midnight Sleigh."

2

Despite the perytons' frantic wingbeats, the sleigh wasn't gaining altitude. Instead of following its traditional high arc over Terra Haven, it zigged and zagged erratically. The people on board . . . I strained to pick out the sleigh's five occupants. Only the driver was visible, and they looked backward as often as forward.

"They're too low," I said.

"Is something chasing them?" Oliver asked when the sleigh swerved, then straightened. "I don't see anything but bell-wings behind them. Should I go check?"

"Not yet." Marcus stepped around me, arm raised high.

A second later, I spotted the message spell spearing from an airship to him. The moment Marcus touched it, the spell unfolded into a circular plane of water, the complicated mirror spell reflecting a wavering image of Kylie's fiancé, Grant. Only, judging by his serious expression, he was speaking as Marcus's Federal Pentagon Defense captain.

"The sleigh is coming in for landing. Make space," Grant ordered.

I glanced around helplessly. Focal Park wasn't designed for a sleigh landing. The perytons would need running room so they could slow down, plus the team and sleigh were at least sixty feet long. The rocky hills, the fiery slopes, the sculpture-filled tiers, and the forested paths of the park were all out of the question. The only place both flat and open enough to accommodate the Midnight Sleigh was the beach next to the river—which was currently filled with people, bleachers, and a whole lot of fire. We didn't have time to dismantle the three-story stands, let alone evacuate the hundreds of people occupying them before the sleigh reached us.

"Any idea what's wrong?" Marcus asked.

"Not yet. I'm sending Seradon to your position. You have three minutes, maybe less."

"Understood."

"Do they need us?" I heard Kylie ask, her voice faint. She must have been standing near Grant, her words projecting through the spell even though her image was out of sight.

"We would be too late," Grant said, his face in profile. "Quinn, we'll need you to—" The spell collapsed on itself before Grant finished his sentence.

"The sleigh is landing," Marcus yelled, projecting his voice through an amplification spell. "I need everyone to stay seated, remain calm, and keep this area clear."

The bleachers erupted in pandemonium. A surge of people broke for the stairs, rushing to the ground Marcus had just asked them to keep vacant.

With ruthless efficiency, Marcus slammed granite-hard wards over the bleachers' exits, then he grabbed my hand and we were running. With quick slaps of water element, he doused the fire pits and flaming pentagram, pulling me across the scorched sand toward the stage. Residual heat wafted across my chilled cheeks.

"Link with me," he said.

I cobbled together all five elements and pushed the bundle toward Marcus. He caught it, folding my magic into his. His familiar magical signature flared inside my mind, a blazing shield encrusted with a dazzling constellation of sparks like cut crystal. Beneath the initial surge of power that personified Marcus lay an alluring core of rosewood. Usually, his strength and beauty stole my breath; right now, it snapped me out of my daze. I twisted, checking for Oliver. He bounded through the sand at my side, a glimmering red shadow. Worried eyes met mine, but I had no reassurances to offer.

Marcus jerked us to a halt at the base of the stage. He pointed to three individuals among the confused throng. "You, you, you—link with me."

I stumbled when three other people's magic joined ours, buffeted by a collage of smoke spires, sunbaked sand, and molten coals that I couldn't differentiate into individual signatures. Fumbling to keep my head and not get lost in the link, I reached for Oliver's boost. It radiated within me and Marcus, and moments later, within the strangers in our link. A bizarre mirage flickered at the edge of my awareness, telling me five gargoyles enhanced our combined magic, not that one gargoyle boosted all five linked people. Dizzy, I stretched out a hand. Oliver's arched wing found my gloved palm, stabilizing me.

Marcus wove the elements with blistering speed, reinforcing containment wards around both bleachers, keeping the crowd securely corralled.

"Please, stay calm. We need to keep this area clear. The

show will continue shortly." Marcus's words rang out over the crowd, and no one hearing his composed tone would suspect the feverish speeds at which he wielded the elements.

Rakes of earth element smoothed the ground between the bleachers. In swift strokes, Marcus's magic plowed away from us, driving a flat strip from the stage toward the park's center, where the sand transitioned to gravel and rocks. Twin glowballs burst into existence at the start of the impromptu landing strip. Another set flared closer, then another set, until a road of light burned across the park, guiding the incoming sleigh straight to the stage.

The perytons were close enough now to make out individual deer. The leader flattened its wings, cutting toward the ground. The second followed, then the third, until the entire team tipped downward, coming in fast. The sleigh rose behind them, caught against the spells and straps connecting it to the perytons, and tipped earthward. A figure so bundled against the cold I couldn't tell if they were male or female stood at the front of the sleigh, a fan of leather reins tight in their fists. The rest of the sleigh's occupants were crowded into the well behind the driver's seat, bent around something impossible to see from the ground.

A spell trailed from the rear of the sleigh, a twisted, fiery train of elements fashioned into complex magical bait for the polar bell-wings. Two figures scrambled to the back of the sleigh, wool coats flapping in the wind. Fire bloomed, shooting white-hot columns straight into the sky. The sleigh's spell disconnected and lifted with the flames, carrying it higher even as the sleigh plummeted.

Silver shimmered behind the sleigh, then ghosted over it as a massive bell-wing took a ponderous flap. I clutched Oliver's wing, my heart in my throat. If the polar moth locked on to the sleigh instead of the ejected spell, it would freeze the people and perytons before they could reach help.

The sleigh rocked and twisted, its descent recklessly fast. Above it, the ejected spell arrowed toward the stars, but the flames carrying it faded too fast. In less than thirty seconds, the columns of fire extinguished, and the spell guiding the polar bell-wings died with it.

The lead moth faltered, coasting on outspread wings. Seemingly oblivious to the Midnight Sleigh, the bell-wing's next flap took it in a slow circle. Behind it, a string of silvery moths stretched to the horizon, with more incoming and no one left to escort them safely beyond our city.

"Get ready," Marcus said, tightening his grip on my hand.

He hadn't stopped working while I was distracted, directing city guards to take control of bleacher exits, reinforcing the warming spells, and layering the landing strip with a net of air and wood to assist the perytons' footing when they touched down. I felt superfluous.

"Should I go stand over there?" I asked, indicating an out-of-the-way spot by the stage.

"You're with me." Marcus flashed me a quick smile, fierce intensity radiating off him. "Oliver, can you boost the sleigh's occupants from here?"

"They're too far."

"Go. Get close, help them, and follow them down."

Oliver burst into a gallop before Marcus finished talking, launching into the air less than five feet in front of us. Dirt and snow sprayed from his claws, and a small sand cloud kicked up beneath his heavy flaps. Marcus blocked the worst of it with a wall of air and simultaneously gave Oliver a boost upward. The gargoyle glowed in the landing lights, his orange-red wings like stone fire, his sinuous body pure grace as he climbed the air. Somehow, the white wreath around his neck held strong.

Oliver's takeoff temporarily quieted the crowds as people in both stands craned to watch his ascent. Quinn's beacon shifted, and I darted a glance in his direction, expecting to see the citrine lion take to the air. Instead, Kylie's ship was in motion, as were the other dirigibles around the park. Message bubbles shot between the ships as they drifted apart, clearing the airspace above Focal Park.

Oliver's boost winked out, and I swayed as the level of magic dropped simultaneously from Marcus and the other three people in our link. Oliver glanced back but didn't slow. The people on the sleigh needed him more than we did. Plus, there were other gargoyles . . .

"Marcus, let me have the link for a moment."

Marcus relinquished control of our combined magic without question, and his trust warmed me. Quickly, I spun two basic message spells, fighting to keep them simple with the full power of five linked people swelling inside me. Speaking into the air bubbles, I kept my requests short and to the point, then sealed them. If I were sending the messages to a human, it would have been a simple matter of tuning the spells to each person's magical signature and letting the elements guide it. Gargoyles didn't have magical signatures, though. Usually, line of sight was required to get a message to them, but I had something better.

Piloting two spells simultaneously and using the beacons in my head for directions took all my concentration. One message shot to the top of the bleachers on the left, finding a small white-and-tan agate ferret with a unicorn's head and stubby wings. I had to tease the other message across the park and up the rock outcroppings of the earth section to a gargoyle I couldn't physically see. I activated each spell, then relinquished control of the link to Marcus, sagging slightly against him.

"What was that?" Marcus asked.

Power expanded inside me, the speed of the ferret gargoyle's response gratifying.

"A request for help." I raised a hand in thanks, amused to see the gargoyle craning over the crowd for a better look at me.

"I didn't even see that one up there," Marcus said.

The far beacon moved in my head. I grinned at Marcus. "Incoming."

The starry sky and low-level fires around the park didn't provide enough illumination to make out more than a glint of sunshine yellow and deep amethyst across thin wings as the far gargoyle glided closer. They landed in a shadow off to one side of the runway, but not before their boost bloomed inside me. A woman behind me gasped as magic flooded our link. I glanced around Marcus. She was the contestant who had made the poinsettia, and judging by the wonder on her expression, she was part of our link.

Oliver's flight path veered, jerking my attention skyward. His carnelian body would have been hard to spot against the sky if not for his white wreath and the sleigh's lights. My friend slowed, pivoting on an outspread wing to dip into the tailwind of the Midnight Sleigh.

"Oliver's got them," I said.

"Not a moment too soon."

The sleigh leveled out, fresh spells bolstering the long runners. The driver collapsed in their seat.

"Brace yourself," Marcus said. "This is going to be fast and dirty."

The perytons careened over the fire section of Focal Park

and dipped into the park's deep basin, teetering on the edge of control. The winged deer flapped out of rhythm, straining for the lit landing strip.

Marcus wove a thick wood-laced air spell, creating a dense headwind. The glowballs along the track rocked and fluttered, and he funneled fresh fire into them without a hitch in the headwind. The lead peryton tossed her head, pawing at the incoming air, but the driver kept the deer on course. Marcus hooked a second spell to the rear of the sleigh, adding an earth-and-wood drag.

I held my breath as the lead peryton touched down. She hit too fast, her slender legs churning in a blur of motion before she tucked them to her belly and relied on her wings to carry her forward. The sleigh blasted past two sets of glowballs. The lead peryton made a second valiant attempt at galloping before being forced airborne again.

Marcus worked frantically, building spells with blinding speed, tugging magic through the link hard enough that black spots flickered at the periphery of my vision. I stood helplessly at his side as eight perytons barreled toward us. Hooves finally connected with soil. Sand and snow flew, the sound thunderous before going eerily silent when the line of perytons tucked their legs and coasted, unable to keep up with their headlong speed. The sleigh hit the snow and bounced. Marcus grabbed its runners with thick bands of wood element, stabilizing it.

I could just make out the driver's grim face, her cheeks ruddy from the cold, her mouth a tense slash. She stood, feet braced against the tall runner in front of her, her body canted backward as she strained to prevent the perytons' helter-skelter landing from becoming a catastrophe.

Another fifty feet vanished behind the sleigh. The lead peryton filled my vision. Sweat darkened the doe's chest and flanks. Steam billowed from her black muzzle, her heavy breaths blending with the gasps of the perytons behind her. White rimmed her large eyes, her terror matching mine. They weren't slowing, not fast enough.

We were going to be trampled.

3

———

I tensed, prepared to leap aside and drag Marcus with me, if necessary.

The driver's gaze swept the bleachers, the stage, and Marcus and me standing in her path. In that split second, I saw her make the calculations. She still had time to pull the sleigh up—

And I read her hesitation.

Whatever the reason for the sleigh's unscheduled landing, it made her willing to risk the safety of everyone on board and all the perytons. And Marcus and me.

"Come on," Marcus urged under his breath. "Trust me."

A golden beacon dropped stone-fast in my head, and Oliver's boost burst through our link, echoed five times over. His wings flashed open, jewel-red in the glowball lights behind the sleigh.

Marcus spun the tide of fresh elements into an intricate new spell and anchored it to the jouncing craft. The Midnight Sleigh hiccupped, its speed cutting in half. With a relieved cry, the driver leapt to her feet and lifted the reins high. Everyone else in the sleigh ducked out of sight. In one choreographed move, the perytons swept their wings up and dropped their hind ends. Marcus grabbed the rear of the sleigh with a fist of air, jerking it down to match the perytons' reduced speed. The driver lurched forward, catching herself against the front of the sleigh without losing tension on the reins.

As one, the perytons landed at the far edge of the bleachers. The thunder of their hooves filled the air as they galloped ahead of the sleigh to avoid being plowed down. The crack of the sleigh's runners slamming into the muddy earth boomed over the hoofbeats. The perytons bore down on us, until all I could see were their widespread wings, sharp hooves, and snorting muzzles. I bent my knees. I didn't have time to drag Marcus out of their path. I would have to tackle him—

Marcus weighted the sleigh's braking spells, digging into the loose soil. With a lurch, the Midnight Sleigh slid to a stop. The lead peryton pawed to a halt less than five feet in front of us.

I collapsed forward, bracing my free hand against my knee, my body limp with relief. The winged deer gasped for air, their labored breathing the only sound in the entire park. Then the crowd exhaled, bursting into cheers.

"Hurry," Marcus said, giving my hand a tug.

I staggered after him, his longer strides propelling us down the line of perytons. Eyes wide, nostrils flared, the eight winged deer huffed and stomped, clearly unnerved by their unorthodox landing and even more alarmed by the cacophony emanating from the stands. Marcus spun me away from the fifth peryton when she reared, wings flapping wildly. I hunched in the safety of his curved body, neither of us slowing, as we ran for the sleigh. The fourth and sixth perytons bleated their annoyance as they were jerked in their harnesses, and the sixth deer kicked out restlessly.

Then we were past the perytons, and Marcus skidded to a stop. He braced my hip to keep me from falling when I stumbled into him.

I gawked at the Midnight Sleigh. Against the backdrop of the sky, it appeared dainty, hardly larger than my bed. Up close, it towered over us, elevated atop a lattice of slender wooden stanchions and sturdy curved runners. The rim of the passenger box was even with my head; the driver's platform stood another foot and a half higher. A mosaic of mirrors decorated its cherry-red panels, and gold cradles topped with curved crystal domes peppered the space between the mirrors, each designed to shield a glowball in flight. When lit, the fiery magic would be reflected and refracted among the mirrors, making the whole sleigh appear on fire. Even now, with the glowballs extinguished, the sleigh glistened in the lantern light illuminating the bleachers.

Oliver landed several feet behind the sleigh and galloped toward us, breathing hard. I reached for him, a thank-you on the tip of my tongue for his quick action, but a prolonged groan of pain from within the sleigh locked the words in my throat.

"This isn't how it's supposed to happen," a tortured voice moaned.

I couldn't see the woman who spoke. The sleigh's high sides and closed doors hid all but the wool-clad backs of two people crouched atop the back benches.

"I told you I could land, Takala," the driver said, leaning over the back of her red velvet seat cushion to speak to the women behind her. A slight quaver in her voice betrayed the relief beneath her nonchalance.

Marcus released my hand and hopped onto the frost-encrusted step beneath the closed door. Leaning in between the people on the back benches, he inserted himself into the middle of the huddle.

"What's the issue?" he asked.

"No issue," the pained female voice said. "I told them, I'm fiiiiiine." A groan distorted her last word.

"She's in labor," the driver said.

"How far along?" Marcus asked.

"Her contractions are coming fast, and they have been for too long," another woman said. "This baby is ready; Takala's body is not."

My heart sank as I translated her calm words: The expectant mother's life was in danger, and so was the life of her unborn child.

"Let's get some help," Marcus said. Magic burst from him, shaping into a message spell faster than I could follow. He spoke into it, then tuned the magic to the nearest healer hall and released it. The bundle of elements shot into the sky, cleared the stands, and zipped out of sight.

"I have to get . . ." The pregnant woman paused to pant, then continued. "Home. The bell-wings . . . I need . . ."

"Takala's our weather shaman," the driver said, softer.

"Do you know the spells necessary to carry on?" Marcus asked.

She gave him a small shake of her head.

My stomach flip-flopped. Guiding the bell-wings was the Nuche weather shaman's responsibility. Left to their own instincts, the polar moths would seek out the nearest heat sources—campfires, chimneys, lanterns . . . the ambient warmth a crowd generated. The longer the moths lingered, the colder it would get, their wings effortlessly altering the elements, weaving air and water into freezing forms. If they mated here, the city would be buried under a blizzard. Terra Haven's citizens would struggle to survive the unnatural winter, and the local farmland would be devastated. The wild creatures living in the valley and nearby foothills would have it so much worse.

The polar bell-wings needed to be guided beyond the temptations of Terra Haven, and only the Nuche shamans knew how to weave the unique spells that lured the moths northward.

Frigid wind gusted across Focal Park, cutting through my adrenaline-generated heat. Giant six-winged silvery moths glided overhead, circling lazily. A stream of bell-wings peppered the southern horizon, floating toward Terra Haven. I huddled deeper in my coat, watching the beautiful, deadly moths amass.

"All right. One thing at a time." Marcus tipped forward, looking toward the sleigh's floorboards. "We'll make sure you and your baby are well taken care of, Takala. Let's get you out of the sleigh and somewhere more comfortable."

"No! No, I don't want to leave."

"Hush, child, we'll be right there with you," one of the other passengers said.

Marcus hopped to the ground and opened the sleigh's door. He had to give it two yanks before the frozen latch snapped open with a crack. Inside the sleigh, Takala crouched on all fours in the foot space between the bench seats, her enormous stomach nearly dragging the floorboards. Pain bowed her spine, and sweat matted dark strands of hair to her forehead. Her eyes slid across Oliver and me, but I didn't think she actually saw us, her attention turned inward. Marcus moved to help down one of the women crouched on a bench seat, and I scuttled backward, out of the way. When I realized I was within kicking range of the nearest peryton, I darted around Marcus to the rear of the sleigh. Oliver hurried to my side, his wide eyes taking in everything.

Two older women exited first, loosening the ties of their hoods and stripping their gloves with calm efficiency. Gray liberally streaked both their braids, and wrinkles lined their dark brown cheeks. Next to Marcus, both short Nuche women looked like children—until a slender girl no more than twelve jumped to the ground. The driver looped the perytons' reins over a hook on the sleigh and swung down from her perch. Between them, they levitated Takala to the ground, carefully setting her down on a pallet of heated air. Marcus disbanded our link and joined with the women, lending his strength to the myriad spells cradling the pregnant woman and warming a bubble of air around us.

Several people darted from the stands, and Marcus coordinated with the guards controlling the wards to let individuals through. When they reached Takala, the spells they weaved marked them as healers. More people converged from the park, and Marcus switched to crowd control, organizing local guards to form a perimeter. I stayed near the back of the sleigh, out of the way.

The perytons pranced restlessly, dragging the sleigh forward several inches. The undercarriage groaned and clacked ominously.

"I think this runner is cracked," Oliver said, shifting his attention from the unfolding drama to inspect the far side of the sleigh. "So are these braces. Are they going to fly this again?"

Reluctantly, I pulled my gaze from the spectacle, wishing I could be helpful, but knowing if I stepped forward, I would just be in the way. Circling the sleigh, I caught up with Oliver and peered at the runner. A hairline crack ran through the wood, almost invisible beneath the grit coating it. I pressed my gloved hand to the stanchion above the crack. The wooden support groaned. I tested the next stanchion. It held soundlessly.

"Can you fix it?" Oliver asked.

"Me?" I glanced around, looking for someone more qualified. Certainly somewhere among the onlookers was a person more adept with wood element, but I couldn't exactly wander through the bleachers asking. Everyone else on the ground was busy. "I'll try."

I started to kneel to study the fractured section but hesitated. Between the flaming pentagram and firepits, Marcus's elemental raking to even the ground, the perytons' sharp hooves, and the warming spells wafting heat across the open field, the frozen soil had morphed into mud. Normally, getting dirty wouldn't bother me, but I had dressed up for the solstice in my most expensive, elegant outfit: a thick red-and-white floral skirt and creamy white angora sweater, with a charcoal wool coat, angora-lined gloves, and a green-and-red plaid scarf layered on top. Black wool leggings and my work boots completed the outfit. Shelling out a third of my month's rent for the beautiful skirt had been an uncharacteristic extravagance, but now I cursed myself for not paying double to have a stain-resistant spell woven into it. Or better yet, an anti-water spell. The mud would soak right into the exquisite fabric.

It was silly to worry about my wardrobe when we had much more important problems, but this was the first nice outfit I had purchased for myself since . . . well, since I had moved out of my parents' house. It symbolized the prosperity and good luck I hoped for in the new year, and it made me feel sophisticated. Most important, in this gorgeous outfit, I looked the part of a gargoyle guardian.

None of which mattered to the next person who attempted to land the Midnight Sleigh on a broken runner.

Sighing, I gathered my coat and skirt close to my legs and squatted. I had to tug excess fabric up between my knees to keep the hems from touching my filthy boots. Off balance, I windmilled my free arm. Oliver shoved his muzzle against my spine, holding me until I grabbed a stanchion.

"Look. Rest on me." Oliver stretched his lean body flat over his short legs and overlapped his wings across his spine, making a living bench.

"That's not necessary," I said, but I ruined my believability by nearly toppling onto my butt in the mud when the sleigh shifted, and I lost my grip. I stood with a huff, shaking out my skirt. "This is silly. I can just sit on the ground."

"No! You look too pretty. Besides, you'll get wet and cold."

As if his words conjured it, an icy wind buffeted the Nuche women's warming spell. My hair blew into my mouth, and I shoved it aside, absently checking on my floral crown with the other hand. When the wind receded, no warmth replaced it. Everyone was too preoccupied with the woman in labor to notice me in the sleigh's shadow—as they should be. Her life and her baby's life depended on the heat they maintained. I would be fine in the cold for a few minutes.

"All right. Tell me if I'm too much." I gathered my skirt and gingerly sat on Oliver's shoulder, careful not to crush his floral wreath.

"I've got you," Oliver said, no strain in his voice. He had picked up the phrase from Marcus, and I smiled to hear him repeat it.

"Thank you." I tucked my skirt around my knees. Cold

seeped into my thighs from Oliver. His quartz body was the same temperature as the air around us, but it was far better than being wet and having my clothes freeze to me. "Let's see what we can do."

I tapped the elements, gratified to feel the boost of the two nearby gargoyles along with Oliver's enhancement. When this night was over, I needed to locate my unknown assistants and thank them personally. Gargoyles had a choice in who they enhanced and who they didn't. Since I had become a gargoyle guardian, every gargoyle I met or requested help from had been eager to boost my magic, and every time, I felt honored and grateful.

Forming a test pentagram, I examined the runner. Any spells that had once protected the long strip of wood were shredded. Tuning the pentagram to wood, I confirmed with magic what my eyes could see: A seven-inch crack ran through the runner, and several more radiated through the stanchions. Unfortunately, diagnosing the problem was the extent of my capabilities with wood. I glanced around once more for help.

Marcus huddled with the healers and the women from the sleigh, forming a circle around the woman in labor. Urgency radiated from every individual. The sleigh's repairs were insignificant in comparison to their life-saving efforts. I could wait, but standing around uselessly held no appeal. Instead, I asked myself what Marcus would do in my situation.

"I'm going to try sealing these cracks with quartz," I decided.

"You brought seed crystals?" Oliver asked.

"I wish." Seed crystals were pure quartz, perfect for patching up injured gargoyles. Since I couldn't predict when I would encounter a wounded gargoyle, I habitually loaded my pockets with seed crystals. Tonight, though, I hadn't wanted the extra weight. Foolish me.

"We'll have to work with what we've got."

What we had were a lot of quartz fragments from glowball containers that shook loose and shattered during the sleigh's violent landing. A handful of shards glittered behind the sled, and more were scattered along the landing strip. Running quartz-tuned earth element lightly through the soil, I collected as many crystalline shards as I could reach with my enhanced magic. In a pile, they looked nearly indistinguishable from the rest of the mud. Carefully, I purified the fragments and molded them into one large seed crystal the size of a grapefruit.

I worked with raw quartz every day, making tiny figurines to improve my dexterity—and as a side business. Compared to healing the living-quartz flesh of gargoyles, manipulating inert quartz was simple. It was one area of magic I had practiced so much I could work it blindfolded. Fortunately, I didn't have to here, but the perytons gave me plenty of challenges. Restless in their harnesses, the winged deer shifted and flapped, jostling the sleigh every couple of minutes. I persevered, wrapping every visible crack and splinter in the runners and stanchions with bandages of quartz, burrowing the stone into the wood on either side of each break the same way I might stitch a wound. Oliver helped, shuffling forward and backward with the sleigh's erratic movements, allowing me to focus on repairs. I finished by replacing the missing glowball containers, redistributing material from the intact cups and reinforcing each quartz sphere with strengthening bands of magic.

Leaning back, I examined my work. The sleigh's mirrors shimmered in the park's lights, reflecting fractured images of my rosy cheeks and red nose. Ice crystals limned the white roses in the wreath atop my head and clung to my eyelashes. A shiver racked me, chattering my teeth involuntarily. I needed to get to warmth soon, but first I ran a critical eye over the sleigh's base. Clear quartz dotted nearly every stanchion and twisted around the runners like ice, but it should hold.

A gust of wind carried the pungent aroma of fresh peryton urine. I scrunched my nose, hiding the bottom half of my face in my scarf. My skin was so cold that my cheek muscles tried to stiffen in place, and I stretched my lips to relax my expression. When I stood, I stumbled on chilled feet. Bracing against the sleigh, I stomped blood back into my toes.

"Is it all fixed?" Oliver asked.

"I think so. Help me double-check?"

While I traced a glowball along every glossy red stanchion and back and forth over the runners, Oliver wormed beneath the sleigh to check for cracks invisible from the outside. Being a long dragon with short legs, his usual bunching walk didn't work in such tight quarters, so he inched side to side. He was halfway through his inspection when the rear peryton spotted him. The doe's eyes rolled wide, and her wings flared.

"Hold up, Oliver. Let me—" I started to jog around the peryton's slapping wings, but my approach alarmed her more. Rearing, she pawed the air, cloven hooves dangerously close to hooking in dangling lines. The doe in front of her pranced in place, ears flattening to her head in agitation.

"Easy, now," I soothed, shooting a desperate glance toward the driver. The bundled woman was preoccupied with the magic and ritual movements of what I thought was a Nuche birthing spell. Whatever she and the others were doing was working. The pregnant woman appeared calmer, no longer fighting against her contractions.

The peryton, however, didn't want to be soothed.

"What should I do?" Oliver asked, holding his statue-like pose.

The rearmost peryton tensed, ears snapping to her skull at the sound of his voice. She punched out with both back hooves, missing the curved front plate of the sleigh by inches. Tremors ran through the harness, agitating the entire team.

"Oh, please, no," I prayed, visions of the perytons leaping into the air and careening driverless and out of control into the city. "Back up, Oliver, quickly."

"I can't back up fast," Oliver whispered.

The rear peryton tensed, forelegs tightening up to leap forward.

4

The reins. I had to grab them—

Air magic teased across the ground under the perytons' hooves. Finger-sized bores of earth element dipped beneath the snow, coaxing dust particles from the topsoil. The fresh aroma of rich dirt gusted on the gentle breeze, enveloping the perytons and sleigh. One by one, the winged deer calmed, until even the skittish peryton closest to the sleigh dropped to all fours and chuffed the air contentedly.

I lowered my arms and stared, dumbfounded.

"It's the scent. They find the smell of the soil comforting."

The voice came from the other side of the sleigh, where a woman swaddled in a thick fur-lined coat smoothed a bare hand down the muzzle of the eighth peryton. Magic sifted from the woman's fingertips, stroking over the doe and circling back, mingling their scents into one. With a last flick of her tail feathers, the peryton relaxed, dipping her head and snuffling the churned soil. Only then did the woman look directly at me, and I recognized her as Raquel,

Seradon's girlfriend. We had been introduced briefly at the Darling Dearest Derby, but with so many people seated between us, I hadn't had a chance to talk with her. I knew her better from Kylie's stories: Raquel was a gryphon rider on the *Terra Haven Chronicle*'s staff and had flown Kylie to a few events.

"Raquel!" Oliver said, having finally extricated himself from under the sleigh.

"Hi, Oliver. Hi, Mika." Raquel strode to the next peryton, running her magic over the doe. I noted her actions had the dual purpose of offering comfort and checking the winged deer for injuries. "I half expected to find Quinn and Kylie here, not you two."

"That would make more sense," I said, knowing how much Kylie loved being at the heart of every unfolding story. "Thank you for preventing a stampede."

"My pleasure. I worked with perytons years ago. They're skittish little things, aren't they?" She half sang her words, her voice nearly too low for me to hear. "Not like gryphons. But what can you expect from prey?"

"There you are, Mika," Marcus said, peering over the back of the last peryton. The doe snorted at him, and he absentmindedly stroked her neck. "Good job on the sleigh."

"Th-Thank you." I shivered.

Marcus frowned, and a personalized heat spell engulfed me. I sighed in relief, my shoulders sagging as tension seeped from my freezing limbs.

"I told you I felt Mika's clever quartz magic," Seradon said, stepping up beside Marcus.

The earth elemental of Marcus's Federal Pentagon Defense squad, Seradon was tall and muscular, with sandy-brown hair nearly as short as Marcus's and smile lines around her brown eyes. I liked her immensely, and not just because she complimented my magic. She treated Marcus like a younger brother, someone to pester and tease when they weren't on assignment, as if she had appointed herself the task of making sure his large—and mostly justified— ego didn't overinflate.

"I expected you here sooner," Marcus said to Seradon. "What took you so long?"

"There was a bit of a crush at the tunnel entrance."

"You weren't in the park?"

Seradon's grin widened at the note of disbelief in Marcus's voice. "You didn't expect me to be squished in the stands, did you?"

Marcus crossed his arms. "These are the best seats, and I got you tickets."

"Yes, that was sweet of you. But Raquel and I were on a rooftop, in a lovely secluded spot Raquel knows. We had hot cocoa and cinnamon cakes, and best of all, a moment of privacy. But I promise we saw the fireworks. Mostly. I mean, have you seen Raquel? You make passingly good art, but that woman . . ." Seradon trailed off, her gaze shifting to rest fondly on Raquel. "You can't compete, Velasquez."

The gryphon rider didn't turn, but I caught a glimpse of her smile as she assessed the next peryton.

Marcus rolled his eyes. "Well, now that you're *finally* here, I could use your help with—"

A knotted spell plummeted through the sky like a meteor, aimed straight for Marcus. He plucked it from the air, sweeping it to the side so it didn't alarm the perytons. At his touch, the spell snapped open, and a watery version of Captain Grant Monaghan glared out. A ghost of Kylie wavered in the background, concern furrowing her brow.

"Report," Grant barked, his voice emanating from the spell.

His brusque command startled the nearest perytons, and they slapped their wings. Raquel shot Marcus a pointed glare. He raised a pacifying hand, striding away from the temperamental deer. Grant's spell floated with him. Oliver and I hurried around the sleigh to join Seradon and Marcus. The heat of Marcus's spell intensified when I gripped his forearm, and I fought the urge to close my eyes in bliss as warmth seeped through my boots to wrap around my frozen toes.

"Our weather shaman is minutes away from becoming a mother and a bit preoccupied with the process," Marcus said, speaking into the spell. "She didn't want to land, but wiser heads prevailed. She's getting the healer help she needs now."

"The tribe sent a shaman who is *in labor* to fly the Midnight Sleigh?" Grant asked, incredulous.

"I'm pretty sure she wasn't in labor when they took off," Seradon said. "And no one 'sent' her. She's the shaman, and she's carrying out one of her sacred duties. Just because she's pregnant doesn't mean she stops being a shaman."

"She's not exactly fulfilling those shamanic duties right now, is she?" Grant snapped. "This was incredibly irresponsible of the tribe elders—"

His words cut off with a grunt. His scowling profile filled the watery spell when he turned his glare toward Kylie, who had obviously poked him in the ribs.

"My darling dearest," Kylie said, and the sweetness of her tone made the hairs on the back of my neck try to stand up. "Do you believe a woman should no longer be in control of her own life when she becomes pregnant? That she shouldn't be allowed to make her own decisions?"

"That's not what I said. She had a greater responsibility here—"

"Perhaps a responsibility she considered so important she insisted on completing it *even though* she is pregnant?" Kylie shot back.

Grant's eyes narrowed. "What about her responsibility to keeping her child safe?" he asked. "Shouldn't a mother put that above any other responsibility?"

I didn't think he was talking about the shaman any longer. I wasn't even sure he remembered we were standing here.

"Of course. Always," Kylie said softly. Her gaze flicked to the spell and the four of us watching raptly, and her tone firmed again. "I'm sure the shaman thought she was making the best decision for her child. Better it be born at home than on the polar bell-wing hatching ground. Besides, if the baby had come a few hours later, the sleigh's flight wouldn't have been affected."

The captain stared a moment longer into Kylie's eyes, his expression unreadable. Then his gaze snapped to the spell. Marcus and I found interesting bits of mud to examine.

Seradon's smile grew, and she lifted a finger to point at Grant and Kylie. "Are you two—"

"So the Midnight Sleigh is grounded?" Grant interrupted, his usual commanding tone reasserting itself.

"For now," Marcus confirmed.

"That's going to be a problem. The temperatures are dropping fast up here, and with the moths so spread out, it's going to get icy down there quickly, too. Heat spells are going to fail."

I had always enjoyed the symbolism of the Midnight Sleigh's passing. As the polar bell-wings' hypnotic current of pulsing wings and reflected moonlight arced over Terra Haven, the moths enhanced the cold winds of winter, reminding us of our vulnerability on the longest night. Then the bell-wings passed, as this night and this winter would pass. In their wake, the warmth of our homes and spells seemed that much toastier. The polar bell-wings' departure made it easier to imagine the spring yet to come and the opportunities in our future.

The Midnight Sleigh's flight heralded in the new year. If the bell-wings didn't fly onward, they would trap us in this winter. Metaphorically, it was depressing. Physically, it could be lethal. Already, a smattering of polar moths circled above Terra Haven, and more diverted in widening circles over the surrounding foothills. To the south, the sky sparkled with the glistening bodies of hundreds of bell-wings fanning out into the valley around the city.

"The silver bells rang; Terra Haven citizens are prepared," Seradon said. "I'm sure they can see something is wrong. They will hold their spells."

"We need a plan to get this migration back on track," Grant said. "In the meantime, we need to corral the bell-wings here, over Terra Haven. Rural residents are more vulnerable. The livestock, the wildlife, the individuals in less-fortified dwellings—we need to protect them. If we don't act fast, people and animals will freeze to death."

"And the airships?" Marcus asked.

"I've sent out orders. Everyone in the air stays in the air unless forced to land."

"What? Why?" I asked. Maintaining heat spells on the ground was difficult enough. For those in the air, it would be twice as hard. It was naturally colder in the sky, doubly so with the bell-wings all around. The ships had little insulation and fewer individuals to maintain spells. Landing was the most prudent course of action.

"It's the heat of the levitation spells," Kylie said. Her eyes lifted, tracking something beyond the range of the spell's mirror image. "The bell-wings are attracted to warmth, and to land, we'll need to release heat. Every time we try to move, they fly closer. We already have ice on the ropes."

My stomach constricted. Enough ice coating a dirigible's ropes could be catastrophic. My brain belated translated bland FPD speak: When Grant said *forced to land*, he meant *crash*. I searched Kylie's watery expression. She gave me a brave smile, but tension crimped her eyes.

"We can't chance a bell-wing alighting on a ship, so we're holding still," Grant said.

"We'll work fast, Captain," Seradon said.

Grant nodded. "I'll coordinate with relay towers and incoming airships. Check back in ten." His spell collapsed into a fistful of water and splashed to the muddy ground.

Seradon gestured toward the Nuche women and healers, got a nod from Marcus, and raced away. The two of them had worked together long enough for the brief exchange to constitute an entire conversation. Marcus squeezed my hand, then gently extracted himself from my vise grip.

"We'll make sure they land safely," he promised. "Stay close but get inside a heat spell. I'll be right back."

I bobbed my head, my heart racing. Yet, my feet refused to move when Marcus sprinted toward the stage. Cold air swirled in his wake.

"Should we go toward the stands?" Oliver asked.

"Not yet."

I pivoted in a slow circle, searching the sky. The airships had extinguished their running lights, likely to reduce the amount of heat they generated. If not for the glow of Quinn's beacon in my head, I wouldn't have been able to distinguish Kylie's ship from the others floating near the west rim of the park. A pair of bell-wings spiraled less than a hundred feet above the ship's canvas balloon. The moths' wings hardly moved, but they didn't need to. The overlapping scales of their wings naturally twisted ambient air and water elements into frost. Gliding didn't alter the elements half as much as a flap would, but ice crystals visibly sparkled in their wake, nevertheless.

Kylie's airship bobbed on a counter current, spinning adrift in a slow circle. Tiny figures moved on the deck. I could pick out Grant simply because he was the tallest, but I couldn't tell what anyone was doing. Assessing the ship's spells or the condition of its ropes was impossible from this distance. Even if I had been on the deck with Kylie, I didn't have enough knowledge about dirigibles to do more than guess at their airworthiness in the best conditions. But the worry in Kylie's expression haunted me. She and the other airborne spectators were running out of time.

"If Marcus and Seradon manage to gather all the bell-wings, it's only going to get colder," I said, dropping my gaze to meet Oliver's worried eyes. "The colder it gets, the more likely those ships will crash. We need to buy them time."

"How?"

"A distraction." My plan formed on the tail of my words, and I quickly outlined it for Oliver. "But only if you agree this is safe for you," I finished.

Oliver craned his neck to take in the sky, eyes narrowing as he thought it through. "I can do it."

"All right. Let's be quick."

Freezing air chased us to the base of the stands, where the heat spell extended past the bottom row of seats. Oliver squelched to my side, the mud sucking at his paws with each step.

"What's going on?" someone shouted.

"Who's going to fly the sleigh?" another called.

I glanced around when no one responded, and my

breath caught to find a sea of expectant faces peering down at me. The audience, trapped in place per Marcus's orders for their own safety, stirred restlessly, their collective attention split between the sky, the Nuche women and healers, Marcus and the contestants on the stage, and now *me*.

Everyone close quieted, waiting for my response. Even the guards reinforcing the stand's spells at the stairs turned toward me.

Sweat broke across my palms inside my gloves. Unlike Marcus, I wasn't used to being the center of attention. People didn't tend to look to me for answers. Gargoyles, yes. But people? No.

"Uh. The FPD is getting it sorted," I said, then purposely turned my back to the bleachers, hoping everyone would realize I didn't have any answers.

"Who are you?"

"What are you doing?"

"Who is your gargoyle?"

The weight of the crowd's attention bored into my shoulder blades. I hunched closer to Oliver, wishing the warming spell extended farther from the stands. Even if I had the authority or the physical fortitude for impromptu public speaking, I didn't have time to disseminate information.

"Spread your wings for me," I said, trying to ignore the shouted questions behind me.

Oliver flared his wings. The crowd hushed, then a murmur of speculation swelled to replace the silence.

"Is that the gargoyle healer who fixed the park? I thought she would be older."

"What family is she from? I heard she's a nobody."

"Doesn't she work for the *Chronicle*?"

"What is she doing down there?"

"What is going on with the polar bell-wings?"

I grasped the elements and drew deeply on all three gargoyles' enhancements, the excess magic forcing me to focus and ignore the people behind me. My first glowball sprang into existence, fist-sized and blinding white. Hastily, I siphoned fire element from it, cooling the light to a softer red-orange.

"Let me know if it hurts."

I wove a strand of quartz-tuned earth into a loop around Oliver's wing, making sure it could flex with his movement, then attached the glowball to the end. The light rested against the tip of Oliver's stone wing, the flame inside licking against a carnelian feather. It would have burned my skin if it were that close, and I anxiously checked Oliver's expression.

"How does it feel?"

"Warm."

"You're not in pain? Not even a little?"

Oliver smiled and shook his head. "Keep going."

I formed a second glowball and attached it next to the first. Glowballs were simplistic fire spells, one of the first every child learned. Tying them off so they continued to burn after I released the spell took a moment of concentration, as did the elemental tether, but neither taxed my magical abilities. In less than five minutes, I draped both of Oliver's wings in a net of fiery lights. Heat radiated from him, warming my cheeks.

Oliver tested his wings with careful flaps. The glowballs held, the tight spells burning strong.

"It's not enough," he said.

"I don't want to make it too hot."

"I could walk through fire and be fine. Keep going."

An inferno bloomed above the stadium, casting warm

light across the churned snow and the perytons' white wings. As far as fireworks went, the sheet of flames lacked finesse and creativity, though its size was impressive: The flaming disc spanned the sky above both bleachers, and its heat radiated all the way to the ground. But it wasn't designed to entertain; someone was trying to attract the polar bell-wings.

I wasn't surprised to realize it was Marcus. He stood on stage, the contestants huddled in a semicircle around him. Pointing to the sky, he indicated a bell-wing drifting closer. Orange light bathed the contestants' serious faces as they nodded at Marcus's words. Then the fiery lake flickered and died, its residual heat evaporating just as fast.

"Maybe our plan won't be necessary," I said, letting the glowball I was building disperse in a harmless puff of hot air.

Marcus hopped down from the stage, and the contestants leapt into action. Arms waved, a space was cleared, and two people stepped into the gap. A spell wove between them, then shot skyward. A column of fire flared thirty feet high. The flames snagged the attention of a pair of polar bell-wings, and the moths swirled away from the heart of Terra Haven to swoop back over Focal Park.

The spell held for thirty seconds before evaporating into the frigid winds. The people who had controlled it sagged into each other and stumbled out of the way. Two more contestants stepped up to take their place. A new ball of fire burst into the sky, pivoting on a flaming string, orbiting slowly above our heads. The spell was a touch showy, but it drew another wayward moth toward the park. The perytons tossed their heads and snorted steamy breaths, clearly unnerved by the fiery displays. Raquel strode from one to the next, twining a nonstop stream of spells through the deer's midst to keep them calm.

Firelight illuminated Marcus's grim expression as he strode toward the sleigh. The fireworks were a stopgap measure. Until the Midnight Sleigh resumed its flight and guided the bell-wings away from Terra Haven, we wouldn't be safe.

"Not all the moths are changing direction," Oliver said.

On the horizon, dozens of giant bell-wings ranged east and west, oblivious to the fireworks. More alarming, new moths were flocking toward the vulnerable airships.

"Back to our plan, then." I formed another glowball and linked it to the elemental ropes on Oliver's wing, then another. In my periphery, Marcus switched directions, bearing down on me. I glanced up questioningly, but he was focused beyond me.

"Who is that?" Oliver asked.

A lone flying carpet barreled across Focal Park, its two occupants huddled low atop its thick surface, their identities disguised by thick coats and fur-lined hoods pulled tight around their faces. A message bundle raced ahead of the carpet. The guard at the perimeter snatched it out of the air, and a second later, a golden beacon ignited above Marcus's head.

The carpet veered into the gap between the Nuche women and the rear of the sleigh, angling for Marcus. It decelerated so quickly that I thought it tossed the front occupant off, until I realized the leading edge of the carpet had folded under, dropping the short figure to her feet. She hit the ground jogging.

I recognized her when she thrust back the hood of her coat, revealing a tanned, age-lined face and intelligent dark eyes: Mayor Mary Lowman. The hem of her serviceable brown coat kicked open as she strode toward us, revealing flashes of a silken teal dress. A dragon's fire opal hung in the center of her forehead, suspended from a gold chain woven into her braided gray hair, and the faint glow emanating from her metallic-orange firebird-feather earrings added a flush to her cheeks and neck. Her companion rolled up their flying carpet and waited at a respectful distance.

The mayor's eyes skimmed Oliver and me, but then Marcus stepped around me, and her attention shifted to him. A barrage of questions swelled from the stands as others recognized the mayor. She lifted a hand in acknowledgment, or perhaps as a gesture for silence. The crowd hushed.

"Mr. Velasquez. Good to see you here. Fill me in on what happened," Mayor Lowman said.

Marcus disbanded the golden arrow above his head with an impatient flick of water element. In succinct sentences, he described the predicament.

"My team is coordinating to get the sleigh back on track," he finished.

"I don't see your team," the mayor said. "I see you and Ms. Seradon."

It was strange to hear Seradon referred to as *Ms. Seradon*, and I vaguely remembered Kylie telling me that Seradon was the earth elemental's last name. I couldn't recall ever hearing her first name. She was always simply Seradon.

"Captain Monaghan is in a dirigible to the southwest, coordinating with inbound pilots and those currently trapped in the sky," Marcus said.

"That's too far away for him to link. All five of you need to be here. Preferably your squad should be aboard the sleigh and on your way out of town."

"That would be ideal," Marcus agreed, "but we're working with what we have."

The mayor's expression grew more pinched, but Marcus continued before she could interrupt.

"Raquel Jervier is assisting us. We've worked with Raquel in the past, and as you can see, she's got peryton experience."

I had resumed tying glowballs to Oliver's wings, but I took a second to peek at Raquel. She strode around the sleigh, examining my patches with a critical eye while simultaneously using brushes of earth magic to soothe any peryton that stepped out of line in its traces. Considering the crowd noises and the rolling flames popping in and out of existence above their heads, Raquel's control of the perytons was awe inspiring.

"What about the Nuche women?" Mayor Lowman surveyed the huddle of women and healers. "Do they all need to assist in the labor?"

"Seradon is checking. But we also have Mika—"

"Who?"

"Mika Stillwater, Terra Haven's resident gargoyle guardian. She's working here with Oliver."

I gave the mayor a shy wave before turning back Oliver. Mayor Lowman's gaze lingered on me, and I fought against the urge to squirm. Sweat dampened my forehead despite the cool air. I attributed it to the heat radiating from the forty-four glowballs affixed to Oliver's wings, not to a fit of self-consciousness at being brought to the attention of such a powerful woman.

Forcing myself to focus on the task at hand, I considered adding more glowballs to Oliver's body. I dismissed the idea when I realized it might impede his ability to land safely. I also wasn't willing to endanger the floral wreath Oliver still wore proudly around his neck.

My vision swam when I straightened. Glowballs weren't difficult to create, but forming so many so quickly had tired me. I braced my hands on my knees to steady myself.

"Give me a test flap," I said.

Oliver swept his wings high and brought them down to nearly touch the ground. The glowballs clung to him like fiery ornaments.

"Harder," I said.

Oliver shook his wings. A warm breeze fluttered my hair around my cheeks. The glowballs danced and shook but held.

"I think I'm ready," Oliver said.

All my fears rushed to the forefront of my mind, and I fought to keep myself from talking Oliver out of this. Instead, I said, "Don't overdo it. If you get tired or want to extinguish the glowballs, come back to me. Or Marcus. Or Seradon. Or just land anywhere there's dirt or snow and drag the spells through the soil. That'll break them up."

"Don't worry, Mika. This is going to be fun." Oliver gave me a toothy grin, his smile made sinister by the firelight flickering across his carnelian muzzle.

Holding his wings away from his body, Oliver trundled awkwardly toward open ground behind the sleigh. The perytons snorted and sidestepped in their harnesses, and Raquel had to work quickly to keep them calm. The crowd behind us quieted.

"What is that gargoyle doing?" the mayor asked. "Mika Stillwater, what did you—?"

Oliver reached the open sand beyond the bleachers. Bunching his hind legs, he launched straight up. His leap didn't clear more than two feet, but it gave him enough height to flap his wings without brushing the ground. In a blur of fire and red quartz feathers, Oliver surged another three feet into the air.

"Marcus, he needs—"

"I've got him." Marcus funneled air beneath Oliver's wings, and Oliver shot into the sky.

The crowd's collective gasp echoed my own. Oliver looked like a gargoyle on fire, his wings living flame, and his long, sinuous body glowing as if lit from within. Even the flowers around his neck took on an amber hue.

A familiar paradox of admiration for Oliver's bravery and fear for his safety constricted my lungs. I swallowed hard.

"Be safe," I whispered.

The arctic winds swallowed my prayer.

5

The latest uninspired firework winked out, and only Oliver lit the sky. He cleared the stadium and kept climbing, canting toward the airships.

"Ms. Stillwater, what is that gargoyle doing?"

"Buying time," I said, not looking away from my magnificent friend.

No one spoke as Oliver neared the first dirigible. A polar bell-wing drifted above the ship's canvas balloon, flirting with the idea of landing atop it. Oliver swooped in front of the moth, heat trailing from his wings. The bell-wing flapped lazily, turning to track him. The six-winged moth dwarfed Oliver, and when it flexed its wings, it temporarily blocked my friend from view. I held my breath until Oliver reappeared, flapping to a higher altitude. The bell-wing followed.

"It's working," I said, then spun toward Marcus. "Will that be enough? Will Kylie and the others be able to land safely with Oliver distracting the bell-wings?"

Marcus squinted at the skyline. "It might. Let me—" He shot a glare toward the stage, where the performers stood idle, gawking at Oliver. "*Next firework,*" Marcus bellowed.

Two people jumped and fumbled to link their magic. Seconds later, a wave of fire spanned the sky above the stage, drawing wayward moths toward us. Marcus turned away, crafting a mirror spell tuned to Grant's magical signature.

I sought out Oliver. From this distance, he looked like a firebird or a mammoth phoenix wheeling and spinning through the stars. Bulky polar bell-wings trailed after him, their numbers growing as he zigzagged above the trapped airships.

"Mika Stillwater." The mayor thrust a gloved hand toward me, and I took it by rote. I expected her to release me after a perfunctory shake, but she caged my hand within hers, anchoring me as she studied my face. A small frown appeared between her brows. "Your name is familiar."

It wasn't a question, but I answered anyway. "You might have heard about me when Focal Park was destroyed. I helped Marcus and the others in my capacity as a gargoyle healer and guardian." I had made a deal with myself to be more proactive in introducing myself to people who might be helpful to future gargoyles in need, and I was proud I hadn't let my natural shyness hold my tongue now. I couldn't prevent the blush that heated my cheeks, though. Had I sounded like I was bragging?

"Ah, that's right." With a nod of approval, the mayor finally released my hand and gestured toward the ferret-unicorn gargoyle perched at the top corner of the bleacher across from us, then to the park at large. "Are you responsible for the gargoyles boosting everyone here tonight?"

Everyone? I continued to feel the enhancement of both close gargoyles, but I hadn't realized they were boosting people outside of those Marcus and I had originally linked with.

"They, ah, well, I asked for their help."

"Smart. And a flaming gargoyle. I never would have considered it, but it's clever. Does that gargoyle know where to lead the bell-wings?"

"No. Oliver is going to try to round them up, but he doesn't know the Midnight Sleigh's path."

"For now, it's enough," Marcus said. He disbanded his mirror spell, but not before I caught Grant's profile and Kylie behind him, giving me quick wave. "Captain Monaghan says more than half the airships have landed, and the rest are in the process. Quinn, a gargoyle traveling with the captain, helped out where he could, but it was a near thing for several of those ships with less-powerful crews. The local healer halls will be mending some cuts and scrapes and minor frostbite, but nothing worse."

"For now," the mayor said, studying the sky. "This could easily turn into a catastrophe."

A pool of fire guttered above the park, temporarily blocking my view of the stars. When it vanished, an undulating sea of polar bell-wings filled my vision. The moths soared on layers of air current, circling like bloated vultures, drawn to the gouts of flames the performers kept in continuous supply. The highest bell-wings glimmered, their wings luminous in the moonlight, but the moths closer to the ground were harder to see in their companions' shadows. I tried to count their numbers, but it was pointless. The fireworks were working, as were Oliver's efforts. I could sense him sweeping in and out of my range, darting through the bell-wings' ponderous flight paths, luring more polar moths to our location.

Frigid winds kicked up, temporarily slicing through the

heat spell. A loud crack like a whip against metal siding echoed through the park. Two more thunderous snaps followed. I jerked around, searching for the source.

"It's the river freezing," Marcus said.

"And the ice sculptures rupturing," Mayor Lowman said, referring to artwork along the river completed today in honor of the solstice.

Marcus and the mayor shared a worried look. In the stands, people began to shift restlessly. Delicate snowflakes drifted from the cloudless sky, moisture spontaneously crystallizing in the chilling air. The guards nearest us called out to members of the crowd, drawing more people into their link to fortify the warming spells.

"Mr. Velasquez, how are your sleigh-flying skills?" Mayor Lowman asked.

Marcus shook his head. "I'm more likely to tangle the perytons in their own traces than achieve liftoff with that team. But Raquel might have better luck."

Hearing her name, the gryphon rider turned our way. Marcus gestured her closer, and she jogged over to us, releasing a teeth-chattering breath when she entered the warmth.

"Think you can drive this sleigh?" Marcus asked.

Raquel's dark eyebrows lifted, and a grin slowly spread across her face. "Me? Drive the Midnight Sleigh? Oh, yes! It's been years since I've had my hands on peryton reins, but I'm sure it'll all come back to me."

"Do either of you know the traditional spells that lure the bell-wings along?" the mayor asked.

Raquel and Marcus shook their heads.

We all looked toward the Nuche women. The opaque ward around Takala dropped as the laboring woman was levitated onto a broad flying carpet. Sweat matted her black hair to her forehead, and she bared her teeth as another contraction tore through her body. Two healers climbed onto the carpet with her, one kneeling at her feet, the other at her head. Delicate elemental weaves coursed over Takala's body, visibly easing her discomfort. The older Nuche women and the sleigh's driver held a secondary spell around the trio even as they climbed atop a different carpet. The polar bell-wing experts were decamping. We would get no help from them.

"We'll wing it," Marcus said. "Heat spells should keep the moths interested. Hopefully, once we get a few in line, the rest will follow. And when we reach the bell-wings' breeding ground, we'll ask the Nuche tribespeople for help and come back for any stragglers."

"That will have to suffice." The mayor huddled deeper in her coat, sidling closer to the bleachers, where the warming spell was thicker. "We can't wait much longer. You need to—"

"Crisis averted," Seradon said, trotting up behind us. "Takala's baby was breech, but the healers are getting it turned around. She and the baby should be fine in a couple hours. And . . ." She stepped to the side, revealing a short figure in her shadow. "I found a weather shaman."

"A shaman in training," the girl corrected.

When she pushed her hood back, I recognized the girl as the preteen who had disembarked from the sleigh. Three braids cinched the girl's shiny black hair tight to her scalp, and thin copper strands secured pearlescent seashells evenly along the outer two braids. Polished rainbow-blue hawk's-eye quartz adorned the center braid, the series of small crescents growing rounder to mimic the phases of the moon. A single, large white quartz disc rested against her bare forehead, an iridescent abalone shell set at its center. I admired the adornments, the quartz artisan in me temporarily distracted by the subtle weave of magic through the stones. They were part of a minor earth spell, one I wasn't familiar with.

"This is Chenoa," Seradon said. "She knows the polar-moth-wrangling spells."

"It's a wildfire tempest spell with cyclonic summer zephyrs woven throughout," Chenoa explained. "And some dry monsoon spells braided with anabatic desert drafts."

Seradon arched a brow. "Is that all?"

"It's complicated, but I can teach it to you. It shouldn't take more than three, maybe five hours."

Marcus and Seradon shared a look over the girl's head.

"I have a better idea," Seradon said. "Why don't you show us from the sleigh?"

Chenoa's eyes widened, and her gaze darted to the Midnight Sleigh, then to the departing Nuche women. "I can't. Apprentices don't whisper the bell-wings."

"Says who?" Seradon asked.

"It's just not done." Chenoa's fearful gaze flicked off me and the others in the circle, looking for someone to agree with her. "Takala didn't whisper the bell-wings until her fourth flight. No one does before they pass their shaman's test."

Seradon's expression was sympathetic, but her tone remained firm. "I spoke with your driver. Keshena said you were in charge of the spell for the last half hour before you landed. Is that true?"

"Yes, but Takala was guiding me."

"Can you replicate the spell?"

Chenoa's breath came too fast, and her eyes were too wide. She flinched when Mayor Lowman reached for her hands, then she clutched the older woman's fingers in her own as if they were a lifeline. The mayor stepped closer, her gaze steady. Chenoa stilled.

"This is a special circumstance," the mayor said. "We need your help. All of Terra Haven does. You wouldn't be in this alone. Mr. Velasquez here, and Ms. Seradon, would go with you."

When the mayor gestured to Marcus, Chenoa's eyes slid up his body, widening as they went. Marcus gave her a dashing smile, and a blush flared across her cheeks. I bit my bottom lip to keep from grinning. It was a potent smile, and I would have been just as red to receive it at her age.

"And Ms. Jervier has volunteered to fly the perytons. You'll be in good hands," Mayor Lowman continued. "But if you don't feel up for the task, we will find another way." She smiled kindly. "It is not up to you to save the city."

Chenoa took a deep breath and squared her shoulders. "I can do it."

"Excellent." The mayor released Chenoa and clapped her hands together. "That's four, then. You'll need a fifth. How about you, Ms. Stillwater?"

Every thought in my head scattered, and I stared blankly at the mayor. "Me?" I squeaked out.

Air travel in ordinary dirigibles scared me, even if most people considered it commonplace. But no one could claim the Midnight Sleigh was a normal aircraft. For starters, it relied on fickle, panickable perytons rather than stable spells. Plus, its sole purpose was to race ahead of blizzard-generating moths. If it slowed down or was overtaken, it would be capsized by the bell-wings.

Chenoa fidgeted beside me, as if my hesitation made her question her own newfound bravery. I shot Marcus a helpless glance. He smiled, but he didn't say a word, letting me make my own choice. My racing heart slowed under his steady regard. Although I knew he wouldn't think any less of me if I said no, I wanted to make him proud.

My gaze slid to the sleigh. I had watched its passing year after year, enchanted by its purpose and its symbolism. I never dreamed I would have a chance to take part in the tradition. It would be incredible—scary and thrilling and like nothing I had ever experienced before or would get a chance to experience again.

My budding fortitude crumbled when I considered my companions. The Midnight Sleigh always flew with five powerful people. Marcus, Seradon, and Raquel were full spectrums, and if Chenoa was a weather shaman in training, she was likely almost as strong. I would be the weakest in the link. What if I held the team back and the polar bell-wings didn't fly true because I couldn't provide enough magic to the link?

"I, ah," I started, reluctant to explain my inadequacies.

Marcus caught my eye and winked. Warmth unfurled in my chest, unraveling the knot that restricted my breathing. If he thought my lesser magic abilities would hinder the sleigh's success, he would say so. Marcus believed I could do this, and I wouldn't let him down.

"I would be honored," I said, my voice shaking.

"Good." The mayor clapped her gloved hands again, and I startled. "I'd like you to coordinate with your gargoyle. Use him to draw any stragglers into your wake."

"We can do that," Seradon said. She wrapped an arm around my shoulders and gave me a brief squeeze, smiling down at me. My own features felt frozen in place, and I knew I looked just as scared as Chenoa.

"Time is of the essence," Mayor Lowman said, gesturing toward the sleigh. "Fly fast and fly true."

Raquel and Seradon jogged toward the perytons.

Marcus beelined for the sleigh. While the women methodically examined the reins and harnesses on each winged deer, knocking ice from the metal buckles and reinforcing spells around the traces as they went, Marcus used the elements to inspect my repairs. Chenoa and I followed more slowly.

I sucked in a startled breath when I passed through the boundary of the bleacher's warming spell, the subzero air sharp on my esophagus. Stinging snowflakes peppered my cheeks and melted against my lips, chilling me instantly. I tugged the hood of my coat over my head, crushing the floral crown I had forgotten I wore.

For a second, a golden beacon appeared in my head, high and faint, at the edge of my range. Then it swooped lower, growing stronger, before whipping with dizzying speed out of range again. Holding my hood secure, I tilted my head back to search for Oliver.

My mouth gaped open. The sky was black with polar bell-wings. Despite their translucent wings, too many huge moths circled overhead to allow moonlight to filter through.

A new firework fountained above the park, blinding me. Shielding my eyes with my free hand, I squinted to see beyond the flames. The light illuminated a churning mass of wings before the fire died, and darkness reigned above the park once more.

My heart pounded against my breastbone. We were going to fly into that swarm?

"They're beautiful, aren't they?"

I shot Chenoa a dumbfounded look. She missed it, her attention on the sky as the next unimaginative firework burned above us. Amber light bathed her face, revealing cheeks still round with baby fat and a nose and chin not yet fully developed. However, I fancied I saw the woman

Chenoa would become in the intensity of her gaze and the determined tilt of her jaw.

"Did you know they live only a week or so after they mate?" she asked.

"I didn't."

"It's such a short life, and yet they reshape the world while they live." She turned to face me, earnestness shining in her eyes. "Takala says we're all like that. We all change the world by being in it and by the choices we make."

"I've never thought of it like that." I searched for something wise or profound to add, settling for a simple, "I'm glad I get to come on this flight."

Chenoa and I shared a smile. Both of us were scared for different reasons, but we were making a choice to change the world for the better. I felt a kindred spirit in the young weather shaman in training.

"Are you with the FPD, too?" she asked.

"No. Marcus and Seradon are FPD. Raquel is a gryphon rider. I'm Mika, a gargoyle guardian."

Chenoa's face lit up with excitement. "The gargoyle on fire? That was you?"

"That was Oliver, my companion. He's there." I pointed, spotting a flicker of fiery wings near the horizon.

Oliver circled from the east, two enormous moths gliding on his tail. I lost sight of him when he surged higher into the crush of bell-wings. He was too far away to offer us his boost, so distant that he didn't even register on my mental map.

"He'll fly closer when we go up." I didn't want to think about *up*.

For a brief moment, I considered asking the two nearby gargoyles boosting everyone to join us on the flight, but I decided against it. The people here might need them to keep the warming spells powered until we drew the polar bell-wings and their freezing temperatures northward.

Chenoa turned to face me squarely. "We should link."

"Good idea," Marcus said, coming up beside me.

I gathered a balance of all five elements and extended it to Chenoa. She backed up a step, hands raised as if to defend herself.

"I'm not—"

"You're going to be in charge of the bell-wing spell. Take the time now to get adjusted to being in control of the link," Marcus said, overriding her protest.

Chenoa took a deep breath, swallowed hard, and accepted my magic. A wealth of power radiated back to me through the link, proving she was a full spectrum. The connection also carried Chenoa's magical signature, a breathtaking flurry of winter wind after a summer squall. No wonder she trained as a weather shaman; she was practically a storm all on her own.

Marcus joined the link next, his solid, fiery signature as familiar to me as Oliver's boost. Chenoa took another deep breath, swaying in place as she adjusted to the increased magic in her control.

Raquel scrambled up to the driver's perch using handholds I hadn't noticed among the sleigh's many mirrors. Deftly, she collected the plethora of reins, weaving them between her fingers in a pattern I couldn't discern from the ground. The perytons lifted their heads, wings rustling, recognizing the signs of an imminent takeoff. I pressed a fist to my midsection, preflight nerves already soaring within the confines of my stomach. Marcus squeezed my bicep, and I nodded to let him know I was all right.

"Up we go," Seradon said, suddenly beside us. She seized Chenoa by the waist and hoisted her into the air.

Chenoa squeaked and grabbed for the sleigh, shimmying up the same route Raquel had taken. Seradon vaulted after her. Both women joined the link, Seradon a core of cool marble ringed in floral fire, and Raquel a headwind cutting across a grassy plain. The rush of collective magic dizzied me, and when my vision cleared, Marcus stood inside the open door of the sleigh, his hand extended down to me.

Heart in my throat, I hitched my skirt out of the way, placed a boot on the iron step, and reached for Marcus's hand. Behind him, the sky seethed with deadly moths. My stomach dropped even as Marcus tugged me into the sleigh.

"Oh gods, I'm really doing this, aren't I?" I whispered.

Marcus grinned. "You really are, my brave guardian."

6

———

Marcus pulled the door shut and bolted it closed. The sleigh shrank around us. Red velvet wrapped the interior—the twin padded benches facing each other, the backrests, and the wall panels. Gold and red paint twined around the rim of the sleigh as if braided. A stylized painting of three silver polar bell-wings transformed the moths into mountain ranges across the back of the driver's box. Even the kickplates beneath the benches were decorated, the geometric red-and-white designs hinting at women and perytons. Everything about the sleigh spoke of the Nuche people's pride in this craft and its purpose.

My gaze bounced too fast around the sleigh, and my choppy breaths clouded the air. Trepidation ballooned upward from my gut, shouldering aside rational thoughts and untethering me from the comfortable bonds of gravity. Already, my head felt light enough to detach from my shoulders, and I clung to the sleigh's side, afraid vertigo would tip me over the edge. Cataloging each adornment of the Midnight Sleigh helped, grounding me in concrete details.

"Do you want to face forward or backward?" Marcus asked, indicating the mirrored bench seats.

"Forward. Definitely forward."

Keeping a hand on me to maneuver in the tight quarters, Marcus swept aside a mound of fur blankets, clearing the rear bench seat. He claimed the right half, then gently pulled me down next to him. I sank into the cushion, tipping toward his greater mass. A generous layer of cushion padded my back, but behind that, nothing existed but a thin brace of wood and empty air. While Marcus layered blankets across our laps, I checked the floorboards, seat, and back of the sleigh for any sort of safety harness, finding none. The vacant bench across from us didn't have any, either.

"Everyone ready?" Seradon called from where she and Chenoa had settled with Raquel in the elevated driver's box.

Marcus draped a muscular arm around my shoulders and pulled me snug against his body, anchoring me against his solid frame.

"Ready," he said.

Chenoa tapped the link, and fire raced around the sleigh's exterior, lighting the glowball sconces with a theatrical flourish. A cheer burst from the stands and spread across the park as others caught sight of the lit sleigh. Alarm and excitement shot through my veins, the weight of the crowd's expectations both exhilarating and unnerving.

Marcus signaled the fireworks contestants, and the dance of flames above us extinguished. At Marcus's request, Chenoa handed control of the link to him, and he draped a thick warming spell into the wells of the sleigh, covering everyone's laps without interfering with our aerodynamics. As if they'd practiced it, Marcus relinquished control of the link, and Raquel took hold. Earth and air magic spun through me, sliding into spells I didn't recognize and didn't attempt to follow.

"This is going to be a steep and bumpy takeoff," Marcus said, leaning close to be heard above the crowd's escalating noise. His voice rumbled against my eardrum, sending a shiver down my spine. Lifting the fur covering our legs, he indicated three leather straps spaced along the seat. "Grab hold of those if you want, or hang on to me. Either way, don't worry; I've got you."

I slid my left hand beneath a strap, curling my fingers around the sturdy handhold. A hearty yank proved it would hold.

"Have you ever done anything like this before?" I asked.

"Have I ever taken the woman I love on a Midnight Sleigh flight?" Marcus grinned. "Never."

His easy affection and focused attention—not to mention *that* smile—befuddled my thoughts in an entirely wonderful way. For a second, I forgot about our imminent ascent into polar bell-wings. Tipping my chin up, I used my free hand to pull Marcus closer. He came willingly, his lips shockingly warm against mine, his kiss tender and exultant at the same time.

The spectators roared their approval, jolting me back to reality. Cheeks burning with embarrassment, I tried to disappear into the red velvet backrest, wishing I could melt down to the floorboards. Marcus's chuckle vibrated the bench.

The sleigh lurched, runners squeaking. The bench shimmied. Another jolt of motion knocked me against the backrest. Icy fear bowled aside my embarrassment. We were moving.

The sleigh bounced and shuddered over the churned earth as the peryton team pranced in a circle, dragging the sleigh around to point south, toward the open bowl of the park. Seradon took control of the link, weaving spells around the sleigh to assist with takeoff. Then Raquel took charge again, ribbons of magic sweeping across the perytons. Chenoa sat between the women, her attention riveted on the polar bell-wings circling ever closer above us.

The perytons lunged into motion, jerking the sleigh forward. I clutched the leather strap and braced my feet against the floorboards. Marcus tightened his grip around my shoulders, pinning me against his side.

The bleachers raced past on either side, the audience a blur of colorful clothes and excited arms waving. The sleigh rattled and shuddered, its wooden frame protesting every bump and jolt. My teeth clacked together, and my vision bounced. The repairs I had made to the sleigh no longer seemed adequate. Even with quartz reinforcements, how could a few slender posts and cracked runners hold up against all this abuse?

We shot clear of the stands and into the open park, gaining speed, and the sleigh's alarming creaking and popping noises intensified. Beneath the racket, the perytons' hooves thundered across the frozen grounds in a heavy, ominous beat.

This was taking too long. Any moment, we would hit rougher terrain, and the sleigh would be torn apart beneath us before the perytons achieved liftoff.

I strained to see beyond the tall driver's box. Seradon and Chenoa remained seated, but Raquel crouched, feet braced wide, arms stretched in front of her as she guided the perytons. With a cry of encouragement, Raquel flicked magic down the traces. The perytons unfurled their wings. A flurry of white feathers filled the air in front of Raquel, just visible above her head, and the snap and flap of the deer's wings drowned out the cacophony of their hooves. I clamped my free hand down on Marcus's thigh, digging my gloved fingers into the fabric of his pants. He winced and shifted my death grip to his right hand.

"Sorry," I said, but the wind swallowed my weak apology.

The lead peryton rose into sight above Raquel's head, ludicrously small in the distance. How was such a fragile animal supposed to keep this entire sleigh and its occupants aloft? The second peryton flapped into sight, blocking my view of the first. Then the third took to the air. Wind whipped my hood aside and stole my floral wreath. I flinched, the brief impulse to try to catch the gift squashed by my overwhelming fear of moving even a fraction and being tossed overboard.

"Hold tight," Marcus said.

The sleigh jerked, then tipped backward. A scream squeezed out from my chest, half strangled by fear constricting my throat. Seradon, Chenoa, and Raquel rose as the front of the sleigh lifted off the ground. The leather strap cut into my left palm, the pain reassuring as gravity tipped me farther backward. I peeked over my shoulder. A blur of ice and mud rushed past, shockingly close. A few more degrees of tilt, and we would be dumped out the back of the sleigh.

The roar of the blades dragging through mud silenced, giving rise to the heavy flap of the perytons' wings. I squeezed my eyes shut, letting out a long exhale—

The seat dropped out from beneath me. My eyes snapped open. Seradon engaged the sleigh's levitation spells, and my shriek cut off with a grunt when the smack of the seat against my butt knocked my teeth together. The ground receded in my peripheral vision, dropping away with stomach-churning swiftness. In quick succession, we surpassed the range of the two gargoyles near the bleachers, and their boosts vanished from our link.

Tentatively, I turned my head to look past Marcus. The horizon hung at an alarming forty-five-degree angle. I tore my gaze from the shrinking people along the high slopes of Focal Park's earth section as more of Terra Haven came into sight. Snow-dusted rooftops and bubbles of heat spells dotted the city. Lights glowed from hundreds of windows, but the streetlamps illuminated empty roadways. Good. People had heeded the warnings and gotten indoors.

Marcus shifted, and I stiffened, my hand spasming around his.

"Look," he shouted, pointing with his chin.

I followed his gaze, turning toward the last gargoyle beacon on my mental map. A small dirigible sank toward the roof of a three-story building outside the park. Kylie jumped up and down on the ship's deck, her blond hair streaming out behind her, her excitement tangible across the empty air separating us. Quinn stood at the railing, the dirigible's lanterns warming his citrine lion body so he appeared to be cast in gold. His boost roared through our linked magic, enhancing everyone at once. Seradon waved, then pointed Quinn out to Chenoa. A handful of ships descended toward the rooftops around Kylie's vessel, oddly close, until I realized their proximity allowed everyone to benefit from Quinn's boost.

Grant strode to the railing next to Kylie and wrapped an arm around her waist. Kylie's parents stood arm in arm behind them, their expressions pure wonderment as we blasted past. I would have been just as awestruck in their place. The Midnight Sleigh in flight was a sight to behold.

Kylie cupped her hands around her mouth and shouted

something. The wind swallowed the sound. She must have realized I couldn't have heard her, because she pointed at me, then at herself, then danced in place and gave me two thumbs-up. A bubble of laughter unexpectedly welled past the fear clogging my throat. Of course. She wanted the exclusive scoop for the *Terra Haven Chronicle* . . . and she was proud of me.

Kylie, Quinn, Grant, and their airship disappeared beneath the rim of the sleigh as we continued to climb. Not long later, Quinn's boost winked out.

I twisted to look for Oliver, keeping a firm grip on the strap and Marcus. I could still faintly sense the gargoyles in the park, and closer, Quinn. Usually, gargoyle beacons floated in my mind's eye at my height or higher. Sensing those lights *beneath* me made my stomach flip. I swallowed hard against the queasiness. I would *not* vomit in the Midnight Sleigh.

A frigid gust knocked the sleigh sideways. My cheek bashed into Marcus's chest, and my arm jolted in its socket when my grip on the strap snapped me back into place. Spells spun through the link, stabilizing the sleigh and forming a cone of protective air around the perytons as a polar bell-wing swept less than ten feet overhead. I ducked instinctively. The moth's widespread wings flared like oversized dirigible sails, filling the sky, and its segmented body stretched twice the length of the sleigh. I gaped, paralyzed between fear and awe.

From afar, the bell-wings appeared a uniform bluish-white. Up close, they were works of art akin to malleable stained glass. Thousands of palm-size scales layered each wing, the thin membranes a kaleidoscope of sapphire, silver, and icy translucence. Natural currents of air and water element twisted among the scales, and the delicate fibers wove spells with each flex of the moth's six wings. Iterations of cooling spells, ice spells, and tiny whirlwinds of snow spells spun off the tips of the polar moth's wings. Most of the spells disbanded into the ether after five or six feet, but a few retained their shape far longer. This was the power of the polar bell-wings: A single moth didn't have much impact, but en masse, they altered the air and weather patterns.

Red-and-gold rainbows danced across the moth's scales as we dipped beneath it, the mirror-like surfaces reflecting the fiery light from the sleigh's glowballs. The bell-wing's long pale legs flexed, ruffling the frost-like fur on its thorax and abdomen. Twin mesh eyes as large as my head tracked us, and tall feathery antennae twitched in our direction. With soft white fur coating the bell-wing's nose, I was struck by how closely it resembled a bunny—an enormous insectile bunny that could freeze me with a beat of its wings.

"She's going to flap," Marcus shouted.

Seradon glanced back, then yelled something to Raquel. Magic pulled through me, fast and hard, burning a soft ache into my temples. The sleigh leveled off, then tipped forward. Arctic wind hit the rear of the sleigh, accelerating us. The park came into view again, a bowl of greenery, sculptures, and earthen mounds. Lincoln River glistened white with ice and moonlight, reduced to a ribbon no wider than my forearm. The bleachers were the size of matchboxes. Terra Haven sprawled in all directions, a grid of wooden and brick buildings defined by cobblestone streets and the circular glow of streetlamps.

The perytons banked, whipping the sleigh behind them. Raquel tweaked the levitation spell to match the curve of our flight, tipping the right side of the sleigh toward the ground. Gravity pushed me across the bench, and I clutched Marcus tighter. His reassuring reciprocal squeeze arrested the panicked screams building in my throat. Then the perytons surged higher, and the sleigh leveled off again. My stomach caught up a second later.

My pulse thundered in my ears. This flight was wild and unpredictable, terrifying and exalting—out of control and almost as if I had wings of my own. My lips trembled, my smile crimped by fear. No amount of flying would ever feel natural, but this was something extraordinary.

I caught Marcus's eye and mouthed, "*Thank you.*"

Surprise bounced his eyebrows, then his lips curved into a soft smile. Dipping his head, Marcus placed his mouth near my ear.

"I wouldn't want to do this with anyone else."

I turned to brush my lips against his. "Me, either."

The sleigh bounced, jolting us apart. A golden beacon swept through my inner map, and I spun on the seat to look behind us. Oliver swooped into sight, a gargoyle aflame. His carnelian body would have stood out against the pale bell-wings anyway, but wrapped in fire, he was impossible to miss.

Tucking his wings to his sides, Oliver picked up speed, closing the gap between us. His boost reached us first, breathing refreshing power into our link. The throb at my temples receded, the level of magic Raquel siphoned through me decreasing.

Oliver didn't slow until he was almost in arm's reach, then he flared his flaming wings wide to coast on the sleigh's tailwind. Over half the glowballs attached to him were extinguished, the spells crushed or broken by his flight. The rest illuminated the grin on Oliver's face, glinting off his sharp teeth and setting his eyes aglow. Miraculously, the sturdy roses of his solstice wreath had survived, ringing his neck in white.

"How do you feel?" I asked, visually searching his stone feathers for signs of burning. His wings moved easily, without the telltale clumsiness of fatigue. I longed to test his health with the elements, but to do so, I would have to split magic from the link, and I didn't dare.

"Incredible!" Oliver shouted back.

"We're going to the mountains," Marcus said, his deep voice carrying easily to Oliver.

"Awesome!" Oliver performed a sinuous midair wriggle. The glowballs on his wings danced.

"You're in charge of stragglers," Marcus said. "Stay in boost range."

Oliver curved his wings and tail, flipping himself in a playful belly roll. While upside down, he gave us an exaggerated thumbs-up with one clawed toe. Marcus skillfully parsed fire magic from the link and rebuilt Oliver's extinguished glowballs. With a whoop of excitement, my friend tipped backward, dropping toward the ground. My stomach plunged with him. Then Oliver pulled out of his dive, using his momentum to rocket skyward. In three wing beats, he cleared the sleigh and kept climbing.

Far below, I heard faint cheers. I peered over the edge of the sleigh. Our ascent had carried us in a long arc, circling around the park to fly north, toward the mountains. The fireworks stage was below us once again, and the people in the stands were going wild over Oliver's antics—and rooting for us, in the Midnight Sleigh.

"You should sit," Marcus said, applying pressure to my forearm where he gripped me.

I glanced at him, shocked to find myself kneeling on the bench seat. I didn't remember climbing up here. On shaky legs, I rearranged myself, burrowing into the seat next to Marcus. He tugged displaced furs over our laps.

"This is *incredible*," Raquel shouted, smiling at Seradon over Chenoa's head.

Polar bell-wings crowded the air in front of us. Like sentient airships, they glided on icy air currents, dipping and twisting lazily. Sporadic shafts of moonlight cut through gaps between those higher up, highlighting furred thoraxes and jewel-like scales of bell-wings closer to us.

To the right, a massive moth dipped out of the collective, wings fluttering in mesmerizing pulses. Dozens of delicate frosty whirlwinds spiraled from its wingtips, rolling into palm-sized snow flurries. Another polar moth sailed from our left, mimicking the first bell-wing's minute flutters as it cut close overhead. Raquel adjusted the sleigh's spells, cocooning us from the turbulent air. Tiny snowflakes brushed my cheeks, and then we were past the aberrant pair. I twisted to watch them meet, giant wings beating the air faster as they began their mating dance. Their stronger flaps lifted them, and in seconds, they disappeared into the crush of bell-wings above us.

"Now, Chenoa," Seradon said, the wind whipping her words past me.

Tentatively at first, then with growing confidence, the young weather shaman unfurled a spell from the rear of the sleigh. Myriad threads of air and fire twisted together, soft and bulging in some places, spiked and spiraling in others. Drawing deeply on our linked magic, Chenoa added layer after layer, feeding all five elements through sections and funneling down to only fire or air in others. I stopped trying to follow her work, marveling instead at the size and scope of the spell as it grew, forming a complex burning-hot polar bell-wing siren song.

The nearest moths pivoted toward the spell, giving chase. Seradon, Chenoa, Marcus, and I twisted in our seats, watching the rest of the flock. Only Raquel kept her eyes on our destination, where tiny sparks glinting along the mountain slopes denoted the Nuche people's enormous bonfires. Oliver ranged from side to side behind us, spinning in taunting circles to draw wayward moths in our direction.

"Come on, take the bait," Marcus urged.

"Add air here, fire here, a touch of wood and air here," Seradon said, tapping a sliver of magic against the indicated branches of the spell.

I swayed as magic siphoned through me. Chenoa pulsed elements into her labyrinthine spell where Seradon directed.

"That's it," Seradon said. "A bit more . . . Nice! Good threading with the wood."

Invisible flames shot through Chenoa's spell, and the air behind us shimmered with the intensity of the heat. A handful of polar bell-wings farther away wheeled toward us, flapping ponderously into line behind the sleigh. More and more fell in behind them, until even the stragglers chasing Oliver caught sight of the sleigh and bypassed the flaming gargoyle to join the migrating stream.

Seradon let out a victory whoop and clapped Chenoa on her shoulder. The young woman allowed herself a faint smile, but her attention never wavered from the complicated spell.

The sleigh climbed, seeming to accelerate as we whipped at the end of the perytons' traces. The outskirts of Terra Haven slid below us. Gray meadows and black groves undulated across the foothills, the monochromatic landscape dotted with clusters of lantern-lit homes and miniature solstice fires. The sleigh bobbed, and my stomach lurched. When I looked up, we were higher than the polar moths.

My breath caught. I'd only ever seen the bell-wings from below, with the luminescence of the moon shining through their wings. I didn't think they could be more exquisite, but I was wrong. The tops of their wings shimmered with the blue-white adularescence of polished moonstone, and when they flapped, snowflake patterns flared white across each wing's surface.

Polar bell-wings fanned out behind us as far as I could see, forming an aerial winter river that once again swept across the land, passing but not lingering, as their migration was always intended to flow. Oliver swooped above and around the edges of the bell-wings, playing as much as herding the colossal moths. Even from afar, his delight was unmistakable.

Taking a deep breath, I tried to imprint the moment in my memory: the taste of ice on the crisp air, the musk of peryton sweat and earthy aromas of the fur blankets, the gentle warmth of Marcus's spell across my lap and legs, and the hotter heat of his body pressed to my side. The stars shone like grains of quartz in the midnight sky, and the moon hung close enough to touch if I dared reach for it. The region's entire polar bell-wings population sailed in our wake, as enchanting as they were deadly.

A year ago, I would have missed out on this opportunity, too scared to try.

Now, though, I had Marcus and Oliver in my life, and that changed everything.

I uncurled my fingers from the leather handhold and reached for Marcus. He ducked his head so I could speak closer to his ear.

"My life hasn't been the same since I met you. It's so much more wonderful than I ever dreamed it could be."

His smile bloomed slowly. "I could say the same about you. Happy winter solstice."

The kiss he planted on my lips curled my toes inside my boots, and pure effervescent joy zinged through my veins.

The new year stretched out in my mind's eye, full of love and adventures, and I couldn't wait to experience it all with Marcus and Oliver at my side.

SPECIAL BONUS

Receive the ebook *Lured* for free!

Join Rebecca's VIP List and receive *Lured*, a short tale
featuring fan-favorite characters from the
Gargoyle Guardian Chronicles.

https://www.rebeccachastain.com/newsletter/

Turn the page for an exciting excerpt from

FLIGHT OF THE GARGOYLES

Book Four of the
USA Today bestselling
Gargoyle Guardian Chronicles series.

AVAILABLE NOW!

To protect gargoyles, Mika must journey
far from safety…

EXCERPT: FLIGHT OF THE GARGOYLES

BOOK 4 OF THE GARGOYLE GUARDIAN CHRONICLES

"*That's* our ride?" I squeaked. I checked Marcus's expression, hoping I had misheard him. His self-satisfied smile did nothing to ease the queasiness swelling in my stomach.

The shriek of tree branches clawing against wood made me jump. I spun to face my nightmare. A flimsy dirigible caromed between the cottonwoods lining the street, scraping its bottom against the upper canopies. Broken branches clattered to the cobblestones, splintering against the hard stone, and shredded leaves swirled into the air as the pilot pivoted the airborne abomination to thread the gap and descend toward the street. I cringed as nearby house wards snapped into place, anticipating my landlady's irritation even as I wished I could duck out of sight behind a ward of my own.

"It couldn't be more perfect," Marcus said. "It's quick, it's free—Patrick owes me—and best of all, it's going our way." He cupped an arm around my shoulders and pulled me against his warm side. "I didn't think we could reach the everlasting tree in time, Mika, but with this, we have a chance."

I tucked my head against his shoulder to hide my horrified expression. I wanted to see the everlasting tree, but . . . flying? Why did it have to be *flying*?

Up until a few days ago, finding the cure for local comatose gargoyles had consumed my focus. The everlasting tree's impending once-a-generation blooming hadn't been important—at least not once I determined I couldn't rely on it as a means for curing the gargoyles. Although the magical tree granted answers to seemingly impossible questions when it bloomed, no one knew exactly when the tree would release its knowledge. I hadn't been willing to leave the lives of the fading gargoyles to chance.

Now, with the comatose gargoyles on the mend and the tree yet to bloom, I had still resigned myself to missing the momentous experience. The everlasting tree was too far away. No trains stopped anywhere close to its grove, and even if we rented the city's fastest horses or powered up an air cart right now, it would take well over a week to reach the tree. Besides, we had only just returned to Terra Haven. My bags were still packed, my clothes still wrinkled from being slept in the night before. I had already decided to wash away the disappointment of missing the everlasting tree with a long soak in my bathtub.

I never considered flying. It was expensive and extravagant, and most important, terrifying. But Marcus Velasquez, a Federal Pentagon Defense warrior who never met a challenge he didn't tackle head on, wasn't scared of something as trivial as being suspended thousands of feet in the air on little more than a few planks of weathered wood, poised to fall to his death.

I glanced past Marcus's shoulder to Ms. Zuberrie's

house, where I rented a room. Home. It was so close. My travel-frayed nerves needed a dose of the serenity that could be achieved only by being surrounded by my belongings. And my gargoyles.

I had sensed them from several blocks away, each a glowing bundle of energy inside my head, but nothing compared to seeing them in person. The four gargoyles talking animatedly on the eaves of the Victorian were as different as any collection of gargoyles—Lydia, a plump pink, purple, and orange agate swan with lion's feet; Anya, a sleek dumortierite-and-aventurine panther with wings that stretched nearly as long as her tail; Herbert, a compact dumortierite-veined rose-quartz armadillo with a toucan's beak and stubby wings; and Oliver, a slender carnelian dragon with eagle wings. Anyone unfamiliar with the quartet would never suspect they were siblings from the same clutch. Only Quinn was missing, having accompanied my best friend, Kylie, to the everlasting tree days earlier.

I barely had time for more than a cursory check of each gargoyle, assuring myself their living-quartz bodies radiated robust health, before Marcus whisked me back to the street. Oliver remained behind to share our recent adventures, but when he caught my gaze, whatever he saw in my expression made his wings unfurl in alarm. With a flick of his tail, he launched from the roof. His carnelian wings fractured the sunlight, bathing Marcus's face in an ominous crimson and flaring bloodred outlines around our shadows.

"What is it?" he asked, landing with a clatter of quartz paws.

I reached for Oliver, taking comfort in the smooth curves of his stone mane beneath my fingers.

"Nothing," I said. At least nothing that would make sense to him.

"Ahoy!" a male voice called from above.

Marcus released me to wave back. Thick coils of air and earth magic wove from his fingers and hooked the sinking dirigible, anchoring it to the street as it landed. Marcus wielded the bands of elements effortlessly, but it would have been just as easy to imagine him stopping the airship with sheer physical strength. Even in civilian clothes, Marcus looked the part of a warrior. It was partially his military-short black hair and partially his anvil jaw, but mainly it was the breadth of his shoulders and the muscles cording his body beneath his white cotton shirt and khaki trousers. Happiness glinted in his blue eyes as he strode toward the ship with his usual energetic grace, exhibiting none of the travel fatigue that clung to me.

If the dirigible hadn't loomed behind him, I might have possessed room in my brain to be self-conscious. Marcus was a powerful full-spectrum fire elemental who tenaciously defended Terra Haven from deadly monsters—human and otherwise. I, on the other hand, was a mid-level earth elemental with a quartz specialty. I could heal gargoyles, but until recently, I spent the majority of my time holed up in my room, fussing over commissioned quartz projects. On a good day, I appeared ordinary and insignificant. With my snarled braid, rumpled clothes, and teetering equilibrium, today wasn't a good day.

"Come on, Mika," Marcus called, waving me forward.

I fluttered a hand in his direction, my smile a grimace. *Let's go,* I urged my feet. *Before Marcus realizes I'm a complete coward.*

My boots remained fused to the cobblestones, my feet transformed into granite blocks.

Movement atop the ship gave me an excuse to jerk my gaze from Marcus's puzzled frown. A lanky black man strode across the airship's deck with the loose-kneed gait of a lifelong flier. Canary-yellow pants bagged around his thighs and cinched his calves just above lace-up leather boots. A form-fitting lime-and-yellow-striped shirt clung to his lean torso. What the outfit lacked in aesthetics it made up for in visibility, which was likely the point. With no regard for the neck-breaking drop to the cobblestones, the man leaned over the nominal railing and grinned down at Marcus.

"You're lucky you caught me before I left town, Velasquez. Another ten minutes, and I would have been gone."

"You would have turned back for me," Marcus said.

The pilot scoffed. "You? No. Her?" His gaze landed on me, and a slow smile pulled up the corner of his mouth. "You know how I feel about redheads. Those flaming locks are a siren song for my eyes."

Marcus grimaced at the mention of a siren. "Patrick, meet my girlfriend, Mika. Mika, this is my childhood friend, Patrick."

My stomach flipped. This was the first time Marcus had introduced me as his girlfriend, and I liked the way it sounded. Clumsily, I got my feet unstuck and shuffled toward the dirigible. Marcus retreated to meet me halfway, his eyes searching mine. I gave him a tremulous smile.

Patrick whistled. "Girlfriend, huh? You don't look big enough to have wrestled Velasquez into submission. You must have hidden talents or some really impressive"—his eyebrows waggled—"magic."

"Did I mention he's got the wit of a sixteen-year-old?" Marcus asked, shooting his friend a glare.

I forced a noncommittal noise past my numb lips. This close, it was impossible to ignore the airship or its striking resemblance to a diseased fish. Convoluted rigging secured faded chartreuse cloth sails against the bloated cabin like crumpled gills, and spells netted the entire ship in a distressing mesh of air and fire elements. Beneath the magic, more than one scrape cut through the flaking yellow paint, exposing raw wood. Six fragile ropes attached the slipshod craft to a slender cigar-shaped balloon, its canvas a sun-bleached exaggeration of Patrick's eye-popping green-and-yellow-striped top.

"Patrick, this is Oliver," Marcus continued. "He and Mika are a team. Oliver, you can ignore everything Patrick says. He's just a means to an end."

"Ouch." Patrick pretended to clutch his heart, but his eyes lit upon Oliver with open curiosity. "I would never disparage a gargoyle, especially not one as handsome as you, Oliver. Now, what are we waiting for? Come aboard, and we'll be off."

My stomach burrowed toward my toes, a ricochet of bile climbing my throat. Patrick flipped a rope ladder over the railing. Eyes unfocused, I watched dust motes explode from the twisted hemp when it smacked the side of the dirigible, and I carefully did not move. If I so much as twitched, I was afraid I would run and not stop until I locked and warded myself in my apartment.

Marcus tossed his bag to the deck, then my satchel, followed by my bag of seed crystals.

"Oyá's grace! What do you have in here? Rocks?" Patrick asked, staggering when he slung the strap over his shoulder.

"Close enough," Marcus said. He gestured me toward the ladder. "Come on. I'll steady it for you."

"Is it just me, or does this ship look like a death trap?" I asked, attempting to sound nonchalant but hoping Marcus would take a second look at the flimsy construction of the dirigible and agree.

He frowned. "You know there's nothing dangerous about it, right?"

"About this ship in particular or any airship?" Surely he understood that bobbing along in a wooden box supported by a hodgepodge of brash spell work, hot air, and fraying ropes was the definition of *dangerous*.

My calves knocked into Oliver, and I teetered, off balance. The gargoyle flared his wings in confusion. His bright eyes darted from my face to Marcus's, then back to me.

"I don't see anything bad. What am I missing?" Oliver reared onto his hind legs, spreading his stone wings wide. Unwittingly, he boxed me in, and I fought a flash of panic that insisted I push past him and flee to open ground.

If only I could escape my fear that easily.

"Nothing." Marcus rested a reassuring hand on Oliver's wing. "Mika, have you ever been on an airship?"

I bit my lip and shook my head. Air travel had never been in my budget. Besides, my fear of heights had always far outweighed any reason for launching myself into the atmosphere.

Until now.

Oliver settled on all four feet, folding his wings. With a soft whine, he twined his tail around my leg in silent support.

"Did you just refer to *Grasshopper's Grave* as a death trap?" Patrick asked, leaning over the edge as if he were going to dive headfirst to the cobblestones.

Marcus dropped his face into his palm.

"*Grave* is in its name?" I asked, my voice an octave too high.

"Patrick, you're not helping," Marcus growled.

Patrick tipped farther over the edge, one deep exhale away from toppling. His serious expression caught mine, the haunted depths of his tawny eyes aging him far beyond his twenty-something years. "It was two years ago on this very day. My first mate, a slight woman, not unlike yourself, Mika. She was so nimble on the ship, we called her a grasshopper. She could make any jump from any wing or rigging. Until one day . . . well, one day, she didn't." He scuffed his feet in a mock jump, then windmilled his arms to catch his balance.

I screamed, short and sharp, grabbing for the elements. Oliver's boost sang through me, and I whipped every ounce of air I could hold toward Patrick to shove him upright. My magic barely touched him, and he rocked back on his heels, having never needed my assistance. His head fell back, and his booming laugh echoed down the street.

Incredulous, I spun on Marcus. "That wasn't— I'm not— I can't—" I sputtered.

"Seriously?" Marcus asked, his head tipped back to glare at Patrick. "What's wrong with you?"

The pilot raised his hands. "Hey, she started it with that *death trap* insult."

Marcus shoved a hand through his thick hair, fisting a clump, but when he focused on me, his expression softened. "He's got a terrible sense of humor—"

"You think?"

"But he's a good pilot." Marcus took my hands, shaking them gently until I unclenched my jaw. His gaze searched mine, earnestness radiated from his blue eyes. "I wouldn't have set up this flight if it wasn't safe."

"I know," I said, not sounding the least bit convincing. But it was true. I trusted Marcus with my life. Not only that,

I loved him. With Marcus, I would always be safe—even on a perilous flying contraption like this.

My head knew it, my heart knew it, but my insides still quaked.

"It's a Message in a Bottle dirigible," Marcus said. "It's fast, safe, and reliable. The company wouldn't have it any other way."

I nodded. He wasn't saying anything I didn't know. Message in a Bottle had a long-standing reputation of excellence. I had used the company's services a few times around the holidays, and every spell-recorded message I sent had reached my parents and sister. I had never heard of one of their ships crashing.

"We also pride ourselves on being on time," Patrick interjected from above, "so if we could get go—"

Marcus's nostrils flared, and cold fire ignited in his eyes. When he glanced upward, Patrick's teeth clicked together.

Was I really going to do this? Was I going to spend multiple days dangling in the sky aboard an *airship*?

I crouched, embracing the need to get closer to the ground. Oliver dipped his head to peer at me. Sun soaked into the deep-red hues of his quartz scales, warming him beneath my hand. Breathing deep, I centered myself in his clean scent and comforting presence.

Marcus squatted in front of me, his wide frame blocking the bottom of the hovering dirigible from sight.

"Any other mode of transportation will be too slow," he said softly.

"I know."

"You can't make decisions based on fear. You have to follow what's in here." He tapped my breastbone over my heart.

Shame washed through me. I was supposed to be a

guardian of gargoyles. Protecting gargoyles was my duty, and if I worded my question for the everlasting tree cleverly, its answer could help countless gargoyles. I should have been like Marcus, doing everything in my power to get to the tree before it bloomed.

Yet here I hunched, knees quaking, scrambling for a reason to stay behind.

Marcus dropped his hand to my knee, and I blinked his face into focus. Why couldn't I be fearless like him?

It's an airship. People fly in them every day. I can do this.

And if I couldn't, what would Marcus think? The possibility of disappointing him made me ill. And Oliver . . . My friend stared at me with love and trust radiating from his dragon eyes. He expected me to behave like a gargoyle guardian. I couldn't let him down.

"Is *Grasshopper's Grave* really the ship's name?" I asked, stalling.

"No. It's *Breezy Bunny* or something like that."

"*Happy Hopper*," Patrick yelled over the side.

"And the woman who . . ." I dove a hand toward the ground to imitate her horrid death.

"Never existed," Marcus said.

I nodded. My head bobbed too many times, but Marcus didn't comment. I let out a shaky breath and forced myself to my feet.

"All right. Let's go."

Keep reading *Flight of the Gargoyles*. Pick up your copy today!

To help a baby gargoyle, Mika will risk **everything**.

CATCH UP ON THE

SPELLBINDING

GARGOYLE GUARDIAN CHRONICLES

TODAY!

"I love this series!"
–Tome Tender

"Nonstop nail-biting action"
–Kam's Place

RebeccaChastain.com

ACKNOWLEDGMENTS

This three-book bundle is a project of love: for my characters, for this magical world, and most of all, for you, my reader. After all the death-defying adventures we've survived alongside Mika and Kylie, I wanted to celebrate the lighthearted, everyday moments often bypassed in their action-packed novels. What better time to drop in on our leading ladies than during the winter solstice?

It turns out, life is never dull for Mika or Kylie. Originally, I planned to write a single *short* story. It was to be a tiny glimpse of the winter solstice, a few dozen pages long. Then Mika and Kylie stepped onto the page, and one adventure wasn't enough. They demanded three. And neither of them were satisfied with a short story.

I hope you enjoyed these three tales. I had a lot of fun writing them.

Of course, none of the stories in *Magic by Starlight* would have been written without you picking up my earlier novels. Thank you for reading the Gargoyle Guardian Chronicles and Terra Haven Chronicles series and asking for (sometimes demanding) more gargoyle stories. I'm happy to oblige!

I'm also grateful for my beta readers, who read through each story as I finished them and gave me so much thoughtful feedback. These holiday adventures would be less-detailed, flatter versions of themselves without the input of Jillian Cori Lippert, Seana Waldon, Renea Kania, Rebecca Moore, and Sarah Gibson.

Although I would sometimes love to publish my unedited manuscript just to share some of the hilarious typos I miss, I'm thankful for my editor, Crystal Watanabe, and the polish she gives my words.

While I adore being an author, it comes with its own challenges. For instance, this bundle was supposed to be an easy, light project that I finished in a month. Eleven months later . . .

Mom, thank you for listening to me whine and for encouraging me anyway. If at any time I start dreaming about writing another "short" story, you know what to do!

Last, but never least, thank you, Cody, for believing I could complete all three of these stories even when I doubted myself. I won't hold it against you that you laughed for so long and so hard when I said this would be "a quick trilogy."

ABOUT THE AUTHOR

REBECCA CHASTAIN is a feminist, animal advocate, and nature devotee. She believes empathy is a hero's trait and love is a motive, an inside job, and a transformative energy that shapes each person's world. She is the *USA Today* best-selling author of the Gargoyle Guardian Chronicles series, the Terra Haven Chronicles series that begins with DEAD-LINES & DRYADS, and the Madison Fox urban fantasy series.

If given the opportunity, Rebecca will befriend your cat.

**Visit RebeccaChastain.com
for free stories, bonus materials, updates, and so much
more!**

DIVE INTO A NEW **EXTRAORDINARY SERIES** FILLED WITH **ELEMENTAL MAGIC** & **HEROIC GARGOYLES...**

"Fun and exciting"
–evOke Magazine

"Deliciously intense"
–The Book Drealms

"Fantastic"
–The Lily Cafe

RebeccaChastain.com